The Book of Skulls

The Book of Skulls

Book 1 in the Doctresses series

David Hutchison

Flying Sheep
Publishing

First edition

ISBN 978-1-8380280-2-2 (Paperback)

Flying Sheep Publishing.

We Can Do This

Liz Tries to Check Florian's Wound

Charles Sews Florian's Wound

Professor Atticus Tests Poison

Death of the Burry Man

The Portobello Egyptologist

Molly

Phrenology Head

Séance

Hector and Campbell

The Book of Skulls

www.davidhutchison.info

Dedicated to my family and friends.

Table of Contents

Chapter 1 Death in Leith...1

Chapter 2   Liz...4

Chapter 3 Campbell...11

Chapter 4 Medical School..17

Chapter 5 Jack..34

Chapter 6 Riot...37

Chapter 7 Mugging..50

Chapter 8 The Alienist...61

Chapter 9 Carnousty's Boarding House 63

Chapter 10 Innocent Railway 66

Chapter 11 Atticus...74

Chapter 12 Burry Man 76

Chapter 13 Asylum 88

Chapter 14 Delivery 93

Chapter 15 Autopsy 99

Chapter 16 Portobello Egyptologist 106

Chapter 17 White Hat 109

Chapter 18 Molly 113

Chapter 19 Hector 119

Chapter 20 Phrenology...124

Chapter 21 The Royal Infirmary 131

Chapter 22 Leith Surgery 143

Chapter 23 Séance 147

Chapter 24 Calton Hill...155

Chapter 25 A Secret Revealed..157

Chapter 26 Gray's Anatomy 165

Chapter 27 Rabbit Stew 176

Chapter 28 The Book of Skulls 194

Chapter 29 Ceremony...218

Chapter 30 Back to London 223

Chapter 31 Christmas in Edinburgh 229

Chapter 1   Death in Leith

Port of Leith, Edinburgh, 1875.

The seaman's mission was a rather dilapidated building, situated next to Leith Docks. In the temporary examination room at the back, stood stocky French sailor Henri Blanc, trousers at his knees. He rubbed a shiny bump on his shaved head: a nervous habit.

The youthful Dr Paul Love completed his examination and shrugged. "You can pull your breeks up!" The doctor washed his hands in a porcelain basin.

"*Docteur?*"

The doctor dried his hands on a towel and gave Henri his best reassuring smile. "All clear."

"*Eh bien.* I thought the scab... I was with a *putain* in London," said Henri.

The doctor shook his head and said, "Sometimes a scab is just a scab."

"*Dieu merci!*"

"Hold on!" The doctor opened up his medical bag and took out a small bottle of greenish liquid. "Here."

Henri read the label. "*Rose's lime juice.* Do I rub it in?"

The doctor laughed. "God no! Just drink it. Vitamin C. It will help your skin."

Henri smiled and nodded. He took out his small leather fisherman's purse.

The doctor shook his head. "No it's fine. The company sends me free samples."

Henri grinned. "*Merci beaucoup.*"

A few minutes later Henri left the mission, and with a happy gait crossed over the Victoria Bridge. He stopped to watch a swan as it rippled through the reflection of the setting sun, bathing Leith Docks in a bloody glow. *La vie est belle!* He turned down the quayside and headed for The Sandport Bar.

The bar was chockablock with early evening customers, chattering and laughing over the musical scratchings of a pair of old bodachs, fiddling in a corner. Henri shoved his way up to the bar counter and ordered a drink.

Quite a few *Pernods* later... Henri was having a great evening, here in his favourite Scottish pub, and it looked like he was going to get laid too. She was giving him the eye; that pretty mademoiselle across the bar; raven black hair and revealing red dress. She winked again, and then strode purposefully off out of the bar.

Henri quickly downed his *Pernod* and rushed out after her. The street was empty. Where had she gone? He went down Quayside Lane. Ah! There! He caught a glimpse of her red dress as she turned off up another lane. Henri rushed up to the entrance. A bit dark. *Eh bien!* He knew well enough what he was getting. He strutted up the lane like a cockerel in a henhouse. She was leaning against a doorway, half-way up. He strode up to her and staggered slightly. He grinned. She pulled him close to her.

"Mon bijou!" said Henri and kissed her. He put one arm around her waist and with the other reached down to pull up her petticoats.

"Oh sir!" gasped the woman as she stroked her hands across his shaved head.

Suddenly Henri was grabbed from behind. Strong hands twisted around his throat. He tried to push the assailant off. He attempted to plead with the woman for help, but he couldn't speak. She just stood there and looked back at him.

"For God's sake Lachie do it quickly!" said the woman, Bridy Scott.

She stepped aside as her man, Lachie Merry; a face bearing the visual and mental scars of an ex-soldier, squeezed harder on Henri's neck. The Frenchman kicked out in a last desperate attempt at freedom.

"Bastard!" shouted Lachie as Henri's boot connected with an old war wound on his shin. Lachie gave Henri's neck a cracking twist. The Frenchman sunk dead to the pavement.

"I'll keep a look out," said Bridy. She ran to the end of the lane and stood guard.

Lachie pulled the body closer to a gaslight. He got out a long surgical knife and began to quickly cut through the Frenchman's thick neck. After a few minutes the head had been roughly severed. Lachie pulled a sack from his coat pocket and dumped the head into it. He dragged the body by the feet back down the lane towards the docks as Bridy came rushing back.

"Someone's coming!" whispered Bridy.

Nice shoes, looked like his size, damn! He didn't have time to untie them. Lachie let go of his victim's feet.

"This way!" said Lachie.

He and Bridy ran up the lane and disappeared around the corner. Elsie, an elderly fish-seller in traditional stripy dress, came up the lane, staggering a bit after a good few too many gins. She swerved to miss a lamppost, tripped up over the body, and fell to the ground.

"Sharn!" she muttered, and sat up. She looked down at the tramp that she'd fallen over. It was only then that she noticed that he had no head. Elsie screamed and screamed.

Chapter 2　Liz

Liz noticed a small bloodstain as one of the sheets floated to the surface of the washtub. Damn it! She put down the dolly and picked up the washboard. She pulled the edge of the sheet out of the water and sprinkled some borax on the stain. Liz rubbed the sheet up and down the washboard for several minutes. She paused and swept a stray lock of her frizzy red hair from her light brown forehead. There, that blood stain was almost out. She scrubbed a bit more. Gone. Liz let the sheet slip back into the water and hung the washboard back on the wall. She spread out her fingers, sore from scrubbing the laundry. Soap bubbles dripped from her wrinkled fingers. She'd have to look after them better if she were ever to become a doctor. Liz picked up the dolly and plunged it back down into the tub, giving the sheet a final stir. She twisted the sheet around the dolly, hauled it out of the soapy tub and plonked it into another tub of clean water. She swirled the dolly around and thoroughly rinsed the sheet.

Liz went out of the small laundry room and into the drying green of Foundling Orphanage. It wasn't much in the way of a drying green; just a strip of gravel hemmed in by tall buildings on all sides. She stared up at the bleak smoky London sky. It looked like it was going to rain. She opened out a hand. A few raindrops splattered on it. Damn! She'd have to hang the sheets up inside again. Liz went back into the laundry room.

The door to the kitchen opened and Carrie the assistant house mistress, generous in size but not in nature, sauntered in.

"Get a move on!" she snapped. Her large nose twitched like a rat with hay fever.

Liz sighed and dragged a sheet out of the tub towards a large mangle.

"Has the post arrived?" asked Liz.

"Who would be sending you a letter? Oh yes! I forgot. The African king. Your father. Left you here by mistake, your Highness," said Carrie, doing a mock curtsy and almost falling over in the process.

"You know fine what I'm waiting for," said Liz as she turned the mangle and fed the sheet through it.

"A good smack if you don't get those sheets done," snapped Carrie.

"Please?" said Liz.

"Oh very well!" said Carrie. She withdrew a letter from her pocket and handed it out. Liz tried to grab the letter. Carrie snatched it away.

"Your hands are wet. Finish this lot and then you can come and get it," said Carrie. She strode off out of the kitchen.

Liz swore under her breath. She got back to squeezing the water from the sheets, all the time wondering what the letter would say. An hour later she had washed all the sheets and hung them up to dry on the pulleys that covered the ceiling of the laundry room. Her mind felt as if it had been washed and mangled too after the waiting. She went into the main hall and across to Carrie's office. She knocked on the door .There was no answer. Liz tried the door. It opened. She went into the room. The letter was propped up against a half-eaten pork pie on the writing desk. Carrie was snoring in a burst armchair next to the fire. Liz sneaked up to the desk and grabbed the letter. Carrie woke up and tried to get up but Liz ran past her and out of the door.

Liz ran through the hall and up the stairs. Carrie rushed into the hall and made to climb the stairs after Liz, but then smiled to herself and headed to the laundry.

Liz reached the third landing and the attic dormitory, which she shared with six other girls. It was empty. Liz rushed in and flopped down on the floor with her back to the door. She saw that the post mark was from Edinburgh. Liz pulled the envelope open and unfolded the letter. She scanned it quickly.

"Yes!" shouted Liz. She read the letter again, this time more slowly.

The door banged from behind. "Open this door at once!" shouted Carrie, panting out of breath. Liz dragged a nearby chair and wedged it under the door handle. She rushed across to her bedside cabinet. She pulled out her battered copy of *Gray's Anatomy*, placed the letter amongst its pages and replaced it in the cabinet.

Carrie pushed the door open and the chair fell over. She stomped up to Liz. "You shouldn't have come into my office without my approval," snarled Carrie, her face red with anger and the stair climb.

"I don't care. I'm going to Edinburgh Medical School!" said Liz.

"No you're not!" said Carrie. "You've got those sheets to clean."

"I've done them," said Liz.

"No you haven't. Come and I'll show you!" Carrie grabbed Liz's arm and strode off out of the room. She half-pulled Liz down the stairs. She crossed the main hall, opened the kitchen door and pushed Liz in. The sheets were lying on the floor.

"You'll have to wash them again," said Carrie.

"You did it. Didn't you!" said Liz.

"What a bloody cheek you dirty mongrel!" shouted Carrie. She slapped Liz across the face.

At that moment the house mistress Miss Dante came into the kitchen. A tall Italian in her fifties, with a stern no nonsense face, black hair with a white streak, pinned up in a bun. She was the closest thing that Liz, and the other girls, had to a mother figure.

"What's all this... *trambusto*?"

Carrie said, "Liz hasn't done the laundry properly, miss."

"I see. Go now Carrie," said Miss Dante.

"But..." said Carrie.

Miss Dante arched an eyebrow and stared at Carrie.

"Yes miss," said Carrie. She gave Liz a filthy stare and stomped out of the room, banging the door behind her.

"You don't mind her. Poor Carrie can't help causing trouble. Ever since her *bambino* died she's been ..." Miss Dante shrugged. . Liz nodded. Miss Dante bent down and helped Liz pick up the sheets.

"I've been accepted to the Edinburgh Medical School," said Liz.

"*Stupendo*! After all that *studiando*, you deserve," said Miss Dante. "*La prima ragazza* to university."

"I don't know how I'm going to pay the fees," said Liz.

Miss Dante said, "I didn't want to ... *spera*...hope..until you pass. Now I can tell you I had a chat with our *benefattore*, how do you say it?"

"Benefactor?"

"*Si*! Our benefactor Dr Charles. He who gave us money for the books. He has fund for residents that go to university. *Non son molti soldi*. It should help pay for expenses."

"Oh thank you. That's wonderful!" said Liz. She did a little jump for joy and nearly knocked the sheets out of Miss Dante's arms. "Sorry!" She took the sheets from Miss Dante and plunged them back into the tub.

"It only for fees. He not pay accommodation," said Miss Dante.

"I'll get a job," said Liz.

"*Un lavror di governo*.... governess job? You've plenty experience teaching *i giovani*. I enquire for you. My cousin lives in Edinburgh. She has a good idea," said Miss Dante.

"Yes that would be great," said Liz.

***

A few hours later and all the sheets were clean and hanging on the pulleys. Liz went to the main room. Two of the younger children had turned up for reading classes. Liz spent the next hour helping them. Liz was very tired when she heard the gong for dinner. She made her way to the large dining room and queued up with the other girls for their food. She sat down at a table next to her friend Jane; a serious seventeen year old girl with long blonde hair and a withered hand.

"I'm going to Edinburgh," said Liz.

"You got in?" asked Jane.

Liz grinned and nodded through a mouthful of mutton pie.

"Congratulations," said Jane. She didn't seem that happy.

"What?" asked Liz.

"It's just that's it's a big upheaval going all the way up to Scotland. And for what? They probably won't let you graduate," said Jane.

"I've got to take the chance," said Liz.

"Miss Dante has asked me if I want to stay on and help run the place. I'm sure that she'd let you too," said Jane.

"I don't want to be stuck here for the rest of my life," said Liz.

"Nothing wrong with good old London Town," said Jane.

"Course not. I don't really mean a place. I mean a career as a doctress," said Liz.

Jane laughed and patted Liz on the back. "Women can't be doctresses or doctors or whatever you call them."

"I've already told you. They can, and have. Look at Elizabeth Blackwell. Qualified in 1849 in America," said Liz.

"That's America for you," said Jane. "Besides with your looks you'd probably be sold into slavery."

"They can't do that anymore," said Liz.

"Don't be too sure. They'd find a way," replied Jane. Liz shook her head.

"Well, then there's Elizabeth Garrett Anderson. 1865, here in England,"said Liz.

"Oh, but didn't she cheat. Went through the apothecaries or something?" said Liz.

"It doesn't matter. She's a doctress," said Liz.

By the time Jane and Liz went back to their attic room most of the other girls were already in their beds. Liz changed into her nightdress. She took the letter out from the pages of her dog-eared medical book in the side cabinet. She reread it. Liz could hardly believe it. All those years of trying to fit in a few hours of study here and there between hours of manual labour. Now her life was going to change!

Carrie marched into the room. Liz quickly put the letter back into the book. Carrie scowled at the girls.

"Have you all said your prayers?" asked Carrie.

"Yes miss," all the girls replied.

"Well you know that if you haven't you'll go to hell. That's as sure as devilled eggs. Lights out!" she said. She turned out the gaslight and went out of the room. In the darkness Jane spoke up. "I'll miss you."

"I'll come back and see you, or you can visit me in Edinburgh. It's Scotland, not Mars," said Liz.

"It might as well be," said Jane. "Night!"

Liz said, "Night, Jane." She stared up at the skylight above, too excited to go to sleep. Dark thunderclouds gathered in the sky. Rain spattered onto the glass, gently at first, then began to drum down hard. Liz pulled the blanket close around her shoulders and smiled to herself.

***

Liz had taken ages to get to sleep so when the morning bell rang she was still half asleep. Jane shook her awake.

"Come on Liz! Remember we're on duty section this morning and you know how bad I'm at frying eggs," said Jane.

Liz sat up and stretched. "I'll be down in a minute."

Jane nodded and went out the door with the other girls. Liz leaned out of bed and opened her bedside cabinet to have another read of her letter. The cabinet was empty. Liz jumped out of bed. She looked behind the sick bowl and rag at the back of the cabinet. She still couldn't find the book and letter. She looked under the bed. It was gone. Who would have taken it? It didn't really matter about the letter but her *Gray's Anatomy* was her prized possession. She didn't think that Carrie would have sneaked into the bedroom and taken it but that was a possibility. Liz didn't like to think of any of her roommates as thieves but that Jessie Banks had stolen her ribbon last year. She strode over to Jessie's bed and looked in her cabinet. Just an old pair of scuffed shoes. She felt at the back and brought out a toothbrush. It looked very much like the one she had lost a few months ago. She definitely didn't want to claim it back if Jessie had been using it, but she wasn't going to let her off. Liz gave her nose a good pick with her pinky and brought out a small bit of snot. She rubbed her pinky across the dark bristles of the brush. That would teach the cow! Liz put the toothbrush back into the cabinet and replace the shoes. She checked all the bedside cabinets but there was no sign of the book and letter. Liz sighed and got dressed.

Jane had already burnt half a dozen eggs by the time Liz arrived in the kitchen.

"You have the gas way too high," said Liz, turning down the heat.

"Sorry," said Jane. "I told you I can't cook eggs."

"Keep an eye on the porridge then," said Liz. Jane nodded and gave the pan of porridge a stir with her good hand.

"Did anyone come into the bedroom last night when we were asleep?" asked Liz.

"I don't think so. Why?" asked Jane.

"Someone's stolen my book and letter," said Liz.

"That's awful. Does that mean you won't be able to go to Edinburgh?" asked Jane.

"No. Course not. It was just a confirmation. But my *Gray's Anatomy*. It's a valuable book. I'll not be able to afford to replace it," said Liz.

"Oh well. Perhaps it'll turn up," said Jane.

Later that evening Liz smiled to herself as she watched Jessie brush her teeth. She thought of telling Jessie what she'd done but the secret knowledge was satisfaction enough on its own. After Liz got undressed and into her nightclothes she checked her bedroom cabinet again. She was surprised to find her book was lying on the top shelf. Liz took it out and flipped through the pages. The letter was there too. She picked up the letter and noticed a single strand of long blonde hair sticking to it. She turned around and saw Jane watching her. Liz thought about confronting Jane, but at that second the door was pushed open and in barged Carrie.

"Lights out girls!" Carrie turned down the gas and the room was plunged into darkness. She pulled the door closed behind her. Liz's eyes adjusted to the darkness and she looked up to the skylight. The moon came out from behind a cloud.

"Jane?" said Liz.

"What?" asked Jane.

"I'm glad the book turned up again," said Liz.

The moon slipped behind the cloud again.

"But I..." said Jane.

"Doesn't matter now. Night," said Liz.

"Night," said Jane.

***

Several days had passed since the letter incident and Liz had been busy. She'd taken in an old green dress given to her by Miss Dante and it now fitted her quite well. She looked at herself in the foxed mirror of the massive old-fashioned wardrobe. The green went with her dark skin and red hair. She needed to look presentable if she was going to become both a governess and a student. She thought that she'd pass, just. There was a knock on the door and Miss Dante entered.

Miss Dante smiled and said, "*Bellissima*! You make a good job with it. Better on you than ever on me."

"Thanks for giving it to me. I didn't have to alter it much at all," said Liz.

Miss Dante handed Liz a note. "The address for the Hughson family. My cousin say they give you lodgings for teaching *i giovani*...young ones."

"Oh thank you," said Liz.

"You change your mind, you are welcome back here. We always do with some help teaching," said Miss Dante.

"That's good to know," said Liz. "I'd better finish getting ready. I'm catching the Scotchman at ten."

Miss Dante smiled and left the room.

Liz pinned on her hat. It looked rather silly but Lily, one of the younger girls, had made it for her last year. She picked up her travel bag from under her bed and went to the door. She stopped and had a last look around the attic bedroom. The seven iron single beds, made up to perfection, each covered tightly with a red tartan blanket. If a penny was dropped on it by Carrie and it didn't bounce you had to make the bed up again. It wasn't much to call home but she felt a bit sad. She went off down the stairs. The rest of the girls were waiting to see her off. Carrie had made then stand in line. Jane came forward and presented Liz with an umbrella.

"We heard that it rains all the time in Scotland so we clubbed together and bought you this," said Jane.

"Oh thank you. Thank you everyone!" said Liz. She gave Jane a hug. Carrie frowned. Lily broke line and hugged Liz. Carrie was about to shout at her to get back in line when Miss Dante came into the hall. The other girls saw their chance and they all ran up to Liz and hugged her. Carrie tutted and called the children back.

Miss Dante handed Liz a small package. "A book for your journey."

"Oh thank you!" said Liz. She gave Miss Dante a hug.

Miss Dante looked rather embarrassed, but also happy. Liz waved to everyone and then went out the front door. The children rushed to the door but a scowling Carrie pulled them back.

It was raining, so Liz put up her new umbrella. It made a most satisfying snap. She wiped her tears away and smiled to herself. This was it! An adventure. She strode off in the direction of King's Cross station.

Chapter 3   Campbell

Liz arrived at the station with twenty minutes to spare. The place was crowded and it took ages to find her carriage. She was used to people staring at her because of the dark colour of her skin and her red hair but the flamboyant young man with sandy hair who sat down opposite her was overdoing it a bit. She took her book from her travel bag and began to read through it. The young man read the title and shrugged.

The journey was fairly uneventful until a long stop at York for a toilet break. The more well off passengers headed off to the station restaurant. Liz sat on a seat on the platform and ate her packed lunch. The young man came up to her.

"Mind if I sit here?" he asked.

"It's a free country," said Liz.

The man sat down. He unwrapped a pie and took a bite.

"I couldn't help noticing your reading material. *Wonderful Adventures of Mrs. Seacole in Many Lands.* Not a book I see many young ladies reading."

"Well, perhaps they should," said Liz.

The man shrugged and took another bite of his pie.

"Isn't she one of Florence Nightingale's cronies?"

Liz put down the book and stared at the man.

"She's an independent woman who overcame racial prejudice and nursed the sick in the Crimea," said Liz.

"An inspiration then?" asked the man.

Liz nodded. "It was a gift, but yes. I'm going to Edinburgh to study medicine," said Liz.

"Oh! That's a bit of a coincidence. I'm a medical student. Second year at Edinburgh," said the man.

"Really?" said Liz. "I'm Liz Moliette." She held out her hand. The man shook it eagerly and said, "Campbell Prebble. Nice to meet you Miss Moliette."

"Liz."

"Campbell," he smiled.

"I'd love to know more about the Medical School. What's it like?" asked Liz.

"Oh, it's very hard work. You know I was always top of the class at school. Considered myself a bit of an intellectual. As soon as I got there I was bottom of the class. So many clever students. Mind you a lot of them don't seem to know much about life," said Campbell.

"What do you mean?" asked Liz.

"All those privileged types. Crying for their nannies. Anyway how about you? I thought they'd stopped women from entering?" said Campbell. "Sophia Jex- Blake's contingent and all that. How they were treated was disgraceful!"

"Oh do you know her?" asked Liz.

"No. That was before I started. I heard that she's trying to get her degree abroad," said Campbell.

"Yes I heard that," said Liz.

"So why all the bother to study in Edinburgh if you might not be allowed to sit the exams?" asked Campbell.

Liz shrugged. "I can't afford to go and study abroad. Mind you I can hardly afford to do it here. Anyway by the time my exams come round the university might have changed their tune," said Liz.

Campbell nodded. "It's possible. I did hear something about the College of Physicians in Dublin were going to allow women to sit the exams."

"Oh! I didn't know about that!" said Liz.

There was a blast of a whistle nearby.

"That's us. We'd better get back on the train,"said Campbell.

Liz and Campbell scrambled for their carriage.

Over the next five hours Liz found out that Campbell originally came from Inverness and that he'd been down in London staying with friends. He'd just managed to pass his exams and was hoping eventually to become a surgeon. In turn Liz had told him about her upbringing in the Foundling Orphanage and how she'd struggled to educate herself. She also learned a few choice words from Campbell such as the Scots word *dreich*, describing a bleak, dreary day and her favourite, the Gaelic word *bùrach*, meaning a mess.

As the train was coming into Princes Street station Campbell got her travel bag down from the shelf and passed it down. "Thanks," said Liz. She looked out the window. It was all grey and misty.

13

"Bit dreich!" said Liz.

Campbell laughed.

"So where's the castle?" asked Liz.

Campbell stared out the window and pointed to a grey smudge in the distance. "Somewhere over there. You can't see it because of the haar."

"What's a haar?" asked Liz.

"Hmm. It's a sea mist rather like fog really. All mixed up with smoke," said Campbell.

"It's quite exciting. Mysterious," said Liz.

The train shuddered to a stop. Campbell opened the door and let Liz out first. She stepped onto the platform and looked around.

"It's called the Wooden Shack," said Campbell.

"What do you mean?" asked Liz.

"The station. It's all wood. See!" Campbell gestured around the station. Sure enough the whole building was made of wood. "One of these days it's going to go up in flames."

"Oh I see," said Liz.

"So where are you staying?" asked Campbell.

"With the Hughson's in Dean Village. Do you know where that is?" asked Liz.

"Oh it's not far from my lodgings," said Campbell. "I'm staying at Mrs Carnousty's in Queen Street. I'll walk you down to the Dean Bridge then you'll be able to find it from there."

A boy selling newspapers called out, "Grizzly murder, grizzly murder. A man beheaded. Read all about it. Get your copy of *The Reekie* here!" Campbell stopped to buy a paper.

"What kind of place have I come to?" asked Liz as she looked over Campbell's shoulder as he read the article. Campbell folded the newspaper under his arm. "It was probably just an accident. Often happens in Leith docks. Come on."

Liz followed Campbell out of the station.

"What's that?" asked Liz, pointing to a gothic structure looming up though the haar covering Princes Street Gardens.

"That's the Scott Monument. You know, the author Sir Walter Scott?" said Campbell.

"Oh yes," said Liz, "I've read *Ivanhoe.*"

"You can climb up inside it. I'll take you some day,"said Campbell. He looked at her dress. "Mind you, the steps are narrow."

"I've got another outfit that's not so cumbersome," said Liz.

Campbell smiled and nodded, "I don't know how you women put up with it."

"We don't have much of a choice," said Liz.

Liz and Campbell crossed Shandwick Place and went along Queensferry Street which led downhill to the Dean Bridge.

"Have you heard of Christian Caddell?" said Campbell.

"No?" said Liz.

"It was a few hundred years back in Moray, a bit further north. She dressed as a man so that she could do a man's job. A witch pricker," said Campbell.

"Gosh! What was that?" asked Liz.

"Someone who used a needle-like instrument to test for the devil's mark on witches. The tool had a secret mechanism in it so it could be retracted, making it look like the needle couldn't draw blood," said Campbell. "There was good money in it. For every witch discovered you got six pounds. It's said that she discovered ten witches."

"Doesn't sound that ethical," said Liz.

"It wasn't. All those women were burnt to death," said Campbell. "She was eventually caught."

"Was she burnt too?" asked Liz. "That would be poetic justice in a way."

"No. She was banished to Barbados," said Campbell. He stopped at the beginning of a stone bridge. "Okay. This is Dean Bridge. Built by Thomas Telford. Our Scottish Bridge of Sighs. Come on." He walked onto the bridge and stopped halfway across. He pointed to the green valley far below. A burn twisted through it. "That's Dean Village to your left."

"It's beautiful," said Liz.

Campbell turned and pointed across the bridge. "I stay over to the right, up the hill a bit." He walked back to the beginning of the bridge and pointed to a track that went downhill to the left of the bridge. "You get down that way. I'll see you around at the Medical School, no doubt."

"Thank you. I do hope so," said Liz.

"Goodbye," said Campbell. He tipped his hat and Liz smiled back. She made her way down the road as Campbell waved and strode off in the opposite direction.

Liz was happy, thinking that she'd now met a new friend. Edinburgh was going to be great! The haar had lifted and she thought how wonderful the place looked. Liz almost lost her footing as she slipped on a large dollop of horseshit. She righted herself and carried on to the bottom of the street.

The Hughson's home was a rather imposing building overlooking the Water of Leith. Liz pulled on the doorbell. After a minute a petite maid opened the door slightly and peered around.

"Hello?"

"I'm Miss Moliette."

The maid smiled and opened the door fully. "So you're the new governess. I'm Gladys. Come in. They're expecting you." She ushered Liz into a narrow hall covered in badly made but earnest tapestries. Liz stopped to look at one of a pig in a blue dress dancing in a meadow.

"They're madam's," said Gladys. She shrugged and carried on down the hall. After a short while she stopped and knocked on a grand oak door. "Enter!" was the muffled reply. Gladys opened the door and popped her head round. "The governess has arrived."

"Well show her in then!" said a gruff voice.

Gladys ushered Liz into a spacious room overlooking the burn. A pregnant woman with dark bags under her eyes, sat at the window, working on a tapestry. A stocky older man with a grey moustache got up from a chair.

"Miss Moliette," said the man. He came across the room and shook Liz's hand. "Edgar Hughson." He turned to his wife at the window. "Helena dear. This is the new governess!" Helena looked up from her tapestry and gave a timid smile.

"Helena's cousin said that you are here to study medicine?"

"Yes I am," said Liz.

"Rather strange thing for a woman to study I must say." He shrugged. "I was assured that you can teach Latin, French and mathematics?"

"I can," said Liz.

"You can have the old cook's room. It's nothing fancy but I'm sure that it will suffice. Evening meals will be included. In exchange I'd like you to give the children lessons between six pm and seven pm during the week and all day Saturday. Sunday, you're free to do as you like. Would that fit in with your studies?"

"I'm sure that will be fine," said Liz, just as two children rushed into the room; a blond boy, chasing a younger brown-haired girl, with a butterfly net. Gladys came in after, face red from trying to catch up with the little ones. The children chased each other around the room.

"Settle down!" shouted Edgar. He grabbed the net off the boy and propped it up against a chair. "Children, this is Miss Moliette, your new governess." The children stopped running, came over and grinned shyly at Liz.

"This is Milton and this is Tabitha," said Edgar.

"Nice to meet you," said Liz. "I do hope we'll have fun studying together."

Edgar frowned. "Learning's not meant to be fun. They need discipline."

Liz tried to keep calm and level-headed. She smiled at the children. They looked back at her, then nervously at their father.

"It's getting late. Off to bed now!" said Edgar.

"Oh please father. Just a while longer!" said Tabitha.

"No! Off you go now," said Edgar. Tabitha put a gurn on her face and marched off. Milton grabbed his net and followed his sister out of the room.

"See, definitely lacking discipline," said Edgar. "Their mother spoils them." He looked across at Helena but she seemed to be engrossed in working on her tapestry.

"I think that's all for now. Gladys can you show Miss Moliette her room!" said Edgar.

"Yes sir," said Gladys. "Come this way, miss," she said to Liz.

The cook's old room was a small space off the kitchen, but it had a nice view of the garden and the Water of Leith.

"So how long have you been working here?" asked Liz.

"Just the year, miss," said Gladys as she straightened the cover on the single bed.

"The children are a bit of a handful but they are little darlings."

"How about Mr and Mrs Hughson?" asked Liz.

"Oh you'll not get a peep out of her. It's me that has to organize all the household stuff. She's what do you call it? Delicate," said Gladys.

"And Mr Hughson. What's he like? Seems a bit strict to me," said Liz.

"Oh that's just his way," muttered Gladys. "You'll get used to him. There's some bread and cold meat set aside for you in the kitchen. Come and I'll show you where it is."

Chapter 4 Medical School

Liz was too nervous to eat any breakfast. She'd put on her green dress, although second-hand it was better quality than her other one and she wanted to make a good impression on her first day of university.   She set off early and soon reached Princes Street. There was no haar this morning and Edinburgh Castle stood proudly jutting up on a rocky plateau towering over Princes Street Gardens. She stopped at the Scott Monument. Sir Walter seemed to stare at her thoughtfully with his white marble eyes. The edifice enclosing him was really a rather fine structure. She hoped that she and Campbell would go up it someday soon.

She took out a small map and checked the direction. She headed east to North Bridge; the bridge that linked the New Town to the Old Town. As she crossed the North Bridge she could see out to the Firth of Forth on her left and Edinburgh Castle on her right. In ten minutes she found the entrance to the College off South Bridge. She went up the steps and into the quadrangle. There were several male students rushing back and fore, looking busy. To her left was the entrance to the Playfair Library. She passed the library and saw a sign for registration. She followed the arrow on the sign to an entrance on the south west corner of the quadrangle. She wasn't sure where exactly to go so she stopped a chubby young man.

"Excuse me. Can you tell me where to register?" asked Liz.

The man looked her up and down and laughed. He marched off. Liz frowned. What was wrong with the chap?   A young Indian woman came out of an entrance. Liz went up to her. "Excuse me. Where do I register?" asked Liz.

"Oh! I'll show you. I've just done it," said the woman. She went back into the building and Liz followed her.

"I'm Liz Moliette," said Liz.

"Amuyla Patel," said the woman. "So pleased to meet you. I was beginning to wonder if I was going to be the only woman here. Come this way."

Amuyla turned left and went down a corridor towards a set of swinging doors. A group of young male students jostled past them.

"Hey!" said Liz. One of the men looked back at her and spat on the floor.

"Charming!" said Amulya.

The men went through the doors without looking back, letting the doors fly back at the women.

"I get the feeling that we're not wanted," said Amulya.

"Well, that's just tough on them," said Liz.

They entered a large hall with rows of tables at one side. Lines of male students waited to register. Some of them jeered at the women. From another door out strode Campbell. He waved and came up to the women.

"Oh so you made it Liz. And who is your friend?" He smiled at Amulya.

"Amuyla Patel," grinned Amuyla.

"Campbell Prebble," smiled Campbell.

Liz nodded to the line of men. "Nice to see at least one friendly face amongst these," said Liz.

"Oh take no notice. I'm not popular either. Didn't go to the right school you see, or something like that," said Campbell.

Amulya pointed to a table with no queue.

"That's where we women register."

Campbell said, "Well, I'll leave you ladies to it. I'm off to see the timetable." He waved and went towards the sliding doors.

"I'll wait with you then we can go and see our timetables," said Amulya. Liz nodded and they went to the table where university administrator Mr Krimi, a doddery seventy year old, sat in front of a register.

"Good morning miss. Name?" said Mr Krimi.

"Elizabeth Moliette."

He looked down his list. There were only two names. Amulya Patel and Elizabeth Moliette. He ticked off her name. He turned the register around and pushed it across the table.

"Sign here please," said Mr Krimi.

Liz signed next to her name.

"So where do we get our timetables from?" asked Liz.

"They are up on the wall in the building opposite but it's not as easy as that," said Mr Krimi.

"What do you mean?" asked Amulya.

"You will have to ask the individual lecturers for permission to attend mixed classes. If they do not agree you will have to sort out separate classes," said Mr Krimi.

"That doesn't sound very fair, but not unexpected," said Liz.

"I'm sorry it's not up to me," said Mr Krimi.

Liz sighed. "Come on Amulya, we'd better get started."

The women went through the swinging doors, back along the corridor and outside into the quadrangle. They followed the string of male students heading to the opposite building. Inside, a wide corridor, a wall was lined with boards and timetables pinned to them. Some of the male students gave the women dirty looks as they tried to get to the timetables. Liz held out her umbrella and ploughed through the crowd. Amulya took out a notebook and fountain pen. Together the women went over the classes that they had to attend for the first term.

***

By the end of the day Liz and Amulya had visited seven lecturers, of which three had objected to the women having mixed classes. They had organised separate class times with these three lecturers.

"I don't know how I'm going to pay the fees for these separate classes," said Liz.

"Don't worry about it for the moment. I have extra money and I need to take these classes anyway," said Amulya.

"That's really kind of you. I think if we went to the press we could force the university to let us have mixed classes," said Liz.

"I'd rather not cause a fuss just when I'm starting. Let's get through the first term and then reassess the situation," said Amulya. "Anyway we've got one more lecturer to see." She checked her notebook. "A Dr Love, how interesting."

After a few false starts the women found Dr Love's office. Amulya knocked on the door.

It was opened by a rather handsome man, thought Liz, in his late twenties with a well-groomed brown beard. He smiled.

"Ladies, what can I do for you?"

"We're looking for Dr Love," said Amulya.

"I am Dr Paul Love," replied Dr Love. He grinned.

"Oh!" said Amulya.

"Younger than you expected?" asked Dr Love. Amulya blushed.

"Where's my manners. Ladies do come in," said the doctor. He opened the door wide and ushered the women to a couple of seats.

He lit his pipe and took a draw.

"So what can I do for you?" asked Dr Love.

"We're the new medical students. Are you willing to have us in your anatomy classes?" asked Liz. "I mean as in mixed classes."

"I don't see a problem with that. Has Professor Atticus been at it again?" asked Dr Love.

"What do you mean?" asked Liz.

"The professor seems to think that women are too disruptive in mixed classes. On the other hand I prefer it. In fact I have found the men behave rather better," said Dr Love.

"Oh that's good to hear. I wish more lecturers had your attitude," said Amulya.

"We've had to arrange separate classes with three lecturers," said Liz.

"Let me guess. Listern, Paycock and Christen," said Dr Love.

"How did you know?" asked Liz.

"All cronies of Professor Atticus," said Dr Love.

"Well thank you," said Liz as she got up.

"Yes thank you, Dr Love," said Amuyla.

The doctor got up and opened the door for them.

"I look forward to seeing you in my classes," said the doctor. Liz and Amulya smiled as they left.

The women walked back into the quadrangle.

Liz stopped and said, "That was a pleasant change."

"Yes. He was rather charming," said Amulya. "Come let's go and have some lunch. I hear that The Dragonfly Tea Room is excellent."

The tea room was busy so they didn't manage to get a table overlooking the castle, but the mural of *A Midsummer Night's Dream* that took up one wall opposite them was fantastic.

"I wish that I could do something like that," said Amuyla. "I've tried but I'm no use at it. It's a copy of Paton's one in the Scottish National Gallery."

The waitress came round and they ordered fruit scones and a pot of Earl Grey.

"So where about are you staying?" asked Liz.

"Oh a lodging house on Buccleuch Place. It's quite nice," said Amulya. "How about you?"

"Dean Village with the Hughsons. I'm working there as a governess part-time," said Liz.

"Dean Village. The baby killer lived there!" said Amulya. "Yes. Mary .... I can't remember her name. Took in unwanted children, you know out of wedlock. Said she'd find a good home for them for a hefty fee.

Turns out the only homes they got was a hole at the bottom of her garden. She was caught and hanged."

"Oh that's really horrible," said Liz.

"Over a dozen bodies were found in her garden," said Amulya.

"Oh no!" said Liz. She noticed that Amulya was grinning.

"Got you!" laughed Amulya.

"You made that up?" asked Liz.

"I was only joking. Mind you it could happen. I've heard all sorts of rumours," said Amulya.

"I think I was born out of wedlock," said Liz, quietly.

"Oh I'm so sorry! What a dolt I am. Please forgive me," said Amulya.

"You weren't to know," said Liz. "Perhaps my parents were married. I don't know. I grew up in an orphanage so I assumed it was something like that."

"You don't know anything at all about them?" asked Amulya.

"Nothing. Maybe I'll find out one day," said Liz.

"Well I must apologise again. The thought of working with cadavers has twisted my sense of humour," said Amulya.

Liz shrugged.

"On that note, I'd really like to visit Surgeons' Hall and see the pathology collections. I have to be back at Dean Village by five though, to give the children their lessons."

"Good idea. That gives us a few hours. I heard that there are some excellent examples of brain tumours there. I'd like to study them," said Amulya. "Eventually I plan on becoming a brain surgeon. What do you want to specialise in?"

"I don't really know yet. I think I might like to know more about forensics," said Liz.

"I don't even know what that is," said Amuyla.

"It's using science to detect crime," said Liz.

"Sounds interesting," said Amulya.

The tea and scones arrived. The women were hungry and made short work of the food. Afterwards they made their way to Surgeons' Hall. It was just up the street from the New College and was a rather grand building in the classical style.

"I think it was built by Playfair; the same architect that made the library," said Amulya.

They showed the guide their registration cards and were admitted into the collections in the main hall. Amuyla was immediately taken with an interesting example of a brain tumour.

"This is exactly what I was looking for!" said Amuyla as she stopped at a glass cabinet. Floating in a jar was a brain, distorted down one side. She took out her notebook and pen and tried to draw it.

"I'll have a look around and come back shortly," said Liz.

"Fine," said Amuyla.

Liz went down the hall and studied glass cases full of medical instruments. She didn't know what most of them were for. She had so much to learn. After about an hour of walking around the collection she came back to see how Amulya was getting on.

Liz saw that Amuyla hadn't exaggerated in saying that she wasn't artistic.

"Oh! That's ... mmm,"

"Rubbish! I know," said Amulya.

"I could sketch it for you if you like?" said Liz.

"Oh would you?" said Amulya.

"Sure."

Amulya handed over her notebook and pen. Within a few minutes Liz had drawn a very acceptable copy of the brain tumour. She handed the notebook back to Amulya.

"Wonderful. Thank you!" said Amuyla.

"Well I'd best get back to Dean Village," said Liz.

"I enjoyed today. I'm so glad you're here too. I really felt like giving up this morning before we met," said Amuyla.

"Me too," said Liz.

They made their goodbyes and Liz headed back down South Bridge and along Princes Street. She looked up at the statue of Sir Walter Scott as she passed. A pigeon shat on his head. That's what happens when you become famous; an eternity of birds shitting on your head. She smiled to herself as she continued along to the end of street, and then down the hill towards Dean Village.

The door was opened by Gladys.

"I've rounded the wee dears up and they're waiting for you in the drawing room."

Liz nodded.

"Now where was that again?" asked Liz.

"Down the hall and to your left. I've set the blackboard up," said Gladys. "Dinner will be ready in an hour. Venison."

"Lovely, thank you," said Liz. She hurried down the hall. The door to the drawing room was open and the children were playing with toy soldiers on the floor. There was a long mahogany table in the centre of the room. On it were several slates with wooden frames, a small box of white chalk and some rags. Gladys had set up the small blackboard next to the fireplace.

"Milton, Tabitha. Come up to the table please!" said Liz. She chose a nice new piece of chalk and went across to the board. Over the next hour Liz found that Milton had a much better grasp of maths than the children that she had taught back at the orphanage. Liz thought that she'd need to do some serious studying to make sure that she kept challenging him.

However Tabitha was completely different. She seemed not to get basic concepts and was very slow to respond.

Liz had her dinner in the kitchen with Gladys. She was quite pleased not to be sitting at a formal dinner with the Hughsons. Helena didn't seem to want to do anything apart from working on her tapestry and Edgar always seemed to be in a foul mood.

Over the following weeks Liz settled down into a routine. She would meet up with Amulya in the morning at the quadrangle and attend several classes. Her favourite were the physiology classes with Dr Love, not so much because she enjoyed this sub-discipline of biology, but that the doctor was so charming.

***

For the next few months everything went well. Liz stayed in Edinburgh over the Christmas break. She didn't have anywhere else to go and she wasn't keen on going back to the orphanage. Luckily Amuyla elected to stay in Edinburgh too, so the two women wrapped up well and went for long walks. They visited the strange man-made caves at Gilmerton Cove, climbed Berwick Law, and at low tide had a look around Cramond Island. Campbell even took the ladies for a trip up the Scott Monument; Liz borrowed one of Amulya's narrower skirts for the occasion and just about managed to fit up the steps.

Classes began again in the middle of January. Liz found the practical classes enjoyable and Amulya helped her with some of the things that she'd never covered before such as chemistry. Things changed in spring.

Liz had had a hard day and was trying to concentrate on tutoring the children. It had been a struggle studying for her upcoming exams and to keep on top of the classes for the children. Amuyla had turned out to be a gifted mathematician and had helped Liz out.

"Two hundred and forty!" shouted Milton as he added up the sum on the blackboard.

"Correct," said Liz. She rubbed her forehead. She could feel a headache coming on. Suddenly a piercing scream came from somewhere at the back of the house. Just as Liz had decided to go and see what was up the door was flung open and Gladys burst in.

"Oh miss, miss. Please come quick!" implored Gladys. She grabbed Liz's hand.

"What is it?" asked Liz.

"It's Mrs Hughson," said Gladys.

Tabitha and Milton got up from the table.

"What's wrong?" asked Milton.

"Is Mummy alright?" asked Tabitha.

"Children stay here!" said Gladys.

"Why?" asked Milton.

"Just... because!" replied Gladys.

She went to the door. "Hurry!" she said to Liz. She waited until Liz passed through and then turned back to the children. "I'll come back and tell you what's happening shortly. Be good!"

Gladys pulled the door shut behind her. "Come on!" she said and ran down the corridor. Liz rushed after her. Gladys made for the sitting room. Helena was lying moaning on the floor, Blood trickled from her lip. Edgar was standing over her. Liz noticed, with disgust, that there was blood on his fist. Liz pushed past him and bent down to Mrs Hughson.

"Mrs Hughson, Helena. Are you alright?" asked Liz.

Helena screamed and clutched her swollen belly. "It's coming, it's coming!"

Liz took Helena's pulse. It was way too fast. She gently felt Helena's stomach through her dress.

"She's going to have it. It's too soon," said Gladys.

"Send for the doctor!" said Liz. Gladys rushed out of the room.

"Get those cushions!" Liz snapped at Edgar. He looked at his fist and seemed dazed.

"Mr Hughson!" said Liz.

"She spoke back," said Edgar Hughson. "She spoke back!" he huffed and marched off out the door. Liz patted Helena's hand. "Hold on."

Liz got up and gathered cushions off the settee. She came back and arranged the cushions on the floor to make Helena more comfortable. Helena moaned and clutched her stomach.

"Has he hit you before?" asked Liz. Helena nodded. Liz suddenly wondered if this had happened when Helena was pregnant with Tabitha. Might that account for Tabitha's slowness? Liz felt a surge of anger.

Half an hour later Dr Florian Blyth followed Gladys into the room. The doctor was slightly built, well-dressed with wavy red hair and a pencil moustache.

"You're not my doctor!" said Helena.

The doctor kneeled down beside Helena.

"Mrs Hughson I'm Dr Blyth. Dr Bell wasn't available. Now where's it hurting?"

Helena touched her stomach. "All over here."

Florian noticed Helena's bruised chin and swollen lip.

"How did that happen?"

"I ... fell," said Helena. Liz shook her head at Florian.

Florian gently touched Helena's stomach. Helena flinched.

"How many months?" asked Florian. "Eight?"

"I'm due in May," gasped Helena. She gave out another moan and shifted on the cushions.

"Can you get up?" asked Florian.

Helena tried to move. "No!"

"Righto, you help to lift her with me!" said Florian to Liz.

Florian moved round and put an arm under Helena's. Liz did the same on the other side.

"And one, and two and three. Lift!" said Florian. Helena screamed as they hoisted her off the floor and across the room to the settee. Gladys quickly gathered the cushions off the floor and arranged them around Helena.

"We need to remove your clothes and give you a proper examination," said Florian. Helena nodded. Liz helped Florian to remove Helena's dress. A lot of blood had seeped through her petticoat and bloomers. As Florian removed the soiled undergarments Helena gasped as she saw the blood. "The baby. Will the baby be alright?"

Florian touched Helena's stomach. "The contractions are coming."

Helena screamed, "Something's wrong!"

"Try to keep calm. It might not be as bad as it looks," said Florian. Liz took Helena's hand and smiled encouragingly at her. Florian examined Helena's vagina. "You're starting to ... your cervix is fully open."

"It's never been... arrgh... like this before!" shouted Helena. She gritted her teeth.

The doctor felt around Helena's stomach and frowned.

Florian said, "The baby's head is in the wrong position."

"What does that mean?" moaned Helena.

"A possible breech birth. Very dangerous for both you and the baby," said Florian.

"Oh my god!" gasped Helena.

Florian pressed gently around Helena's stomach.

"Arrgh!" moaned Helena.

Florian grabbed a cushion and adjusted it under Helena.

"I'll try again," said Florian. "You okay?"

Helena nodded. The doctor pressed around Helena's stomach.

"Oh!" cried Helena.

"I'm sorry. I can't move your baby into the correct position," said Florian. "Mrs Hughson. What's your first name?"

"Helena."

Florian took her hand. "Helena. There is a procedure. It's risky but I think it's you and your baby's only chance."

"What?" asked Helena.

"A caesarean birth. I make a slit in your abdomen and uterus. Then lift out the baby that way. It will hurt like hell and be dangerous but it could be worse if I don't," said Florian.

"Oh my god! Have you done this before?" asked Helena.

"Yes once. Both mother and baby survived," said Florian.

Helena nodded. "You must do it then."

Florian patted Helena's hand and turned to Gladys. "I'll need hot water and fresh towels."

"Yes sir!" said Gladys. She rushed off to the kitchen.

"Have you any alcohol in the house?" asked Florian.

"There's brandy in the cupboard of that dresser over there," said Helena.

"Could you fetch it miss?" Florian asked Liz.

Liz nodded. She got up and went over to the dresser and found the brandy. She brought over the bottle and a glass. She poured a glass out and held it out to Helena.

Helena screamed in pain. She ignored the glass, grabbed the bottle and took a long slug. Liz looked at Florian who took the glass out of Liz's hand and downed it.

"Waste not, want not," said Florian.

Gladys arrived, carrying a pan of steaming water and some towels over her shoulder.

"That was quick," said Liz.

"I always have a kettle on the boil," said Gladys. She placed the pan on the hearth and brought over the towels. Florian rummaged in a black leather medical bag, took out a long surgical knife, a small bottle of carbolic acid and a wooden box. Florian handed the box to Liz.

"Any good at threading a needle?" asked Florian. Liz nodded and opened the box which contained an assortment of threads and needles.

"The black thread's the strongest. And that needle there," said Florian pointing to a large needle. The doctor went over to the pan of water and poured some carbolic into it.

"What's that?" asked Liz.

"Carbolic acid. A tip from one of Dr Lister's lectures. Cuts down on infection," said Florian. "Don't know how, but it does help. Give your hands a quick dip in it. When you've threaded that needle dip it in this too." Liz nodded. Florian and Liz quickly washed their hands. Florian picked up the knife, dipped it in the water and went back across to Helena. "Are you ready?"

"Yes," said Helena.

"I'll be as quick as I can," said Florian and then looked around. "Find her something to bite down on."

Gladys searched the room. She rummaged in a wicker basket on the table and pulled out a long leather strap with a padded section and small holes in it. It looked like a sex toy that the Marquis De Sade would use.

"My Shetland grannie's knitting belt. Will it do?"

"Perfect!" said Florian.

Liz offered Helena the brandy. She took another long slug. Gladys handed her the knitting belt. Helena pushed the padded part between her teeth. Liz and Gladys took each of Helena's hands.

"Ready?" asked Florian.

Helena nodded. Florian quickly made a horizontal slit across Helena's abdomen. Helena gave out a muffled scream as she bit down. Florian sliced again and cut through to the womb. "I can see the head!"

Florian handed the bloody knife to Liz. Florian carefully pushed several fingers into the open wound and the top of the baby's head appeared. Helena shuddered. Florian manoeuvred around to make sure that the umbilical cord was free from the baby's neck. Helena let out a muffled scream.

"Sorry!" said Florian, and moved another hand into the wound. The baby's head and shoulders came out of the wound. Florian took a grip under the tiny arms and gently lifted the baby out of the womb. The doctor placed the bloody baby onto Helena's chest.

"It's a girl!" said Florian.

Helena spat out the belt and clutched her baby as Florian removed the placenta.

"Cut the cord!" said Florian to Liz, who was in a bit of a daze, standing with the bloody knife.

"Och!" said Florian, grabbed the knife off Liz and cut the cord. The baby started screaming.

Gladys took the baby from Helena and gave it a clean with a towel, as it continued to bawl.

"Here's your beautiful baby girl," said Gladys as she handed the cleaned baby back to Helena.

"You might want to bite down again," said Liz as she held out the belt. Helena gave the baby back to Gladys and bit down on the belt. Liz fished the threaded needle out of the water and handed it to Florian.

Liz felt queasy as she watched Florian quickly stitch up Helena's uterus. How was she ever going to be a doctor? At one point Helena passed out with the pain. In a few minutes all the stitches were in place. Helena was in a half-asleep stupor. Gladys had cleaned up the blood and was rocking the baby in her lap. Florian covered up Helena's lower half with a towel.

Florian looked in the medical bag and pulled out a small rubber tube.

"What's that?" asked Liz.

"A catheter," said Florian and turned to Helena. "I'm going to insert this into your bladder to drain urine so you won't have to move." Helena nodded. "If you could raise your knees please." Florian quickly inserted the catheter. "There that's it. Well done! You can put your knees down." Florian stood up. "Well I'd best be off. Try to keep as still as possible. We don't want those stitches to split. I'll come back tomorrow morning to check on you and if you're able to move around without too much pain then we'll take it out."

"Oh thank you doctor," said Helena.

Florian nodded to Helena and then looked at Gladys and Liz. "Let me know at once if any more bleeding starts." Liz and Gladys both nodded. Gladys handed the baby to Liz.

"I'll show you out doctor," said Gladys.

"Goodnight ladies," said the doctor and left with Gladys.

Liz smiled down at the baby. "Have you got a name for her yet?"

"I think I'll call her Flora, after the doctor," said Helena. Liz gently placed the baby onto Helena's chest.

"Hello Flora," said Helena. She looked up at Liz. "Could you fetch the children? I'd like to introduce them to their new baby sister."

Liz smiled and went off to the drawing room. Edgar was seated in a corner reading a newspaper. The children were sitting silently on the floor. Liz could see that they had been crying.

"I heard Mummy screaming!" said Tabitha.

"Your mother is in pain but she's going to be alright. You have a new baby sister," said Liz.

"Oh!" said Milton.

"A sister!" gasped Tabitha.

"Can we see her?" asked Milton.

"Yes but you mustn't stay long. Your mother is very tired and if she is to get better she needs rest," said Liz.

The children looked up at their father. He nodded. Tabitha and Milton rushed past Liz, out of the room.

Liz stared across at Edgar. "What did you do, hit her?"

"A girl!" Edgar shook his head.

"What happened?" asked Liz.

Edgar Hughson tapped the tobacco out of his pipe and got up out of his chair.

"Don't you dare question me in my own house, you're dismissed!"

"What?" asked Liz.

"Get your things and get out of my sight!" snapped Edgar.

"Too right I will!" said Liz. She marched out of the drawing room and slammed the door shut behind her. What an idiot! She went to her room and packed her bag. There really wasn't that much to pack anyway. As Liz folded her brown dress there was a knock at the door. "Yes?"

Gladys opened the door. "What're you doing miss?"

"He sacked me," sighed Liz.

"But you helped to save the mistress!" said Gladys.

Liz shrugged and tied the belts on her travel bag.

"I suppose I questioned his authority. Oh well."

"What will you do now?" asked Gladys.

"I really don't know but please look after Mrs Hughson," said Liz.

"I'll try," said Gladys. She came over and gave Liz a hug.

"Say goodbye to the children for me," said Liz as she broke off from the hug. She picked up her bag and went out the door, down the corridor and out the front door.

She didn't look back as she made her way up the track towards the bridge. Liz walked out into the middle of the Bridge of Sighs and looked down on Dean Village. What a mess she had made of things. Poking her nose in other people's affairs and now what was she going to do? It would be so easy to just jump off and end the struggle. She put down her travel bag and peered over the railings.

"Miss?"

Liz turned round. Milton was holding out her umbrella.

"You forgot this."

"Oh!" said Liz. She took the umbrella from him and gave him a hug. Milton was a wee bit embarrassed, not used to hugging.

"I'd best get back. Don't worry I'll look after Mummy," said Milton.

"You do that!" said Liz.

"Bye!" said Milton. He waved, ran along the bridge and back down the track to Dean Village.

Liz picked up her bag. She straightened herself up and tucked her umbrella under her arm. She marched up the hill. In half-an-hour she'd crossed the New Town to the Old Town. She went up to the door of Fifteen Buccleuch Place, a four story Georgian sandstone building, and pulled on the bell. Sally, the rather untidy young maid, opened the door.

"Miss Moliette?" said Sally.

"Is Miss Patel in?" asked Liz.

"Yes. Come in," said Sally. She opened the door wide and ushered Liz into the spacious hall with really awful wallpaper. Liz followed Sally up the grand staircase. They reached the landing and a series of doors. Sally went to the end door and knocked on it.

"Miss Moliette to see you miss!"

Amuyla opened the door and saw the look on Liz's face.

"What's wrong?" asked Amuyla.

"Can I stay with you tonight?" asked Liz.

"Of course. Come in and tell me about it," said Amuyla. She ushered Liz into her room.

She turned back to Sally, who was hovering at the doorway.

"Sally be a dear and make us tea."

"Yes miss," said Sally. She rushed off.

Over a pot of Earl Grey, Liz related the events of the evening to Amuyla.

"I'm very impressed with this Dr Florian Blyth of yours," said Amuyla. "I've only heard of that procedure being successfully carried out a few times."

"Yes and I just froze like an idiot! You know it's nothing like working on a cadaver. All that blood," said Liz. "I don't know if could be a doctor."

"Don't be stupid. Of course you can! And you stood up to that pompous Mr Hughson," said Amuyla. "I thought it would be different here, but it's not. We can't vote. The man is always in charge. We have to change this!"

"But how?" asked Liz.

"Have you heard of the Suffragette movement?" said Amuyla.

"No. What's that?" asked Liz.

"It's about empowering women. A friend in London went along to one of their meetings. We should attend one," said Amuyla.

Liz sighed. "It's a great idea but I'm so busy studying that I couldn't take anything else on at the moment."

"Fair enough. Perhaps once we graduate?" said Amuyla.

"If they let us," said Liz.

There was a knock on the door and Sally came in.

"Is there a spare room going here?" asked Amuyla.

"Yes, I think Mrs Randers was expecting someone but they cancelled. I could ask but she's just retired for the evening," said Sally.

"Don't worry, I'll speak with her in the morning. Miss Moliette is going to stay over with me tonight," said Amuyla.

"Very good miss," said Sally. She gathered up the teapot and cups onto the tea tray. "Is there anything else I can get you?"

"No thank you Sally. Good night," said Amulya.

Sally left the room and closed the door behind her.

"But I have hardly any money. Not enough for a deposit anyway," said Liz. "I'll have to go back to London."

"No you don't!" said Amuyla. "I can loan you the money until you get on your feet again."

"Oh I couldn't do that," said Liz.

"Look I'm being selfish too you know. I don't want to be the only woman studying here,"said Amuyla.

"Thank you!" Liz sighed.

"Don't worry about it. Anyway it's about time to go to bed," said Amuyla.

"Well thank you. I'll sleep on the settee," said Liz.

"No. There's plenty of room in my bed," said Amulya. The women got undressed and changed into their nightdresses.

"You have that side," said Amulya. Liz got into bed. Amuyla crossed the room and put out the gaslight. She got into bed. "I hope that you don't snore."

"I don't think so," said Liz.

An hour later Liz was still wide awake. She was finding it difficult to sleep with Amuyla's snoring.

***

Campbell checked his pocket watch by a gaslight on Regent Terrace. Twelve thirty a.m. He turned off the pavement at Greenside Parish Church and made his way to the steps leading up Calton Hill. There were no lights on the steps but it was a clear night with plenty of moonlight. On one side was a high stone wall that backed onto private gardens and on the other was a steep slope covered in bushes. Campbell meandered up the steps. Towards the top he saw a figure leaning against the wall. Campbell ambled past the man, who had a cap pulled down, hiding his face. Campbell felt excited. He went up the steps for another twenty feet then stopped. He leaned against the wall and took out his pipe. He pushed a bit of tobacco into it and lit it with a match. He took a draw on the pipe and looked back down the path. The man was still there. He was definitely on the trawl, thought Campbell. After a few seconds the man slowly came up the steps. He stopped level with Campbell.

"Got a light?" asked the man.

Campbell thought that the voice sounded familiar but he couldn't place it. He handed the man his box of matches. As the man struck the match to light his pipe Campbell suddenly got a glimpse of his face. It was fellow pupil Wilton Grimes with his blond hair and athletic build. At the same time Wilton recognised him.

"You!" said Wilton. "What you doing here?"

"Same as you," said Campbell.

"Oh well," said Wilton. He handed the box of matches to Campbell and took a drag of his pipe. He reached out and rubbed Campbell's crotch. He unbuttoned the flaps of Campbell's trousers. He slipped his hand in and took hold of Campbell's penis. Despite his personal dislike for Wilton, Campbell couldn't help be turned on and he began to stiffen. Wilton chuckled and bent down on his knees.

It was all over in a minute.

Wilton got up and wiped his mouth with a handkerchief. "See you around." He walked off up the steps.

Campbell buttoned up his flaps. The usual feelings of guilt flooded his mind as he walked back down the steps.

***

In the morning Amulya went downstairs and introduced Liz to her landlady Mrs Randers.

"Where do you come from?" asked Mrs Randers, a neatly dressed big woman.

"London," said Liz.

"Oh I thought maybe one of the colonies. We had a girl from Barbados last year, although the least said about her the better," said Mrs Randers. "Anyway I was saving the room for someone but they haven't turned up. Come and see it."

Amulya and Liz followed Mrs Randers up the stairs to a door on the landing above Amulya's room.

She unlocked the door and ushered the women in. It was a lovely spacious room with tall windows overlooking the back garden.

"Five shillings a week, includes a breakfast and an evening meal. There is a small separate charge for laundry," said Mrs Randers. She paused to think. "What else?" She nodded to herself. "Rules. The main door is bolted at nine p.m. If you need to stay out later you can be assigned a pass key. No male guests under any circumstances. We have our reputation to think of."

"It's a beautiful room," said Liz.

"Thank you. There is a small deposit and one month's rent in advance," said Mrs Randers.

"I'll pay that for now," said Amulya. "Miss Moliette will pay me back when she gets the wages for her new job."

"A job, I thought you were a student?" asked Mrs Randers.

Liz tried to think of something quickly.

33

"Oh just some private classes. Some fellow students need extra maths tuition."

"Don't you take maths too seriously. Look at that Countess Lovelace. Some mathematician she was. Frittered away the family fortune betting on horses!" said Mrs Randers. "Anyway the room's free if you want it."

"Yes thank you," said Liz.

"Breakfast will be served in the dining room shortly," said Mrs Randers. She went off back downstairs.

"I'll see you down at breakfast. I've got a few notes to go through. Remember we've got that anatomy exam today," said Amulya.

"I almost forgot about that!" said Liz.

Liz didn't take long to unpack her belongings. She made her way downstairs and Sally showed her to the dining room. Amulya was already at the table eating a plate of kippers and reading the local newspaper *The Reekie*.

Amuyla looked up when Liz came in. "Perhaps you could get some tutoring work? Campbell said that a few of his classmates were struggling with their maths."

"I'm not sure how a female tutor would go down with them. They're not all as liberal as Campbell," said Liz. "Besides I'm nowhere as good as you in maths."

"I'm sure before they came here they probably had women tutors, you know governesses," said Amulya.

Liz shrugged.

"I'm not looking forward to this anatomy exam," said Amulya.

"Why, I thought you enjoyed anatomy?" asked Liz.

"No, it's not that. When I was in the library yesterday I overheard that Wilton Grimes talking about some demonstration planned for today *"to show females their place"* he said."

Liz said, "He's just peeved that he's to share an exam class with women. What a prat!"

Chapter 5   Jack

The extinct volcano of Arthur's Seat floated above the haar creeping across Duddingston Loch. A murder of crows flew over the soft mist, swooped down and alighted onto the gnarled yew tree, next to the Innocent Railway tunnel. Below, a bald man in plain clothes, carrying a battered leather satchel, scampered along the railway line and disappeared into the mouth of the tunnel.

Once inside the tunnel the man, Jack Fox, slowed down to let his eyes adjust to the gaslight. He moved purposely up the tunnel, glancing back every few yards. Finally he was satisfied that he had found the exact position. He knelt down on the iron rails and opened up his satchel. He withdrew a sketchbook, a tin of pastels and a wee rag. He quickly thumbed through his sketchbook and came to a blank page. He picked up a pastel and began to sketch out the scene, the semicircle of light in the distance outlining the blackened stone walls of the tunnel. He grinned maniacally as he drew a demonic figure crawling down the walls. A light scuffling noise sounded behind him. He turned around and peered down the tunnel. Some of the gaslights further down were out. Probably just rats, he thought. He liked rats. People said they were dirty creatures but they were wrong. He'd tamed one back in his cell. Called it Percy. It was probably missing him now. This was the time that Percy was usually fed. A few oats rolled in mutton fat.

Jack raked through his box for a vivid cadmium red. He found it and began to fill in the demon's eyes. A shudder shook the rails. Jack quickly finished the eyes. He grabbed a cerulean blue and briskly crosshatched the sides of the tunnel. The tremor of the rails increased. This must be what it's like in those countries where they have earthquakes, he thought.

Outside, the crows flew off the yew tree as a steam train sped past, their squawking protests drowned out by a tooting whistle.

The train rushed into the tunnel, blocking the light. Another swift stroke of pastel and Jack threw himself back against the sides of the tunnel. The train swooshed past, the noise of brakes squealing in his ears. Jack grinned as he examined his sketch. The best one yet! Suddenly a strong rough hand reached out from behind and clamped over his mouth and nose. Jack was pulled back. He struggled to remove the hand but it wouldn't budge. He tried to wedge around to see his attacker but he was held in a vice-like grip and his air was running out. He was being burked. The word sprung up into his dying mind. Burked as in Burke and Hare, the body snatchers. The method Burke had used to smother his victims. Jack's last thought was of his rat Percy looking at him with his wee hungry eyes. Where are my oats rolled in mutton fat?

Lachie checked for a pulse on Jack's throat. Satisfied that his victim was dead, Lachie hiked the corpse over his shoulder and carried it out of the tunnel. He looked around but couldn't see much through the haar. He noticed a dark shape to his left, a clump of gorse bushes. He headed round the back of the bushes and laid the body on the ground, face up. He took a sack from his shoulder and pulled out the surgical knife. It was a real beauty and he had no intention of giving it back to the doctor when the job was done. He bent down and closed Jack's eyes. Staring eyes bothered him when he had to do his work. A few deft slices removed the scrag around the neck and he was able to get a good view of the bones that made up the cervical vertebrae. He slipped the knife in between the joints and decapitated the body. He lifted up the head and popped it into his sack. Lachie rubbed his bloody hands in a patch of dry grass. He got up and looked around. There was no one in sight but the haar had reduced visibility to thirty feet anyway. He listened out for sounds of anyone approaching. It was all very quiet. He hoisted the sack over his shoulder and went back down round the bushes. He crossed onto the railway line and looked back to the tunnel.

He laughed. "Innocent Railway. They'll have to give it a new name." Lachie moved off the tracks and into the woods.

We Can Do This. © David Hutchison.

Chapter 6   Riot

A dirigible, advertising *MacLeod's Ouija Boards*, passed across the sky and was swallowed up by the persistent haar. Like a hungry spectral feline the chilling sea fog licked the tops of the fine buildings, hunting for treats. It stealthily twisted around the classical columns of Surgeons' Hall towards the chanting crowd below.

"No doctresses! No doctresses!"

A tramp tipped out a wheelbarrow of turf clods onto the pavement. Eager students scrambled to gather up the dirt, to use as missiles.

Liz and Amulya stood on the opposite side of Nicolson Street and faced the crowd. Liz glared at the protestors. She recognised some of her fellow students; white male privileged types. It looked as if they'd brought in reinforcements, wastrels bribed with cheap drink no doubt, judging by the state of some of the men.

She scanned the crowd. Was that Wilton Grimes, posh runt of the litter? Yes! Look at the dimwit. Lifting his *No Doctresses* placard up and down, conducting the chanting crowd.

Liz thought that perhaps she should feel scared. After all a rowdy mob of men stood between her and her goal. But Liz was too angry to be scared. Years of growing up in the orphanage had taught Liz how to look after herself. After all had not the *Edinburgh Seven*, women pioneers Sophia Jex-Blake and her group of female students, marched through a barricade, a riot at this very same spot a few years ago?

Liz tapped her umbrella on the cobbled road and turned to Amulya. She looked scared stiff, her anxious brown eyes seemed to swallow up Liz.

Liz channelled up her anger and gathered up her strength, "We can do this!" She grabbed Amulya's hand. "Think of the *Edinburgh Seven*!"

Amulya whimpered, "But I'm not brave like them."

Liz squeezed Amulya's hand. "Nonsense. We can do this!"

Amulya gulped, "I'm ready."

As Liz and Amulya were about to step down from the pavement a horn blasted and a horse drawn tram rushed past.

"Idiots!" the driver cursed at the women. Liz shook her umbrella back at him, "Idiot yourself!"

"Liz!" Amulya patted Liz on the shoulder.

This time Liz made sure to look both ways along the road. She grabbed Amulya's hand again and they stepped off the pavement. They marched across the road. Wilton moved forward and waved his placard to block the women from the gates to Surgeons' Hall. Some of the crowd held up clods, ready to pelt the women.

Reporter Hector Findlay, early thirties, blond beard, suddenly darted in front of Wilton and his crowd. Hector was never without his beloved pen and notebook, and these he brandished in the air like weapons.

"Please let me take a note down of the names of you brave gentlemen. *The Reekie* will endeavour to print your names on tomorrow's front page," declared Hector.

Hector moved forward. "Now who's first? Master Grimes is it?"

Wilton swore under his breath and moved to the side. The crowd reluctantly parted as the women moved through them towards the tall wrought iron gates set in a sandstone portal. Liz tried to open the gates but they were locked. Wilton barged past Hector and spat on Liz's back.

"Foreign whores!" he snarled at Liz and Amulya.

Liz turned and brandished her umbrella. "How dare you! You toe rag!"

Wilton held up the wooden placard and tried to hit Liz, but she fenced him off with her umbrella. Hector grabbed onto Wilton. Wilton turned and punched Hector in the face. Hector stumbled. Wilton went to punch Hector again but this time Hector grabbed Wilton's fist and twisted his arm.

Wilton screamed, "You bastard!"

Some of the crowd began to throw clods. One knocked off Amulya's hat. Hector picked it up and handed it back to her.

"Thank you sir," said Amulya as she shook the dirt from the purple feathers.

Campbell darted from The Surgeons' Hall building and rushed through the formal gardens to the gates. He fumbled with the key. The lock was notoriously stiff. It gave way ungraciously and Campbell wrenched the gate open with all his slight might.

"Come on, come on!" shouted Campbell as he ushered the women and Hector through the gates. Some of the crowd tried to pass through but together Campbell and Hector managed to force the gate shut again. Campbell locked the gate and smiled, just as an earth clod hit him on the chest.

"Who did that!" screeched Campbell. He glared at the crowd.

Wilton peered through the bars of the gate at Campbell and winked. Campbell scowled back. Hector quickly picked up the clod and rubbed it in Wilton's face.

"Who's laughing now!" grinned Hector.

"Bastard!" shouted Wilton.

Hector turned and followed Campbell and the women through the garden towards the main door of the building. They entered through the impressive door into a hallway. Portraits of prominent surgeons looked down on them.

"Oh thank you Campbell and Mr?" said Liz.

"Hector Findlay of *The Reekie*," grinned Hector. "It was my pleasure." He took Liz's hand and kissed it. Liz nodded and said, "Liz Moliette."

Amulya held out her hand, "I'm Amulya Patel." Hector winked at Amulya and kissed her hand. Amulya blushed.

Campbell cleared his throat. "Hurry ladies. The exam is about to start!"

As Liz and Amulya rushed up a staircase to the exam hall, Hector shouted, "I hope to speak to you later. I'd like to write an article on women in medicine for my paper."

Amulya waved but Liz pulled on her arm and they both disappeared through a door on the landing.

"I'm Campbell Prebble. Maybe I can fill you in? I've been chaperoning the ladies for a while now. There are still a few of us male students that are gentlemen." He held his hand out. Hector shook it firmly and grinned.

"I do think that we should wait until the crowd disperses," said Campbell.

"Yes that's probably a good idea," said Hector.

"I'll show you some of the collections, if you like," asked Campbell.

"Yes! That would be most helpful for my article," grinned Hector.

"Body parts or instruments?"

"Oh body parts first!" replied Hector.

"I see. A man after my own heart," laughed Campbell.

"Follow me then," said Campbell. He patted Hector on the shoulder. Campbell went down a corridor and up a staircase to the next floor, followed by Hector.

***

Light flooded down from the ornate circular window in the ceiling of the Playfair Hall. Yet more ubiquitous portraits of learned men adorned the pale blue walls. Invigilator Dr Love looked up from his desk as the women came through the doorway.

"Ladies we were just about to start. I'm glad you could make it!" said Dr Love. Behind him around forty male students sat at desks with papers face down in front of them. Most of the students grimaced at the women. Liz and Amulya headed for some empty desks at the front.

Dr Love stood up and strutted out from behind his desk. He looked up at the ornate clock on the wall. He paced back and fore in front of his desk as he gave out instructions. "Ladies and gentlemen, please turn over your papers. You have two hours. No talking or conferring. Anyone finished early please hand your paper to me and leave quietly as not to disturb the other students. Thank you."

Liz turned to smile at Amulya but she was already engrossed in the exam. Liz looked around the room. She caught Dr Love's eye and he smiled at her. She smiled back and turned over her paper. Yes he is very handsome, thought Liz, but really she should be more interested in his supposedly extensive book collection. She suppressed a giggle. Anatomy wasn't her best subject. It had taken some effort to get the anatomy classes organised that she and Amulya had needed. The university had not let the women have mixed classes. Some of the students, especially that Wilton Grimes and his Professor Atticus, had come up with ridiculous excuses. *"It would be immoral to allow women in mixed classes. They would be corrupted by seeing a naked man,"* and other such nonsense. Especially when you took into account that women could already attend mixed anatomy classes in other countries. Luckily Liz had found a private lecturer willing to give classes to her and Amulya. But at a cost. Liz would have to find some way of paying back Amulya. The grant from the orphanage was really stretched. If money hadn't been a problem she'd have surely bypassed Edinburgh and gone straight to study in Paris or Dublin where they seemed more willing to take on female students. Only the previous year the famous *Edinburgh Seven* had left. The original first female students had gone abroad to finish their studies after the university had reneged on their commitment to let them graduate. The hope that Liz and Amulya kept in their hearts was by the time it came for them to graduate that the university would have seen sense. Anyway it was no use thinking of that now. She told herself to stop daydreaming and get on with the task in hand. Liz looked at the first question and attached diagram. She panicked as she tried to remember the names of the different bones that made up the human hand. She always got mixed up between distal and proximal phalanges.

***

Hector followed Campbell down the corridor. "Are we lost?" said Hector.

"It's just round the next corner," said Campbell. Sure enough round the corner Campbell stopped at a door. He took out a key and unlocked it.

"Here we are!" said Campbell as he ushered Hector into the small room. The room was dark, until Campbell lit a gas lamp. The light showed up a dusty display case at the far end of the room. Hector walked across and peered into the case. He turned at the sound of the door locking behind him.

"Why did you do that?"

"I don't want us to be disturbed," shrugged Campbell.

"Whatever's in this case must be very secret then," retorted Hector as he rubbed the dust off the case. "But this is empty!" Hector turned to Campbell and was shocked when Campbell pulled him towards him and kissed him full on the lips. Hector pulled away. "What the hell are you doing?"

"Don't be such a coward. I could tell you liked me straight away," grinned Campbell. "No one can see us."

Hector was silent for a few seconds as he stared at Campbell. Suddenly he grabbed Campbell and kissed him back. Kissing passionately they frantically undressed each other in a whirlwind of pent up lust.

***

Dr Love glanced at the clock.

"Ladies and gentlemen, your time is up. Please put down your pens. Remain seated while I collect your papers!"

There were sighs and fidgeting amongst the examinees. Liz turned to Amulya and they shared a smile.

Dr Love marched down the rows of desks, his shoes made an echoing tapping, as he collected the papers. He returned to his desk and locked the papers in a drawer.

Dr Love said, "You are free to leave now."

Amulya got up and ran across to the window. She peered out across the garden and towards the gates. The place was clear of rioters. She went up to Liz.

"They've gone!" said Amulya. "It's safe to go."

Dr Love came across to Liz. "Can I have a moment of your time?" he asked.

"Of course," said Liz. She turned to Amulya and said, "I'll catch you up."

"Fine. I'll get you outside," replied Amulya as she headed off out of the exam room.

The hall was suddenly empty apart from Dr Love and Liz. He came up to her.

"I was meaning to ask you, are you able to help out with my free surgery on Thursday?" enquired Dr Love.

"I should be able to. Where is it?" asked Liz.

"At the seamen's mission in Leith. It's at the back of the Custom's House," said Dr Love. "Dinner afterwards?"

Liz beamed, "That would be nice, Dr Love."

"Please, there is no one here so just call me Paul," laughed Dr Love.

Suddenly the door was flung open and Professor Atticus barged in. A stringy tall man in his seventies, his pupils were hugely enlarged, giving him a haunted look. Liz thought, he's been at it again. It was an open secret at the university that the professor had a predisposition of experimenting with poisons on himself. Liz raised an eyebrow at Dr Love.

The professor gave Liz a disdainful shrug as he strode up to Dr Love.

Liz said, "I'd best catch up with Amulya," and quickly made her escape. Professor Atticus looked back at her as she left, as if she were something distasteful that had stuck to his shoe.

"Professor, can I help you?" asked Dr Love.

The professor stared at Dr Love, as if in a daze.

"Professor Atticus?"

Professor Atticus snapped out of his trance. He pulled out a piece of paper from his pocket and thrust it at Dr Love.

"Those infernal female students should have never been allowed to matriculate. I'm gathering a petition to send to the senate. Will you sign?" The paper wobbled in the professor's quivering hand.

"No!" Dr Love shook his head.

"Why ever not my good man?" bemoaned Professor Atticus.

"The women make exceptional students. Consistently outperforming the men," said Dr Love.

Professor Atticus replied, "Become midwives or nurses, yes, but doctresses. Did you know that the female's brain weighs four ounces less than the male's?"

The professor's eyes seemed to become even darker. He began to shake.

"Are you feeling alright professor?" asked Dr Love.

The professor wiped his eyes with a handkerchief. He held out the paper to Dr Love again but Dr Love shook his head.

"Pah!" grumbled the professor. He thrust the paper into his pocket, turned and stomped off in the huff.

***

The haar had lifted at last and the midday sun shone down into the courtyard of the Edinburgh Medical School. Liz followed Amulya across the cobbles.

Midway across Amulya grabbed Liz's hand and said, "So is Dr Love living up to his name?" She winked at Liz.

"Don't be ridiculous! He wanted to see if I'd help at one of his surgeries again," replied Liz.

"Oh?"

"And asked me to dinner after!" Liz grinned.

Amulya laughed.

"No really. It's not like that at all! I've heard that his book collection is astounding."

Amulya laughed. "Pull the other one!"

Liz grinned.

Amulya shrugged. "So dinner at his house?"

"I assume so," said Liz.

"Then you'll meet his sister," said Amulya.

"I didn't know he had a sister," said Liz. "He's never mentioned her. What's she like?"

"I've never met her before but I've heard she's some sort of invalid. A rare bone disease. Never goes out. Poor thing," said Amulya.

The two women walked across the courtyard and up the wide stone steps into the foyer. Several male students were gathered around the notice board where the latest mathematics exam results had been published. One of the students with a particularly nasty gurn on his face spat on the ground in front of Amulya. Liz rapped her umbrella on the stone floor and stared at the man.

He said, "Come on boys. It smells like a whorehouse here." The men moved off.

Amulya was biting her nails. "Forget about them," said Liz. "I'd be surprised that they could even read the board, let alone pass an exam."

Amulya cheered up and smiled. They searched across the board for their results.

"I passed!" shouted Amulya.

"Well done!" shouted Liz.

Amulya found Liz's results and pointed to them. "You're going to be the first woman to win the Hope Prize!"

"Me?" asked Liz.

Amulya ran her finger up and down the scores on the board. "See. The highest score!"

"Yes!" Liz brandished her umbrella in the air. It just missed Professor Atticus as he marched past.

"Sorry!" said Liz.

The professor scowled and paused, was about to say something, thought better of it, and pranced off. Liz tried not to laugh when she looked across and saw Amulya grinning.

Liz moaned, "I could really do with the prize money though. I still owe you that money I borrowed for the rent."

Amulya shook her head, "Don't worry about it. Let's celebrate! How about I buy you a birthday lunch?"

Liz suddenly realised that she'd almost forgotten that it was her birthday. Money worries were starting to blind her to everything.

"I'm sorry I can't. Got to see the administrator. How about if I see you back here for the Hope Award ceremony in an hour?"

"Alright," agreed Amulya.

Liz marched off down the corridor. Amulya had a look at the other notice boards. Stuff on lodgings and that sort of thing. Then she spotted an advertisement for an interesting job. She read it, looked around to make sure no one was watching her and unpinned it.

***

Liz knocked on the door of the administration office.

"Enter!"

Mr Krimi nodded to Liz. As she sat down he put on his lunettes and opened up a ledger. He searched down a list of figures.

"Miss Moliette, you are a term behind with your fees!"

Liz frowned, "But the orphan fund have always paid up before. Have you contacted them?"

Mr Krimi nodded. "I wrote to them several weeks ago and have had no reply. I'm afraid if the fees aren't paid by the end of the week you'll have to leave."

Liz said, "What am I going to do?"

Mr Krimi shook his head and said, "I'm sorry. I can't help you."

***

Amulya was waiting for Liz at the notice board when Campbell appeared.

"Hello Amulya. Did you pass?" grinned Campbell.

"Yes. So did Liz. In fact she got the top marks!" replied Amulya. "You're looking awfully pleased with yourself. Did you pass too?"

Campbell shrugged. As he turned to look at his mathematics results Amulya saw that the back of his trousers and jacket were covered in dust.

"I passed!" exclaimed Campbell.

Amulya used a handkerchief to rub the dust of the back of his jacket.

"What are you doing?" Campbell turned around.

45

"You've got dust or something all over your jacket. Here you'd better do the backside of your trousers," said Amulya.

"I must have been hit with a clod there too," laughed Campbell.

"That reporter, Hector Findlay was interesting. Did he say when he wanted to interview us?" asked Amulya.

Campbell took out a card. "This is his address. He asked me to give it to you."

Amulya smiled and took the card.

Liz appeared over Amulya's shoulder. "Who's the card from?"

"It's Hector's. I mean Mr Findlay the reporter. Remember he said he wanted to interview us?" said Amulya.

"Come on let's go or we'll miss the ceremony!" said Campbell.

Campbell and the two women rushed out of the foyer and down the steps.

The main courtyard has been laid out with chairs facing a flower bedecked platform at the far end. Most seats had already been taken but there were some free at the back. Liz, Amulya and Campbell settled down in the back row. Campbell took out a tiny pair of scissors and began to trim his nails as they waited for something to happen.

Professor Atticus walked up to the platform and addressed the crowd. "Gentlemen..." he looked at the ladies in the crowd, "... ahem... and ladies. We are here again to award the Hope Prize. As you know it is the prize for the student with the best marks overall for the past year. It is a money prize but of course the prestige is priceless. Anyway without further ado we'll get onto it. Gregor?"

An eager young man ran up to the platform and handed an envelope to the professor. He ripped it open.

Amulya grabbed Liz's hand and grinned.

Liz smiled and closed her eyes. Let it be me! Let it be me!

"And the Hope prize this year goes to... Wilton Grimes!" exclaimed Professor Atticus.

Liz snapped open her eyes. She angrily tapped the ground with her umbrella as the crowd clapped.

"Wilton Grimes! Even I've beaten that toady in mathematics," stated Campbell, in disbelief.

"Unbelievable! I looked at the board. You had the most points Liz!" exclaimed Amulya.

"That prize money would have paid off my fees!" said Liz.

Wilton jaunted up the steps. He shook the professor's hand and was handed a certificate. He held it up in the air to the crowd. He beamed a smile across directly at Liz.

Sickened to the heart, Liz stood up. She marched out of the courtyard, quickly followed by Amulya and Campbell.

"Let's go to the Green Man. I need a drink after that!" said Campbell,

"Yes, I'll come for one, as long as you don't mind having to sit in the patio area with a woman?" said Amulya.

"Course not!" said Campbell.

Amulya grinned.

"Oh I nearly forgot. Here!" Amulya handed the job note to Liz. "Dr Blyth's looking for an assistant."

"Dr Blyth?" asked Liz as she read the note.

"I had him for a class last year. He's rather pompous but he knows his stuff," said Campbell.

"Since Dr Bell's left he's taken on his police work as well as the extra lectures. Any use?" asked Amulya.

"Any use! I'm off to see Dr Blyth right now. He's the one that did the caesarean operation on Mrs Hughson. Unless there are two Dr Blyths in Edinburgh!" exclaimed Liz. Her head swam. It would be an amazing experience. And police work too. She'd heard about forensics. It was something that she'd wanted to specialise in since ever thinking of doing medicine. Not only a doctress but a police surgeon.

"I thought the name sounded familiar," said Amulya.

Liz scanned the address. "I'll catch up with you later." With that Liz sped off down the corridor.

***

A body lay on a marble table. Dr Florian Blyth, sleeves rolled up, cut around the skull with a scalpel. There was a knock at the door. Florian ignored it and carried on with the cut. There was another knock at the door.

"Blast!" Florian threw down the scalpel, crossed the room and wrenched the door open.

"Yes! What is it?" the doctor quipped.

Liz got a whiff of an unpleasant smell emanating from the room. Perhaps this wasn't such a good idea? "I'm here about the assistant's position," she said meekly.

"Oh! Wait? I've met you somewhere before haven't I?" asked Florian.

"I'm Liz Moliette."

Florian looked Liz up and down. There was definitely something familiar about this young woman.

"We met at Mrs Hughson's," said Liz.

"Oh of course, I recognise you now!" Florian nodded without smiling, but let Liz in.

"How is Mrs Hughson?" asked Liz.

"She's doing well. The baby too. I saw them this morning."

47

Florian stepped aside and let Liz into the lecturer's office/dissecting room.

"Can you draw?" Florian asked Liz.

"I've done the odd still life. Flowers mostly," said Liz.

Florian dragged a stool across the room to the corpse on the table. Florian patted the stool.

"Sit!" commanded Florian.

That got Liz's goat. "I'm not a dog!" she said, under her breath.

"Sorry, I thought you wanted the assistant's job? Your trial starts now!"

Liz grimaced but she sat on the stool. It crossed her mind that it might be like the fat falling into the fire. She brushed that thought aside. The doctor rummaged in a drawer and handed Liz a board, a piece of paper, ink and a fountain pen. Florian looked at Liz's gloved hands.

"I think you'd draw better without your gloves," declared Florian.

"Of course," muttered Liz. As she removed her gloves Florian noticed a mark on Liz's right thumb. All of a sudden Florian became rather breathless and flustered.

"It's stuffy in here." Florian went to the window, opened it and took in a few breaths of fresh air. Florian closed the window. "To work!" Florian strode back across the room and picked up the scalpel. The doctor removed the top of the skull and examined the brain tissue.

Liz felt a bit squeamish but she took a few deep breaths and got over it. The doctor was too engrossed to notice.

"Tumour on the frontal lobe as I suspected! Draw this bit here and take notes," said Florian.

Liz started to sketch the brain.

***

Several hours later it was getting dark so Florian lit a gas lamp. Florian gathered Liz's drawings and tacked them up on a wall. Six drawings of the skull and brain with notes.

Florian stood back and stared at the wall. "You won't be asked to paint the Sistine Chapel any time soon but they will suffice. So why do you want to be my assistant?"

"Because I eventually want to be a doctor," said Liz. "I've always imagined my father would have wanted me to be one."

"Oh and is he a doctor?" enquired Florian.

"I don't know. I'm an orphan. I never knew my parents," said Liz. "I don't even know my family name. The orphanage named me after the wife of a benefactor."

Liz was almost certain that Florian was blushing.

"Are you alright Dr Blyth? Shall I open the window?" asked Liz.

"No, no. Thank you I'm fine. It's rare to meet a woman that wants to be a doctor, or should I say doctress? "said Florian.

"Either is fine by me. I've heard some actresses like to be called actors. Anyway I'm not hopeful they will ever let women graduate here," sighed Liz.

"Yes. It was shameful how they treated Miss Jex-Blake and her group," replied Florian. "Why didn't you try Paris or even Dublin? You can graduate there."

"Money. That's why Amulya and I stayed on. Well not Amulya. Her parents wanted her to study in Edinburgh. Anyway we thought by the time we finish they'd have sorted out graduation for women," replied Liz.

"Amulya?" Florian lifted up the brain with a large pair of forceps and placed it into a jar.

"My housemate and fellow student," grinned Liz. "She told me about this job."

There was a sharp rap on the door. Florian nodded to Liz. She went to the door and opened it. Professor Atticus stood in the hallway, holding up a pen and his noxious petition. The professor barged past Liz into the room.

"What is she doing in here? This is no place for a woman!" screeched Professor Atticus.

"Can I help you?" asked Florian.

"Dr Blyth. I need you to sign this petition. The female students are causing utter chaos. It must be stopped!" declared Professor Atticus.

"Yes, it must be stopped!" said Florian.

Liz looked on in despair. She found it hard to take in. Why had he caved in so easily?

The professor smiled and held out the petition. Florian batted the paper away.

"Yes! This persistent misogyny must be stopped!" shouted Florian.

Florian gestured to the wall of brain sketches and turned to Liz. "You passed the trial."

"That's wonderful!" gasped Liz.

Florian turned to the professor. "Meet my new assistant, Miss Moliette!"

The professor had most of his teeth but if he had had false ones that would have been the point where he swallowed them. He stomped out of the room, leaving the door swinging open. Florian went and closed it.

"Did you see his pupils? Dilated. Experimenting with poisons again no doubt!" said Florian.

"That would explain it... what would you like me to do now?" asked Liz.

"That's it for today. We'll work out a proper timetable around your studies tomorrow. I also help out as a police surgeon but that's as when I'm needed so I don't want to bother you with that for the moment," said Florian.

"It sounds exciting," gasped Liz, "a police surgeon."

"It has its advantages," shrugged Florian.

Liz smiled. She put on her outdoor coat and hat. "I'm going to catch up with some friends at the Green Man. If they're still there that is." Liz picked up her trusty umbrella.

"Oh! That's my local. I might pop in for a quick tipple later," exclaimed Florian.

Chapter 7   Mugging

At the top of Crichton's Close in the Old Town a man waited in a doorway, his face hidden in shadow. Lachie Merry in a long black coat, bag draped over his shoulder, crept up the close, keeping to the shadows, away from the gaslight. He stopped half way up and scanned around.

"Psst!" hissed the man in shadow.

"Ah!" murmured Lachie. He headed towards the man and held out the sack. "As you ordered sir."

The man's hand reached out for the bag. Lachie pulled the bag back.

"The money first!"

The man threw a wee bag of coins at Lachie, who then handed over the sack. The man disappeared into the night.

Lachie eagerly opened up the bag and poured the coins into his palm. "Yes!"

***

The Green Man was fairly bustling. The usual crowd of fiddlers fiddling around a blazing fire. Lachie had bought them all a drink and they were playing his favourite reel *Tam Lin*. He was a bit tiddly and happy, tapping his fingers to the beat. He threw some coins from the bag onto the counter and bought another whisky. Diamond Lou, a mature prostitute who'd seen better days, eyed up the coins. She jostled up into the space next to him.

"It's so stuffy in here," she crooned. She leant up against Lachie. "I feel so hot!"

Campbell went past with a tray of drinks, out the doors to the patio garden at the back and to a table where Liz and Hector sat. Campbell held up his glass and toasted Liz.

"Happy birthday Liz!"

"Happy birthday!" shouted Campbell.

Hector clinked his glass with Liz and Campbell. Florian appeared with a drink in hand.

"It's your birthday?" asked Florian.

Liz nodded. Florian was momentarily dazed.

"Many happy returns!" said Florian

"Thank you! Move up Campbell! Dr Blyth come and join us. You look as if you could do with a seat," exclaimed Liz.

***

There was a moaning sound from a doorway up South Gray's Close. Was it a cat in heat? No it was Diamond Lou and Lachie doing a knee trembler. She overdid the fake groaning a bit. Lachie climaxed and moaned. Diamond Lou pushed him off and pulled down her skirt. She rushed off down the close. Merry leant against the wall, panting, trying to get his breath back. He wiped the sweat from his head with his hand. He looked in his pocket for a handkerchief but couldn't find one. He suddenly remembered about his bag of coins. He frantically searched all his pockets. He realised that Diamond Lou had robbed him.

"Bitch!" he cried.

He ran down the close and into the main street, but she had vanished.

***

A dimly lit large stone cellar with a long wooden table in the centre, covered with medical paraphernalia. Along one wall rows of shelves were blocked off into compartments, each filled with a skull. There were four spaces left, one of them occupied by a sleeping cat called Pickle, a plump black and white moggie. A pan bubbled on a gas stove. A man's hand reached forward and turned the gas off. Forceps lifted the skull from the pan onto a tray. A hand dried the skull with a cloth.

Pickle rushed out of the way as the skull was placed in one of the adjoining empty spaces. The man spoke to the cat, "Pickle! We'll have to get you a nice box or something. These compartments will be filled up very soon." The cat miaowed as if in agreement.

His hand flipped through a sketch book of hand-drawn skulls with notes and came to a blank page. The hand filled a fountain pen with ink and then began to sketch the skull.

Pickle came up and tried to get between the sketcher and the skull, as cats do.

"Pickle!"

52

Liz Tries to Examine Florian's Wound. © David Hutchison.

The Green Man had shut and most of the punters had already headed off home along the empty urban canyon of the Cowgate.

"I think you're going in my direction," said Campbell to Hector. "Yes, quite close by in fact," smiled Hector.

"Well I go the same way as Dr Blyth," said Liz.

"Goodnight all!" said Hector.

"Night!" said Campbell.

"Night!" said Florian and Liz, in unison.

Hector and Campbell stumbled up the road together. Liz and Florian headed down the Cowgate. The cobbles were a bit mucky and not all the gaslights worked so they made their way slowly down the hill.

"So have you enjoyed your first day as my assistant?" enquired Florian.

"Yes, I very much...ahh!" gasped Liz as Lachie stepped out of the darkness brandishing a knife.

"Gie's your money!" grunted Lachie.

Florian quickly moved in front of Liz. "Away with you!"

Lachie lunged and stabbed Florian in the chest. Florian gasped and fell to the ground. Lachie bent down and snatched Florian's wallet. Liz lashed out with her umbrella and knocked off Lachie's hat. He grabbed his hat and ran off.

"Dr Blyth?" cried Liz. She got down on the ground beside Florian. Blood was pouring from Florian's chest. Liz tried to unbutton Florian's shirt.

"No! Don't!" gasped Florian.

"Don't be stupid! I need to check the wound" said Liz. She tried again to open Florian's shirt but Florian grabbed her hand.

"I said no!" gasped Florian.

"Alright!"

An empty carriage came towards them. Liz stood up and flagged it down. "We'll get you to the infirmary," said Liz.

"No! Take me home," exclaimed Florian.

The driver got down and helped Liz to take Florian into the carriage.

Fifteen minutes later they arrived at Florian's town house off Causewayside. The driver helped Liz take Florian up the steps to the imposing front door. Liz pulled on the bell knob. Charles Okora, a black manservant in his fifties, opened the door. A small white dog, a Westie Jack Russell cross, shot out and jumped up on Florian.

"Down Psyche!" gasped Florian.

"In God's name what's happened?" asked Charles.

"He was mugged. Stabbed!" exclaimed Liz.

"Thank you, I can manage now," said Charles as he took over from the driver. He and Liz helped Florian into the hallway, which smelt of beeswax and lavender. Charles set Florian down in a chair.

"Miss Moliette you can go now. Charles will attend to me," said Florian.

"But look at you. I should really take a look at that wound!" exclaimed Liz.

"It's just a scratch. Charles will dress it."

"But what if you need stitches?" complained Liz.

"Charles can cope," said Florian.

"Alright but I'll come and see how you are in the morning," said Liz. She was fuming but tried to stay calm.

Charles showed her to the door. Liz walked down the steps as the door closed behind her. She walked off down the street.

Charles carried Florian up to the bedroom. He helped her to sit on the edge of the bed. He removed Florian's jacket and bloody shirt. Florian's chest was bandaged up with towels. Charles quickly unwound a towel.

"Careful!" said Florian.

"Sorry," said Charles. He carefully unwound the next towel. He used a clean rag to clean the blood off Florian's obviously female breasts and around the wound which was below the left breast.

Florian touched her wound and flinched. "I was lucky. Another inch and it would have got my heart."

"It doesn't look too bad. The towels helped," said Charles.

"You'll need to stitch it," said Florian.

"Do I have to?" asked Charles.

"Oh! I'll do it but go and boil some water first," said Florian.

Charles rushed off and came back several minutes later with a small iron pan of steaming water. Florian took a swig of brandy. She dipped a needle and thread into the water and began to sew up the wound.

"Arrgh!" yelled Florian.

"I'll do it!" said Charles.

He took over from Florian and pulled the thread through the first stitch. Florian grimaced. Charles made two more stitches.

"Arrgh!"

"Sorry nearly done dear," said Charles.

Florian took another swig from the bottle. Psyche barked once and then settled down. Charles did one more stitch. He took out a pair of scissors and cut the thread. He put the scissors down on a side table.

Florian looked down at her wound. "Not bad."

Charles said, "Needlework is not my forte."

Florian handed Charles a clean bandage from her bag. Charles wound it around her chest and fixed it with a pin.

"There!" exclaimed Charles. He kissed Florian. "Oh wait!" he said and gently peeled off her fake moustache. Charles bent forward and kissed Florian again.

"Ah, that's better!" he exclaimed.

"Charles?"

"What?"

"That girl Liz, my new assistant..?"

"What about her?" asked Charles.

"I think she's our daughter!" exploded Florian.

"Our daughter? How?" gasped Charles.

"Do you remember when I went to the Crimea?"

"Yes you wouldn't let me go!"

"On the way I discovered that I was four months pregnant."

"What!"

Charles got up and paced back and fore across the room.

"I don't believe this!" he exclaimed.

"So I stayed in London. Had the baby."

"Why didn't you tell me? Didn't I have a say in this?" said Charles.

"I'm sorry," said Florian. "What could you have done about it anyway?"

"I don't know. But you should have told me!"

Charles took the brandy. "I need a drink!" he took a swig of brandy.

"Give me a sip!" said Florian.

Charles passed the bottle to Florian.

"How did she find you?"

"She didn't. She doesn't know," said Florian.

"Are you sure that she's our daughter? I can't believe that I'm saying this. Our daughter!" said Charles.

"Yes!" said Florian. "She has a birthmark on her thumb. Same as my baby's."

Charles shook his head. "It could be a coincidence."

"I gave her up eighteen years ago, today, as soon as she was born. It's her birthday today," said Florian.

"You'll have to tell her!" said Charles.

"How can I?" sighed Florian. "Come to bed. I'm shattered."

"You must be joking. I'm sleeping in the spare room," grunted Charles.

He stormed out of the room and shut the door. Psyche looked up at Florian and gave a wee yelp.

"At least someone loves me," sighed Florian as she patted the dog.

The door opened and Charles popped his head in. Psyche jumped off the bed and rushed across the room and out of the door. Charles pulled the door behind him. Florian sighed.

Charles Sews Florian's Wound. © David Hutchison.

Liz turned into Buccleuch Place towards her lodgings. Her head was buzzing. What was it with Dr Blyth? Surely he wasn't sexist or he wouldn't have given her the assistant job? There was definitely something strange. She walked up the steps to the door of Fifteen Buccleuch Place and pulled on the bell.

After a short wait the door opened. "Oh it's you miss!" said Sally.

Liz thought that Sally seemed more nervous than usual. "Evening Sally. Anything wrong?"

"No miss." Sally stood aside and Liz entered the ample hallway. Liz went up the stairs to the open landing on the second floor. She tried to open her bedroom door but it was locked. Sally came up the stairs. "Mrs Randers emptied out your room miss. Foul mood she was in. Said she was worried that you couldn't pay the rent."

"What?"

"Someone told her you'd lost your funding," said Sally.

"Who?"

"I don't know miss."

"But I do have a job now," said Liz.

Amulya came out of her bedroom on the landing below. Liz came down to her.

"I gave Mrs Randers what money I had on me but it wasn't enough," said Amulya.

Sally said, "I've put your things in the room under the stairs. Mrs Randers says you can stay there until the rent is paid."

"Under the stairs?" sighed Liz.

"Sorry miss. You'd have been out on the street if it hadn't been for Miss Amulya," retorted Sally.

Liz thought of all the worse places that she'd stayed in her life and tried to shrug it off.

"Thanks Amulya. I'll pay you back," said Liz.

"Sorry I couldn't stay to celebrate. I had a headache. Did you catch up with Hector? " said Amulya.

"He walked Campbell home. We were mugged, Dr Blyth and me. He was stabbed!" said Liz.

"Oh how exciting! Sorry, I mean is he all right?" said Sally.

Liz shrugged. "I think so."

"Did you not check or take him to the hospital?" asked Amuyla. "And you, are you alright?"

Liz said, "I'm fine. But it was very strange. He wouldn't let me examine the wound."

Amulya said, "I'm really sick of these men who think we can't be doctors!"

Liz shook her head. "No, he's not like that. He gave me the job."

"But that's wonderful!" said Amulya. "So did they catch him, the mugger?"

"I don't think Dr Blyth wanted any fuss!" said Liz.

"But surely he should report it?" asked Amulya.

"I'll catch up with him tomorrow," said Liz. "Anyway I'd better see this room."

"It's not too bad. Let's have a look!" said Amulya. She started down the stairs. Liz and Sally followed. They reached the bottom of the staircase. Sally opened the door of the tiny room under the stairs. Liz got an overpowering waft of lemon oil.

"I gave it a proper clean out," said Sally, proudly.

The room was very small. Just enough room for a single bed and a tiny dresser. Liz's belongings were piled up on the bed. Liz tried to open the tiny window.

"It doesn't open miss. Sorry," said Sally.

Liz cleared a space on the bed. "It's not so bad."

"Sorry Mrs Randers wouldn't let me share my room with you," apologised Amulya.

"Me too!" sighed Liz. That Mrs Randers was a real scrooge, she thought.

"Sally. Have you got a file?" asked Liz.

"I bite my nails miss so I don't have much use for one," replied Sally.

"No, not a nail file. One of these things for filing metal down," said Liz.

"Oh there might be one in the toolbox in the cellar miss. I think I saw the gardener fixing the railings last week. Do want me to see if it's there miss?"

"Yes please Sally," smiled Liz.

"Whatever do you want a file for?" asked Amulya.

Liz just smiled.

***

It was a right dreich morning. Old Mrs Grey was walking her wee dog Bobby around Duddingston Loch. The path was rather muddy and Mrs Grey, not too firm on her feet even on a dry summer's day, was taking her time. The Skye Terrier was excitedly straining on the lead.

"Bobby. Stop pulling!" commanded Mrs Grey but the dog gave another tug and the lead was jerked out of her hand. The wee rascal shot off the path down to the loch side and scattered a family of ducks.

"Heel Bobby!" commanded Mrs Grey. But it was a forlorn hope. Bobby always did exactly what he wanted. The dog ran off to explore some gorse bushes near the Innocent Railway tunnel. Mrs Grey sighed and hobbled her way up to the bushes.

"Bobby! Heel!"

Bobby had found something and wasn't coming out. The dog barked in excitement.

"Bobby. Have you caught a poor wee rabbit? You bad dog!" Mrs Grey made her way around the bushes. She stood on something soggy, damn! She looked down. A man's hat, covered in mud. Bloody tramps everywhere, she thought. She shuffled round a bit more. Then she saw it sticking out of the bushes, just as a train passed on the track. A man's body, beheaded. Bobby was licking the ruddy neck stump.

The train's shrill whistle drowned out her scream.

Chapter 8   The Alienist

Dr Emrie, chief alienist at the Edinburgh Lunatic Asylum, was an overweight gentleman in his early sixties, with a shiny bald pate. His small silver-framed glasses made his blue eyes look huge as he looked out his window at patients working in the garden below. Behind him diagrams of the human brain vied for space on the high walls between overflowing bookcases. There was a knock on the door and Nurse Steeple, a tall thin woman in her forties with a severe face and red hair, entered with Dr Love.

"Dr Love to see you," said Nurse Steeple. She picked up a tea tray off Dr Emrie's desk.

"Sir?" said Dr Love.

"Ah Paul. Have a seat!" said Dr Emrie.

"Would you like more tea?" asked Nurse Steeple. Dr Emrie looked across at Dr Love, who shook his head. "No thank you dear," said Dr Emrie. The nurse left with the tray. Dr Emrie took a pipe from the desk and lit it. He took a puff and said, "It's been hectic. One of our patients has escaped again."

"Oh, who?" asked Dr Love.

"You've studied him before. The artist," said Dr Emrie.

"Artist?" asked Dr Love.

"The cat painter," said Dr Emrie. He nodded to a small painting of a ginger cat on his wall.

"Ah yes. Jack Fox! I've one of his cat paintings too. I hope that you find him."

Dr Emrie nodded." He usually comes back in a few hours so it's worrying that it's been longer. Anyway what can I do for you?"

"Your letter?" said Dr Love.

Dr Emrie put down his pipe. "Of course. I forgot. Now where is it?" He rummaged through a pile of letters on his desk and pulled one out.

"Ah! Here we go. An unexpected cancellation at the Royal Society! A free lecture slot this Monday. Will I put your name forward?"

"Less than three days away! I don't know if I'll have all the specimens collected by then," said Dr Love.

Dr Emrie shrugged. "The last time a space came up was over two years ago. Grasp the nettle firmly!"

"Yes indeed! Do put my name forward!" exclaimed Dr Love. He opened his case and removed a book. It had a fancy leather cover, embossed with a phrenology head and the title "Outlines of Phrenology". He handed the book over to Dr Emrie. "Thank you for the loan of it. Spurzheim has some excellent theories."

"Quite so!" said Dr Emrie. He got up and looked through his bookcase. He pulled out a thick tome.

"But I prefer Combe's System of Phrenology," stated Dr Emrie. "Would you like to borrow it?"

"You lent it to me back in spring," smiled Dr Love.

"Oh yes. I quite forgot," said Dr Emrie.

Chapter 9   Carnousty's Boarding House

A shaft of light beamed through the half-opened wooden shutter, illuminating the mess of discarded clothes crumpled on the floor of Campbell's bedroom. Hector and Campbell lay entwined on the bed, sleeping. Hector was snoring.

There was a knock at the door and a rattle of the door handle. Hector woke up. He shook Campbell awake.

"Mr Campbell. Breakfast!" shouted Lucia Carnousty, the formidable sixty year old matriarch and owner of the Queen Street guest house.

Hector quickly slid out of the bed and onto the floor. Campbell got up and dragged on his quilted velvet dressing gown. Hector crawled under the bed. Campbell checked that he was out of sight, then opened the door. Lucia marched into the room like she owned the place; which she did.

"Why did you lock the door Master Campbell? Do you think I'm going to rob you? This is not a den of thieves!" exclaimed Lucia.

"To preserve my modesty Mrs Carnousty," smiled Campbell, as he sat on the bed. Lucia put the tray down on the bedside table next to him.

"Ain't nothing that I've not seen already Master Campbell," said Lucia. She crossed the room, flung open the shutters and pulled up the window. "It smells like a brewery in here!"

Lucia turned and stared at the pile of clothes strewn across the floor. She tapped a pair of black leather boots with her foot and picked one up.

"New boots? They must have cost a pretty penny?"

"I was given them yesterday. A present for my birthday," stammered Campbell.

"Oh many happy returns Master Campbell! I didn't know it was your birthday," said Lucia. "If I'd known I would have organised a little party, a soiree. I like to make all my lodgers feel at home."

"No thank you. It's not my birthday yet. In a few months. My mother kindly sent them in anticipation of my birthday," said Campbell.

"I think she got the size wrong. Compared to your other shoes," said Lucia. She tapped a brown shoe lying on the floor. She picked it up and compared the sizes of the sole of the shoe to the boot. Very different sizes.

"Thick socks. She loves to knit me thick socks. That's why she always gets me a size too big. Her socks are wonderful. Striped ones to go with the colours of my dressing gown." Campbell rummaged in a drawer and pulled out a pair of thick purple and light blue striped socks. He held them against his purple dressing gown with the light blue satin trim. "See!"

"Very fetching I'm sure." Lucia crossed the room back to the door. Under the bed, Hector was itching to sneeze. He stuffed a sock over his nose.

"You'd better eat your porridge before it goes cold," said Lucia. She was about to go out of the room when Hector couldn't hold back anymore and sneezed. Lucia turn around.

"What was that?" asked Lucia.

Campbell made a pathetic attempt at a cough. "I think I'm coming down with a cold."

Lucia made as if to come closer. "Or maybe it's the flu," said Campbell. Lucia backed off. She tutted, went out of the door and pulled it closed behind her.

Hector popped his head up from under the bed. Campbell shook his head. Sure enough the door opened again and Lucia looked in.

"Oh I forgot! I've got a séance on tonight so the parlour is out of bounds," said Lucia. "Unless you want to join in. I could give you a special rate?"

"That's alright. I'll probably go to the library later anyway," said Campbell.

"Do you need any laundry done?" enquired Lucia.

"Not today thank you Mrs Carnousty," said Campbell. He got up and went to the door.

"Good morning," he said as he closed the door on her. He turned the key in the lock.

"Phew!" gasped Campbell. He threw himself onto the bed. He rolled over, pulled himself to the edge of the bed and looked down. Hector wriggled his head and shoulders out from under the bed.

65

Campbell moved forward and rested his hands on the floor. He leaned down and nuzzled against Hector's blond beard.

"Do you really have to go to work today?" asked Campbell.

"Yes." Hector wriggled out from under the bed. He picked up his jacket from the floor and flopped down onto the bed next to Campbell. He gave Campbell a kiss then sat up. He took a silver pocket watch from his coat.

"It's stopped again. Doesn't matter how many times I wind it," sighed Hector.

"Come here!" Campbell pulled Hector back down and snogged him. Hector sat up.

"I've got to go," Hector said. "I'll be late!"

Campbell got up off the bed. He crossed over to the dressing table and felt in a pocket of his jacket which was draped over a chair. He pulled out his pocket watch by the tartan ribbon attached to it.

He handed it over to Hector. "Borrow mine until you get yours fixed," said Campbell.

"Thanks," said Hector. He opened it up and read the inscription. *"To Campbell Angus Prebble on his eighteenth birthday. Always laugh when you can. It is cheap medicine."*

Campbell said, "Byron."

"Come here!" said Hector. They started kissing again.

Chapter 10 Innocent Railway

A large crow glided above the grimy High Street and swooped down to its favourite perch, a gaslight next to the police station. PC Urquhart, an earnest young man with curly brown hair, whistled as he ran up the steps. The crow flew off. Urquhart pushed through the main door, nodded to Sergeant Wills on the desk, went round the side and knocked on Inspector Frazer MacLeod's door. He didn't wait, but went straight in. The Inspector was holding a framed photograph of his wife. His green eyes welled up with tears.

"Damn it Urquhart. Don't just barge in!" The Inspector wiped his eyes.

"Sorry, I did knock sir," apologised PC Urquhart.

Inspector MacLeod put the photograph down. "What is it?"

"Sir! A body's been found at the Innocent Railway. Mutilated sir." PC Urquhart whistled.

"Suicide. Hit by a train?" asked the Inspector, stroking his red beard and bushy moustache.

"I don't think so sir. The body wasn't found on the tracks, but behind bushes at the entrance to the tunnel," replied PC Urquhart.

"A train at speed can throw a body pretty far." The Inspector rose and pulled his long coat on. "Ask Dr Blyth to meet me at the Innocent Railway tunnel."

"Yes, sir." PC Urquhart whistled sharply and sprinted off out of the office.

***

After the recent shower the wet cobbles glistened. Liz thought they looked pretty. She slipped on a clump of fresh dung as she crossed the street but managed to steady herself with her trusty umbrella.

"Murder, murder. Read all about it!" shouted a wee boy holding out a clutch of newspapers on a street corner. He tried to thrust one into Liz's hand. She shook her head and turned off Causewayside, down a cul-de-sac towards Dr Blyth's town house.

Visiting in the daylight, she could now see that the area was pretty. Not nearly as nice as the New Town, but way better than anything she'd ever be able to afford. Even though at the moment she was demoted to the room under the stairs, she still remembered when she'd first come to live at Buccleuch Place. A water closet and gaslight, such luxuries. Separate bedrooms, clean sheets.

Liz reached the entrance to Dr Blyth's town house. She climbed the worn steps, pulled on the doorbell and waited. She was about to try the doorbell again when the door was opened by Charles. He looked worn out and gave her a strange look, as if he was seeing her for the first time.

"What is it Charles?" demanded Liz.

Charles blinked, "Nothing, miss." He held the door open. "Come in."

"How is he?" asked Liz, as she entered.

"Stubborn. In other words, back to normal," grinned Charles. He held out his hands and Liz gave him her hat and umbrella. He placed them on the stand. On the previous visit Liz had been too distraught to take in the surroundings. This time she noticed that the hallway was full of macabre prints. She recognised some interesting ones by French anatomist Jacques Fabien Gautier d'Agoty.

"Come this way! He's in his study," said Charles.

Liz followed Charles down the corridor. She passed what looked like an original flayed penguin drawing by William Henry Fisk. Charles knocked on a door.

"Come in!" called Florian.

Charles opened the door and said, "Miss Moliette to see you, sir." He gestured for Liz to enter.

The study had a long ornate desk next to a window overlooking a misty Arthur's Seat in the distance. One wall was lined with bookcases, another with glass-fronted oak cabinets filled with anatomical specimens floating in jars and skulls of various animals, including one of a human. Dr Florian Blyth was lying on a velvet chaise longue next to a small fire. On the mantelpiece a stick of incense gave out a sweet vanilla smoke that rose above to a collection of African masks. Psyche sat on Florian's lap. The dog jumped down and yapped as Liz came into the room.

"Thank you Charles. Come here Psyche! Sit down dear," said Florian, indicating a set of Queen Anne chairs embroidered in hunting scenes. Liz smiled and sat down in the one nearest to the fire.

"Make us tea would you, Charles," said Florian.

"Certainly sir," nodded Charles. He pulled the door closed as he left.

Liz took off her gloves, bent down and patted Psyche. She looked up at Florian.

"How are you, Dr Blyth?" asked Liz.

"Charles patched me up. I told you he would," said Florian. "Come here Psyche." The dog returned to its master.

"You lost a lot of blood," said Liz.

"It wasn't as bad as it looked. I've got a cracked rib and a few small cuts. That's all," said Florian.

"I still think I should have a look at it. An infection might take hold," said Liz.

"Please stop making a fuss, my dear. I'm absolutely fine. Nothing that a few days rest won't cure," grunted Florian.

"Oh well doctor, if you're sure," shrugged Liz.

There was a knock at the door and Charles entered. "There is a policeman here to see you," said Charles. Psyche growled and shot up to the door.

"Here Psyche. Here!" commanded Florian. The dog rushed back and hid under Florian's chaise longue. A whistling sound came from the corridor.

"Some guard dog you'd make!" said Florian. "Well, show him in then."

Charles nodded and PC Urquhart marched into the room.

"Beg your pardon sir." He nodded briefly to Liz. "Miss."

"What is it?" asked Florian impatiently.

"The Inspector needs you," said PC Urquhart.

"Does he, what for this time?" asked Florian.

"A nasty murder. In Holyrood Park," stated PC Urquhart.

"Charles, my woollen overcoat please!" Florian rose out of the chair. "Arrgh!" moaned Florian.

Psyche yelped. Florian slowly sat back down.

"Dr Blyth, are you okay?" asked Liz.

"My rib's giving me gyp. I need to rest for a while yet," said Florian. Charles picked up a tartan rug from a chair and brought it over. He placed it over Florian's legs and chest.

"Thanks Charles," smiled Florian.

"I could go instead!" piped up Liz.

"But it's a body!" said PC Urquhart.

Florian stared at Liz and nodded, then looked up at PC Urquhart. "Miss Moliette is my new assistant. She's perfectly capable."

"But she's a woman!" said PC Urquhart.

"And?" asked Florian.

PC Urquhart blushed. "Well it's just that the body's not a pretty sight, if you know what I mean sir. Fair gruesome it is. Mutilated!"

Liz tried not to show how mad she was getting, "As a medical student I've seen dead bodies before. I've even cut them up and examined them."

PC Urquhart gave out a whistle. "We'll be having police women next, miss."

"Wouldn't that be a good thing?" retorted Liz.

"I suppose so miss. I never really thought about it. Anyway sorry if I've caused offense. I'd be pleased if you'd come along and give us your medical opinion," said PC Urquhart.

Liz smiled and nodded. "Of course."

"Right. I'm glad that's settled. Charles would you show our guests out. Oh and if you could take Psyche out for a walk. I'm going to take forty winks," sighed Florian and smiled. Charles nodded but did not smile back.

"Come on dog!" said Charles. Psyche ran up to Charles. Liz and PC Urquhart followed Charles and the dog out of the room.

***

Dr Love's office in the Medical School was extremely neat and fastidiously clean. Plain oak panelled walls, a walnut sideboard, oak desk and two Edinburgh chairs. The only ornament was on the sideboard, a taxidermy glass dome displaying a mongoose in the act of killing a cobra. Dr Love looked across at Lucia and couldn't help comparing her to the mongoose behind her. But that meant that he was the snake. Unhappy with the thought, he got back to the matter in hand. He pulled out a money box from a drawer in his desk. He placed it on the table. Lucia's greedy eyes lit up. Dr Love took a key from a chain at his waist and unlocked the box. He counted out five florins and passed them across the table.

"I think that's what we agreed on Mrs Carnousty," said Dr Love.

"Oh yes, thank you," beamed Lucia as she quickly picked up the coins and slipped them into a small tapestry purse. "I can't think why you'd want to know about them."

"As I said, it's for my research," said Dr Love.

"These sodomites disgust me. But what can I do? I need lodgers. My séances don't bring enough money in. Perhaps I could arrange a séance, special discount of course, for you and a small group. No more than six people at most. The signals get too confused with more than that," said Lucia.

"That's very kind of you Mrs Carnousty but I'm a man of science. I don't think it would be appropriate for me to partake in such an event," said Dr Love.

Lucia got up and went towards the door. "Well if you change your mind let me know. I do get a fair share of academics. Thursday evening is séance night. Well, most Thursday's unless I'm away visiting my sister," said Lucia.

"Oh wait! Where are Master Prebble and his companion now?" said Dr Love.

Lucia stopped in the doorway. "As I said I didn't see his companion. Master Prebble is usually to be found at the library at this time."

"Thank you Mrs Carnousty," said Dr Love. Lucia smiled and went out the door.

***

PC Urquhart whistled a tuneless ditty as he and Liz walked through Holyrood Park. It was turning into a beautiful day. The clouds had lifted and Arthur's Seat was clear. They passed a flock of sheep grazing on the glistening slopes of Salisbury Crags. Going uphill in a corset was hard going and Liz was glad to have short rest on a bench when they reached the south end of the Radical Road.

Rested, they moved downhill towards the strange rock formation of Adam's Ribs and then veered off down towards Duddingston Loch. They headed down a path towards the south entrance of the Innocent Railway tunnel. As they neared they saw Inspector MacLeod bend down and examine something in the bushes. Next to him a rotund middle-aged man, Archie Porter, was setting up some sort of wooden tripod. Liz tried to overtake PC Urquhart. He grabbed her arm. "It's an ugly site, it is miss."

Liz tapped her umbrella on the ground. She felt like whacking him across the arm but she restrained herself and stared at the policeman. PC Urquhart gave out a nervous whistle and let go of her arm. Liz walked around the bushes and came upon the body lying on the ground. The Inspector was examining the neck of the headless corpse while Archie was bolting a bulky camera onto the tripod.

"Good morning," said Liz.

"Morning," said Archie.

The Inspector ignored her as he rifled through the victim's pockets. "Nothing!" exclaimed Inspector MacLeod. He stood up. "Can we get one of the general position of the body and then one close up of the neck?" said the Inspector to Archie.

"On it!" said Archie. He adjusted the lens.

Liz bent down and examined the body. "The head was removed post mortem," she stated.

"And who are you?" Inspector MacLeod stared at Liz.

"Liz Moliette. Dr Blyth's new assistant. He sent me as he's indisposed," replied Liz.

"Indisposed?" asked the Inspector.

71

"Dr Blyth was mugged last night. Stabbed in the chest," said Liz.

"Damn! How bad is he?" asked the Inspector.

"He seems to be recovering," said Liz.

"Seems?" asked the Inspector.

"He wouldn't let me attend to the wound," said Liz.

Inspector MacLeod nodded. "Florian can be stubborn. So he sent you along to help. Do you have any medical training?"

"I'm almost on my second year as a medical student," replied Liz.

"I thought all the female students had left," said the Inspector. "Something about not being allowed to graduate?"

"Yes, the first group left. I'm hoping that by the time I come to graduate that they'll have sorted it out. I couldn't afford to go and finish my degree abroad," said Liz. "So who's the victim?"

The Inspector sighed. "No idea. We've not found the head."

"Stand back please!" said Archie. He lifted the dark cloth at the back of the camera, pulled it over his head and took a photograph of the body.

"Done" He removed the camera and adjusted the height of the tripod and checked the lens.

Liz moved back to the body. "Judging by the amount of blood he was beheaded here," said Liz.

"You don't say! Can you give me something more helpful, like time of death?" asked Inspector MacLeod.

"Rigor mortis has set in so at least five or six hours. An autopsy could find out more," replied Liz.

"Excuse me," said Archie. He moved the camera and took a close up photograph of the severed neck.

Liz walked around the body.

"Inspector. Look at his shoes," said Liz. "Red mud. Where would that have come from?"

"The tunnel!" said the Inspector. "Perhaps he was attacked there. Let's have a look. Urquhart, stay with the body!"

The Inspector and Liz went around the side of the bushes and walked up to the mouth of the tunnel. As they entered the sooty smell clawed at the back of Liz's throat. She followed the Inspector as he slowly moved along the side of the track.

A little way up the tunnel the Inspector stopped and exclaimed, "Look here. A footprint!" Liz rushed up the tunnel and almost fell over. The Inspector caught her. "Careful miss!"

"Thank you Inspector. I should have worn more appropriate shoes," said Liz. She pulled herself from his arms. She looked down past the Inspector. Water dripping from the roof of the tunnel had created a small boggy patch of reddish mud, and right in the centre of it was a large footprint. Liz and the Inspector bent down and examined it.

"Bigger than the victim's foot," said Liz.

The Inspector nodded. "I count eight hobnails," he said. "Least that's some sort of clue. What do you think?"

"Yes and I'd say it was a size ten shoe so most likely a man," said Liz. "Could you stand here Inspector? Make a mark with your foot." The Inspector did as he was asked. "See how little your footprint goes down. The other footprint belongs to someone much heavier than you. I'd guess at least twice your weight," said Liz.

"Or!" exclaimed the Inspector, "someone carrying a body. So the victim was attacked, probably out of sight in this tunnel, then carried along here and then finished off in the bushes. Great! Let's look further up the tunnel."

As Liz and Inspector MacLeod slowly moved up the tunnel the rails began to shake. From the distance came a hooting sound. Liz and the Inspector quickly flattened themselves against the stone wall. A goods train shot into the tunnel. The noise was deafening as carts of coal whizzed past and the train disappeared down the tunnel. Liz sighed with relief.

"It would be easy to murder someone here. Just push them out in front of a train. I wonder why they took the trouble to take them to the bushes?" said the Inspector.

"They wanted the head intact for some reason," said Liz. "As a trophy perhaps?"

Inspector MacLeod and Liz walked the length of the tunnel but didn't find anything else of interest. They went back out of the tunnel. The Inspector got Archie to come and take a photograph of the footprint. PC Urquhart commandeered a horse and cart to transport the body to the dead house, a squat grim mortuary situated in the small graveyard next to the High Street police station.

Professor Atticus Tests Poison. © David Hutchison.

Chapter 11   Atticus

Professor Atticus's study had the prerequisite looming bookcases of medical tomes. Spaces between covered with diagrams of the human head and botanical prints. The fire was out and the room was damp. The professor went to the mantelpiece and removed the dropper from a tiny glass bottle of yellow liquid. A sharp unpleasant odour filled the air. He looked into the Regency mirror above the mantelpiece and dropped the yellow liquid onto his eye. He blinked and stared in the mirror. He replaced the dropper and picked up the bottle, crossed the room to his walnut desk and sat down.

He checked the grandfather clock on the wall and noted down the time in a leather-bound notebook. For years the professor had been obsessed with the link between different intoxicants and the functioning of the brain. He'd researched the ingredients that so-called primitive tribes had used to reach elevated states: the Incas and the coca leaf, the peyote and the Aztecs, the liberty cap and the Druids.

There was a knock at the door. He shoved the glass bottle and notebook into a drawer.

"Enter!" commanded the professor.

Daphne Blanc, the young housemaid, timidly entered and made an awkward curtsy. "Sir."

"Well what is it lass? Stop dithering!" said the professor.

"Excuse me, begging your pardon sir. Master Grimes is here to see you," stuttered Daphne.

"Well show him in lass!" said the professor.

Daphne ushered Wilton Grimes into the study, then she left. Wilton bowed. The professor impatiently gestured to a seat and Wilton flopped down. Suddenly the professor's face whitened. He turned and vomited into his wastepaper basket.

Wilton got up, walked behind the professor and patted him on the back. "Are you alright, sir?"

The professor sat up and brushed Wilton off. "I think it was the kippers." He wiped his mouth with his handkerchief. He clutched the bell pull and gave it a tug. Wilton went back and sat down.

"How did you get on with the petition?" asked Wilton.

"Eight signatures collected so far. That's out of the ten lecturers that I asked," stated the professor. "I've still a few more to ask."

"Oh who didn't sign?" asked Wilton.

"Dr Green. Struts around as if he owns the place just because his grandfather donated money to the university years ago," said the Professor.

"He's not that great a lecturer either," said Wilton. "Who else?"

"That prissy Dr Love. What a cheek he had! He actually told me that the women were intellectually superior to the men!" bemoaned the professor, "or words to that effect."

"Unbelievable!" gasped Wilton. He slapped the desk and the phrenology bust next to him fell over.

"Careful!" said the professor.

"Sorry sir!" apologised Wilton. He righted the statue.

"Ours is a thankless task. Saving the fair sex from unnecessary ugliness," sighed the professor.

"Exactly. What kind of woman would want to become a doctor? A midwife I can imagine. But a doctor. It's unnatural!" ranted Wilton. The professor nodded. "And anyway the university shouldn't be encouraging mulattos and orientals."

"Grimes! I do not approve of women doctors but I am no racist," said the professor.

Wilton was taken aback. "Sorry, I didn't mean to..."

There was a sharp knock at the door and Daphne entered. "Sir?"

The professor pointed to the wastepaper bin. Daphne gave him a *not again* look. She picked up the basket and left. The professor pulled his notebook from a drawer and thumbed through it.

"The women are taking another anatomy class at Surgeons' Hall tomorrow," said the professor.

"On a Saturday?" asked Wilton.

"Yes. Something to do with the exam hall being double booked. They shouldn't be allowed to sit these extra exams in the summer anyway," grunted the professor. He leaned forward. "It would be unfortunate if something were to happen to disrupt the class," grinned the professor.

Wilton smiled. "Most unfortunate indeed. I'll see what I can do!"

Chapter 12   Burry Man

Someone had crudely scrawled *"foreign whores"* in red paint across the front door of Fifteen Buccleuch Place. Luckily it was some sort of water-based paint rather than the oil-based one that had been used last time. Two days of scrubbing to remove it! Still, it was a hard job to remove and Sally silently cursed as she tried to scrub the words off. Her thoughts were interrupted by the persistent sound of a bell. Someone wanted her inside. She carried on scrubbing. The bell went again. Sally picked up the bucket and went down the stone steps, across the pavement and poured the dirty water into a drain. She went back up the steps, picked up the scrubbing brush and went inside.

In the dining room, Amulya dipped a toast soldier into the runny yolk of her egg, whilst she read a letter. She gulped the toast down and reached out for the bell pull just as the door burst open and Sally appeared with a pot of coffee.

"Where were you? I've be ringing you for ages!" snapped Amulya.

"Begging your pardon miss. I was washing the door down again," said Sally as she filled Amulya's cup with steaming black coffee.

Amulya put down the letter. "What was it this time? No don't tell me!"

"The same again, miss!" said Sally.

"I told you not to tell me!" sighed Amulya.

"Begging your pardon, miss I didn't!" replied Sally.

Amulya shrugged. "I must be going. Hector's asked me to accompany him to South Queensferry."

"Master Findlay. That's nice, miss," said Sally.

"To do an article on the Burry Man. I've always wanted to see the Burry Man!" grinned Amulya.

"That pagan thing. Miss! A grown man parading around in a bunch of burls. It's ungodly," said Sally. "Those folk at South Queensferry should be ashamed of themselves."

"Don't be so holier than thou Sally. You should see the amazing gods we have in India. For instance Ganesha with his elephant head or Lord Brahma with his four faces," said Amulya.

"Stop please!" said Sally.

Amulya laughed. "Did you sew the button back onto my outdoor coat?"

"Yes miss. I've laid it out on your bed," replied Sally.

***

Inspector MacLeod and Liz followed PC Urquhart and Sergeant Wills as they wheeled the body into the plain stone space of the dead house. Several bodies, draped in sheets were already laid out on tables at the far end. By the sickening ripe smell they'd been there quite a while. Urquhart and Wills lifted the body onto a mortuary slab.

"Anything else sir?" asked Wills.

"No thanks," said the Inspector.

Wills left. The Inspector showed Liz the cupboard where they kept what little equipment they had.

Liz removed the clothing off the corpse, helped by a reluctant PC Urquhart. The young constable became particularly uncomfortable when the man's body had all its clothes removed apart from the underwear.

"Miss, it seems wrong you doing this," muttered PC Urquhart.

"Nonsense!" snapped Liz as she removed the man's underwear. She picked up a small grey towel and placed it over the man's genitals. She them turned the body on its side and pushed a thermometer into the rectum. She grinned at PC Urquhart. He gave out a nervous whistle. Liz pulled the thermometer out. She noted the temperature and turned to Inspector MacLeod.

"Between eight and twelve hours," said Liz. She wiped the thermometer on a cloth.

"So you're saying that he died between four and eight p.m. yesterday?" asked the Inspector.

"Give or take a couple of hours," replied Liz.

"Any tattoos, distinguishing marks?" asked the Inspector.

Liz looked along the body. She turned it on its other side, then onto its back.

"Not that I can see," said Liz. She examined the body's fingers. "There is a little amount of blue residue under this fingernail. I don't know what it is."

The Inspector said, "Do an autopsy and see if there is... " Liz interrupted him. "I'm not qualified to do that. You'll have to wait until Dr Blyth is back."

"I thought you wanted to be a doctor. Here's your chance. I'm giving you permission!" said the Inspector.

"Sorry,"said Liz. "That's not how it works."

"Any idea of his age?" asked the Inspector.

"I'd guess between fifty and sixty. I can't be more accurate than that," said Liz.

She examined the neck closely. She got a rag and cleaned the edge of the wound. "The killer used a long knife, possibly a surgeon's knife. Some basic knowledge of anatomy. Cut between the vertebrae."

"A surgeon?" asked the Inspector.

"Possibly. A butcher perhaps," replied Liz.

"Anything else?" asked the Inspector.

Liz shrugged. Then she remembered something. "When I first arrived in Edinburgh, back in September, I'm sure there was something about a man found beheaded."

"Oh? Do you think it's connected?" asked the Inspector.

"I don't know. It might have been an accident or something," said Liz.

"I'll have a look in the police records," said the Inspector.

The door opened and Florian hobbled in, leaning on a walking stick.

"Inspector!" said Florian.

"Dr Blyth. How are you?" asked Inspector MacLeod.

"Dr Blyth, shouldn't you be lying down?" asked Liz.

"Pah! I couldn't stand being cooped up," retorted Florian as she went across to examine the corpse. "So whose body do we have here?"

The Inspector looked up from his notes. "Anyone's guess. No head and there's nothing to identify him in the pockets."

"A knife was used to remove the head," said Liz.

Florian examined the neck.

She opened a drawer and took out a surgeon's knife. "I agree. A surgeon's knife," exclaimed Florian and moved a finger along the knife, then stopped and pointed, "With a nick in it around here!"

"Are you implying that the killer is a doctor?" asked the Inspector.

"They did have some rudimentary knowledge of anatomy," shrugged Florian. Liz nodded her head in confirmation at the Inspector.

"I found some sort of blue residue under the left index fingernail," said Liz to Florian.

"Ah, let's see," said Florian. She examined the finger, bent down and gave it a sniff.

"Oil pastel!" said Florian. "An artist perhaps. Left-handed?"

79

Florian went across to the bench where the victim's clothes were placed. She opened out the jacket and unfolded the trousers. "Standard inmate's outfit, if I'm not mistaken!"

The Inspector came up to the bench and looked over Florian's shoulder. "Not at any prison I know of."

Florian shook her head. "No, not a prison. An asylum. If I'm not mistaken, the Royal Edinburgh Lunatic Asylum."

Florian suddenly grimaced and bent over. "Arrgh!"

Liz quickly brought over a chair and Florian staggered into it.

Florian gasped, "Thanks!" She took a few deep breaths and seemed to recover. "We should pay a visit to Dr Emrie."

"Dr Emrie?" asked Inspector MacLeod.

"The alienist who runs the asylum," gasped Florian. She took out a handkerchief and wiped her head. "On second thoughts perhaps I'll leave you two do the visit."

"Oh! Do you remember something about a beheading in Leith, back in September?" asked the Inspector.

"I wasn't the police surgeon then but I could contact Dr Bell?" said Florian. "Is there a connection?"

The Inspector shrugged. "Probably not but best to check it out."

"Will you be alright, doctor? Perhaps I should look at that wound?" asked Liz.

"A few drops of laudanum will suffice. Off you go!" replied Florian.

"Are you sure?" asked Liz.

"Of course. Now leave me be!" snapped Florian.

The Inspector said, "Miss Moliette would you accompany me to the asylum then?"

"Certainly Inspector," replied Liz.

"Righto! Let's go and see if the police carriage is available," said Inspector MacLeod.

Liz and the Inspector nodded to Florian. They left the dead house together.

***

The Firth of Forth sparkled in the glorious summer sun as ferries crisscrossed this busy stretch of water. There was an air of expectation in the picturesque village of South Queensferry. People bustled about getting ready for the festivities. Oyster sellers were setting up stalls as children helped their less agile parents hang bunting from trees.

In a leafy back garden voices came from an old wooden shed. Lachie Merry dropped silently down from a stone wall, into the garden and crept up to the shed. He ducked past the window, circled the shed until he found a small hole and peered through it. Inside, two young men, Bruce, long scraggy black beard and Douglas, clean shaven, were

80

helping their father Gabriel Aird to adorn his Burry Man costume. Gabriel stood in the middle of the cramped space, his arms outstretched. He was covered in green burrs; prickly seed cases from the burdock plant. Bruce slipped a balaclava over his father's head and tucked it in under the burr-covered cloth shirt.

"Ouch!" cried Gabriel.

"Sorry father," apologised Bruce as he removed the burr that had got caught between the balaclava and his father's neck.

"Here let me do it!" said Douglas. He pushed in past Bruce and accidently planted a burr on the balaclava over his father's cheekbone.

"Hey!" shouted Bruce. "I was doing fine." He glared at his brother.

"Aye right. Look at your hands. They're shaking! I told you! You shouldn't have drunk so much last night," said Douglas.

"Boys!" shouted Gabriel. "Let's get this done. We're running late. Bruce you go and check with your mother whether the garlands are ready!"

"Yes father," sighed Bruce. He went off out of the shed.

Douglas quickly covered his father's head in burrs, leaving the top of the head free. Bruce returned with two long stripped poles, beautiful flower garlands tied onto the end of each. He wore a bowler hat covered in flowers on his head.

"Here they are!" Bruce leaned the poles against the wall. He took the hat off and showed it to Gabriel.

"Your mother has done a braw job," said Gabriel.

Douglas tried to take the hat from Bruce. "I'll put it on him," said Douglas.

"No you won't!" snapped Bruce. He pushed the hat onto Gabriel's head.

Gabriel shouted, "Arrgh!" as a couple of burrs pressed into his scalp. "Be more careful!"

"See what you'd done," snapped Douglas. He carefully removed the hat from his father's head and sorted the burrs. He gently place it on his father's head. Gabriel looked into an old black speckled mirror hanging on the wall. He turned round slowly.

"Mmmh! Looking good. Thanks!" said Gabriel. Both sons smiled.

***

Amulya sipped Earl Grey tea as she sat in the garden of the Hawes Inn. She looked at Hector in his ridiculous white hat that his mother-in-law had given him for his birthday. He had his note book out and was reading from it. "So when the university decided not to let women graduate you still thought you'd apply anyway and it would be sorted by your graduation time?"

"Yes, that's about it," said Amulya.

"So why Edinburgh?" asked Hector.

"My parents wanted me to study here. My father stayed here for a while," said Amulya.

"I forgot to ask the most important question. Why choose medicine. What inspired you?" asked Hector.

"My younger sister died from cholera."

"Oh I'm sorry," said Hector.

Amulya said, "It was a long time ago, when we were children. I faced the reality of death early on."

"That must have been awful," said Hector.

"It's what's given me the drive to study medicine," said Amulya. "That and the fact that If I'd stayed in India I would have been married off by now and no chance of a career."

"Oh so you don't want to get married?" asked Hector.

"My parents have several possible husbands lined up for me but if I get married it will be on my own terms," answered Amulya.

"I know the feeling," said Hector.

Amulya smiled. "I'm going to go back to India, after I learn all that I can here, and set up a hospital like the Medical College in Calcutta."

Hector smiled. "I'd like to visit India someday." He scribbled a few notes then looked up and said, "I think I've covered everything. When do you think I could see Liz?"

"I don't know. She's been all over the place since she started working for Dr Blyth," said Amulya.

Hector put down his port and stood up. He took out the pocket watch with the tartan ribbon and checked the time.

"What's happened to Archie?" said Hector.

There was the sound of a crowd in the distance. Hector went to the bottom of the garden and looked along the street.

"He's coming! The Burry Man! " shouted Hector. Amulya spilt her tea in excitement. She got up and rushed down the garden. It looked as if the whole village, and more had turned out. Gabriel Aird as the Burry Man, waddled down the street, arms extended out, each hand clasping a garlanded pole, held out by his sons on either side. Douglas and Bruce had smartened themselves up in dark suits and polished shoes. Smiling in unison the brothers seemed to have settled their differences.

In front of the procession an eager fat boy rang a bell and chanted, "Hip hip hooray. It's the Burry Man's day!"

As the march got closer the innkeeper, a burly man with a red beard, rushed out with a filled glass and a rye straw. He ran down the garden past Liz and Hector and out of the gate. He ran up to the Burry Man and held the straw up to his mouth. The procession stopped as the Burry Man emptied the glass. The innkeeper grinned as he retrieved the glass and straw. The Burry Man and his assistants continued on the march.

As the innkeeper came back through the gate Hector waved him over.

"Would you like anything else?" enquired the innkeeper, slightly out of breath.

"Who's the Burry Man this year?" asked Hector.

"Oh that's secret sir! I don't want no bad luck coming down on me. Is that all sir?" said the innkeeper.

"Yes, thank you," replied Hector.

The innkeeper began to clear glasses off the garden tables. As the crowd passed Hector refreshed his pipe, lit it and took a drag.

"Come on Amulya! I'm not hanging around here waiting for Archie anymore." He hooked his free arm with Amulya's. They went off to follow the procession.

Archie sat on a bollard on Hawes Pier eating a mutton pie. The grease spilled down his chin. He wiped it off with a finger and then licked it clean. He had already set up the bulky camera on its wooden stand and now he saw the crowd as it moved on from Hawes Inn. He wiped his hands on his trousers and stood in front of the camera. He waved at the Burry Man. "Hey, over here!"

The Burry Man and his assistants must have seem him as they turned and headed towards Archie. At about twenty feet away Archie held up his hand. He came from behind the camera and went up to the Burry Man.

"Great costume! First I'll get one of you all from this angle. If you can keep your positions. I'll shout *prunes* when I'm about to take the photograph and if then you all could keep absolutely still for say eight seconds. Then I'll get you sir and your two assistants to go up the pier a wee bit and that'll give me a nice backdrop of the firth for the next shot. Got that?" The Burry Man nodded.

Archie scampered back up to his camera. He bent down and pulled the dark cloth at the back of the camera over his head. He shouted, "Prunes!" and flipped the lens cap off. He counted eight seconds and then replaced it. "Okay fine. If the Burry Man and his assistants would come round this way!" said Archie. He removed the wet plate and pushed it into the box below the camera.

Gabriel, guided by his sons, waddled past Archie and along the pier.

"That's fine!" shouted Archie. He lifted the camera and tripod and turned it to face his subjects. He inserted a fresh wet plate.

The Burry Man and his assistants stopped and turned around. Douglas and Bruce adjusted the garlanded poles. "We're ready!" shouted Bruce.

"Can you come in a bit on the left," said Archie. Bruce moved slightly. "Yes. That's it. Fine!" said Archie. "Hold it there. Perfect." He pulled the cloth over himself again and touched the lens cap. "Prunes!" shouted Archie. He flipped the lens cap, counted for eight seconds and replaced it.

"Thank you, all done!" shouted Archie.

Hector and Liz wove through the crowd up to Archie.

"I thought we were meeting at the Hawes Inn?" said Hector.

"No I said Hawes Pier. Anyway I got the shot you wanted," said Archie. He stared at Hector's white bowler hat.

"What?" snapped Hector.

"Where did you get that hat?" grinned Archie.

"It was a birthday present from his mother-in-law," laughed Amulya. Archie grinned and said, "Happy birthday!"

The Burry Man with his two assistants Bruce and Douglas came up to Archie. "Thank you for taking the photographs," said Bruce.

"It'll be in *The Reekie* tomorrow," said Archie. "I'll send you copies of the photographs."

"Thanks," said both Douglas and Bruce. The Burry Man nodded.

"I'd like to interview you," said Hector to the Burry Man.

"After the march," said Bruce.

"We've got a few hours to go yet. Best be off now," agreed Douglas.

The crowd parted as the Burry Man and his assistants moved through them and off the pier.

Archie started to pack up his camera. "I'm off to the Hawes Inn for a drink," said Archie. I'll catch up with you in a while. Hector and Liz waved him goodbye and followed the crowd.

***

A few hours later of marching and imbibing the proffered drinks, by villagers hoping to be blessed with good luck, and the Burry Man's bladder was full.

"I need a piss," whispered Gabriel to his assistants.

"There's that wee park and some bushes coming up on your left," said Douglas.

The procession stopped at the entrance to the park. Douglas and Bruce led their father through the park and up to a clump of bushes.

Archie pushed through the crowd with his camera. He came up to Amulya and Hector waiting at the entrance to the park. "What's happening?" he asked.

"The Burry Man is relieving himself," said Hector. "That reminds me. I need to go back to the inn. I forgot something. I'll catch you up."

Amulya nodded. Hector dashed off through the crowd.

***

"We'll come and get you in a few minutes," said Douglas. He and Bruce started to walk back through the park.

Lachie Merry watched from the cover of bushes as the Burry Man's assistants left the clearing. He checked to make sure that there was no one else around. He didn't fancy the problems that burking a man covered in burrs would involve. A slash across the throat would be the easiest way, he thought. An iron bar to the temple would have been his preferred method but he'd been warned about damaging the head. He removed the surgical knife from the bag tied to his belt. Suddenly he heard the rustling of bushes. He froze. A man wearing a white bowler hat passed within a few feet on him. The man stopped, unbuttoned his flies and unleashed a stream of piss. It seemed to last ages. Finally the flow stopped, the man gave it a shake, buttoned up and moved off.

Lachie waited a few seconds and then quietly moved forward. He came to the clearing where Gabriel Aird was in mid-flow. He crept up behind the man and stepped on a twig. Gabriel turned, still pissing.

"What the..!"

Lachie lunged forward and slashed Gabriel across the throat. The Burry Man clutched at his throat. The blood and piss sprayed across Lachie. Gabriel fell to the ground. Lachie quickly pulled the flower-covered bowler hat off Gabriel's head. He ripped off the burr-covered balaclava. He quickly cut through the man's neck, found the vertebrae and hacked between the bones.

***

Douglas and Bruce came down to the gates. "Won't be long," said Douglas.

Archie set up his camera on the tripod.

"Haven't you got enough photographs?" said Amulya.

"I'll take one of you. Stand over there, next to the Burry Man's assistants," said Archie.

"I don't want my photograph taken," said Amulya.

"You can give it to Hector as a birthday present," said Archie.

"Alright then," agreed Amulya. She moved towards the gate next to Bruce and Douglas.

"Do you mind being in a photograph with this young lady?" asked Archie.

"Not at all," smiled Bruce. Douglas didn't look so happy about it. Bruce gave him a stare.

"Yes. Okay," muttered Douglas.

Archie directed Douglas and Bruce to either side of the gate and got Amulya to stand in the middle.

They grinned towards the camera.

"Almost ready," said Archie. He adjusted the angle of the camera. "Keep still!" He bent down and pulled the cloth over his head. He held his hand up. "Prunes!" he said and pulled the lens cap off, waited a few seconds and then replaced it. "Thank you!" said Archie.

Amulya smiled at Bruce and Douglas. She went up to Archie, who was packing up his camera. Hector made his way through the crowd up to them.

"Did you find what you were looking for?" asked Amulya.

"Yes. What's the hold up?" said Hector. Amulya shrugged. She looked towards Douglas and Bruce.

Douglas said, "I'll go and see if he's finished." He walked off through the park up to the bushes.

Lachie heard the sound of someone coming through the bushes. He hurried up and cut through the last of the flesh. The head rolled off to one side. Lachie grabbed it by the hair and dropped it into the sack. He got up and ran back through the woods. He heard a scream and the sound of someone crashing through the bushes towards him. Lachie speeded up. He got to the stone wall and tried to clamber up and over it but it was difficult holding the sack at the same time. He twisted the sack and clamped it between his teeth. He scuffled up the wall and got onto the top just as Douglas burst out of the woods, carrying one of the garland poles.

"Hey you bastard!" shouted Douglas, and launched the pole at Lachie, only just missing its target by inches.

Lachie dropped over the other side and rushed off down a muddy path. He looked back. "Shit!" The man was clambering over the wall after him. Lachie sped down the path and followed it around a corner. He dived off the path and hid in a thicket, heart thumping. He thought, I'm getting too old for this!

Douglas landed on the ground. He saw Lachie running around the corner and gave chase. He got round the corner and saw that Lachie had vanished.

"Damn it!" shouted Douglas. He marched down the path but couldn't see any trace of the man. He turned back and headed back along the path.

***

After hearing the scream from the bushes, Bruce rushed through the park, followed by the bell ringing boy.

86

"Come on!" said Hector to Liz. They rushed through the gate and into the park. They followed Bruce around the bushes to a small clearing.

"Oh my god! Father!" cried Bruce. Gabriel Aird lay on the ground on his back, decapitated. One of the garlanded poles stuck up out of the ground at an angle. Bruce sunk to his knees and held onto the pole. He stared at his father's body. "Why? Who would do this?" he stuttered. His brother Douglas suddenly appeared carrying one of the poles.

"I couldn't catch the bastard!" said Douglas. "He went over the wall at the back. By the time I got over he was gone." He went up to Bruce and laid his hand on his brother's shoulder. "Someone better get the police."

"I'll go!" said the bell ringer. He ran off through the crowd that had begun to gather in the park.

Archie appeared in the clearing, carrying his camera and tripod over his shoulder. "Not another one!" He set up his camera.

"What are you doing?" asked Douglas.

"I'm also a police photographer," said Archie. "This is now a crime scene."

Amulya bent down to examine the body.

"Get away!" shouted Douglas.

"I'm medically trained. Perhaps I can help" said Amulya.

"Help! How can you help? He's dead!" shouted Douglas.

Death of The Burry Man. © David Hutchison.

Chapter 13 Asylum

The police carriage drew up outside the Edinburgh Lunatic Asylum, a looming sandstone building surrounded by trees and gardens. Inspector MacLeod and Liz got out. They went to the formidable front door and knocked. The door was shortly opened by Nurse Steeple. Her piercing green eyes looked them up and down. "Yes?"

"Inspector MacLeod and Miss Moliette to see Dr Emrie," said the Inspector.

"Do you have an appointment? The doctor is extremely busy," frowned Nurse Steeple.

"I am the law, ma'am. I don't need an appointment!" said the Inspector. He brushed past her and into the cavernous hallway that smelled of beeswax and phenol. "If you could please point us in the direction of the good doctor's office!"

"Very well. If you insist. Follow me!" sighed Nurse Steeple. She turned and marched across the hall and down a wide oak-panelled corridor with a polished wood floor, flanked with high windows and velvet curtains. They passed two old ladies in grey smocks, laughing like children as they played hopscotch. A young man, totally naked and reeking of shit, screamed as he ran out of a door in front of them, almost knocking Liz over. Two male orderlies came out and chased down the corridor after him.

"Master Lucas doesn't like bath time," said Nurse Steeple, as she covered her nose.

As Liz passed the room that the young man had fled from, she saw an iron bath tub half-filled with water and lumps of ice. No wonder he doesn't like bath time, she thought. Further back down the corridor the old ladies screamed as Master Lucas ran through their chalk markings in his wet feet. He ran off round a corner, chased by the orderlies.

At the end of the extensive corridor the nurse turned off into another hallway, with an impressive staircase at one end. Above the staircase was a huge oil painting of *The Raft of the Medusa*, obviously a copy but splendid nevertheless. She knocked on a door to her right.

"Come in!" The nurse entered followed by Inspector MacLeod and Liz.

Dr Emrie was sitting at a large desk reading *The Reekie*. The headline read *"Surgeons' Hall Riot Shame Again!"* He put the paper aside and smiled at his visitors.

"Inspector MacLeod and Miss Moliette to see your sir. I told them that you were busy but the Inspector insisted," said Nurse Steeple.

"That's perfectly alright nurse," said Dr Emrie. Nurse Steeple nodded and pulled the door closed behind her. The doctor gestured to some chairs.

"Ah Miss Moliette. The medical student?" asked the doctor.

"Yes sir. But I am here in the capacity of assistant to police surgeon Dr Blyth," said Liz.

"Oh I've not seen Florian for years. We were at medical school together. How is the old codger?" smiled Dr Emrie.

"He's not that well at the moment but he's recovering," said Liz.

"Oh, I'm sorry to hear that. What's up with him?" asked Dr Emrie.

Liz replied, "He's had ..." The Inspector interrupted, "The doctor will be fine after a rest. Could you tell me doctor, are any of your male patients missing?"

"Well there's ...why?" asked the doctor.

The Inspector pulled a photograph from his jacket and handed it to the doctor. It was one of the photographs that Archie had taken of the body at the Innocent Railway.

"My word!" gasped the doctor as he peered at the photograph. "What is this?"

"The body was found in Holyrood Park early this morning. As you can see the man was beheaded, making it hard to identify him. Dr Blyth recognised his clothing as coming from here," said Inspector MacLeod.

"I estimate the victim was around five foot eight inches," said Liz.

"Jack Fox!" sighed Dr Emrie.

"Who's this Jack Fox?" asked the Inspector.

"Melancholia sufferer. He occasionally absconds but usually returns by tea time. We'd better check first." Dr Emrie got up, crossed to the door and opened it. "Come with me!"

Dr Emrie crossed the hallway and went up the staircase. The Inspector shrugged at Liz. They followed the doctor up the staircase. On the main landing they passed Nurse Steeple who was carrying what looked like a dirty wedding dress. Dr Emrie stopped her.

"Has Mister Fox returned?" asked Dr Emrie.

"I don't know. I was checking in on Miss Havisham," said Nurse Steeple. "I'll expect he'll be back in his room by now waiting for his dinner. Will I go and see?"

"That's alright. I'll look in on him," said the doctor. The nurse nodded and carried on down the stairs.

Dr Emrie gestured to the massive painting above the landing. "Did you know that the original artist spent many hours in hospitals and dead houses, studying the dying and the dead just to get the colours right. Such dedication!" he sighed. "This is a copy of course, but that's why I've been rather lax when Mister Fox goes off on his searches for inspiration. He's an artist too. He was a rather famous painter of cats before his illness. I encourage all our residents to pursue their artistic traits as part of their rehabilitation."

"Does it work?" asked Liz as they climbed the next set of stairs.

"Yes we've had some successes. Mister Fox was really improving," replied the doctor.

They turned down a narrow corridor.

"Here we are." The doctor opened the door. The room was small but with a high ceiling. A barred window at one end faced south and let plenty of light in. The only furniture was a metal bed and a table. The walls were covered with pastel sketches, mostly of fantastical cat-like creatures, close up studies of different types of claws and talons, large scale drawings of caverns and underground waterfalls.

Dr Emrie looked under the bed. "Jack?" An empty space. Only a saucer with some oats. "Sometimes he likes to hide under the bed and grab my leg. He's rather like a child," explained the doctor.

Liz went across to the table and looked through the pile of drawings lying on it. One particular sketch caught her eye. It was of a hideous winged cat demon crawling along the roof of a tunnel. It reminded her of the scary Bosch print that had hung in the dining room of the orphanage.

"Inspector. Look at this!" exclaimed Liz. The Inspector, who was studying a waterfall in a stygian setting, came up to her. Liz held out the sketch to him. "What does that remind you of?"

"My mother-in-law," said the Inspector. Liz tutted. "The background." The Inspector shook his head.

"The Innocent Railway tunnel!" said Liz. She took out a white handkerchief and rubbed a small part of the drawing. She held up the blue smudge. "Blue pastel!"

"You're right!" exclaimed the Inspector.

"Have you found something interesting?" asked Dr Emrie.

"Perhaps," said the Inspector.

"So can you confirm whether my missing patient is your victim or not?" asked the doctor.

"We'll have to get back to you on that, doctor," said the Inspector.

"I see," said Dr Emrie. He showed them out of the room.

***

An hour later the Inspector and Liz got back to the dead house. Liz pulled back the cloth covering the body. She used a scalpel to scrape the blue pastel from under the corpse's fingernail and rubbed it onto her handkerchief, next to the sample taken from the drawing.

"Yes. Both cerulean blue!" said Liz.

"Well observed! Then this is most likely Jack Fox. We'll need to pay the asylum another visit."

"I'd like to go and see how Dr Blyth is first," said Liz.

The Inspector pulled out his pocket watch. "Of course. It is getting on. We can leave it until tomorrow."

As they left the building Liz suddenly remember something. "Oh and I can only do the morning tomorrow."

"Why?" asked Inspector MacLeod.

"I've got a class that I can't miss in the afternoon," said Liz.

"Fair enough." The Inspector hailed a carriage coming down the street. "Can I drop you off at Dr Blyth's?"

"It's not far. I could do with the walk," said Liz.

"Are you sure? After that stabbing incident?" asked the Inspector.

"I can't go around being scared of my shadow," said Liz. She lanced out her umbrella at a small piece of wood lying on the ground. She held up the umbrella with the wood skewered onto the sharp spiked end of the umbrella. "Besides I've updated my brolly so I'm not completely defenceless!"

The Inspector grinned. "Until tomorrow then." He got up into the carriage. The driver flipped the reins and the carriage moved off.

Liz sauntered off along the High Street feeling pleased with herself. Suddenly a street urchin jumped out from a dark close and shouted "Boo!"

Liz gasped in fright and dropped her umbrella. The child laughed and ran off.

Liz picked up her umbrella and brandished it at the fleeing child. "You little toe rag!" she shouted. An old lady hobbled past and shook her head at Liz.

***

The carriage drew up outside the Inspector's flat on Leith Walk. As he got out he saw that PC Urquhart was waiting on the step. "Hold on!" the Inspector said to the driver.

PC Urquhart rushed up and said, "Oh sir, I've being looking for you!"

"What is it?" asked the Inspector.

"Another one!" PC Urquhart whistled. "At South Queensferry."

The Inspector turned to the carriage driver, "Can we make it to South Queensferry tonight?"

"Yes sir," said the driver, "the horses can do another two hours easy, but they'll need rest and food after that."

"Hop on PC Urquhart. Let's go!" said Inspector MacLeod, as he got back into the carriage. The PC climbed up beside him and began to whistle.

"If you continue that all the way to South Queensferry there will be another murder tonight!" said the Inspector.

"Sorry sir," apologised PC Urquhart.

Chapter 14 Delivery

Lachie Merry staggered up Crichton's Close clutching a sack. He peered into the shadows.

"Hey? I've got it for you!" he shouted. "Where are you man?"

"Psst!" came a male voice from a dark corner.

Lachie moved up to where the sound came from.

"Sir?" asked Lachie. "Is that you?"

"Keep it down!" said the voice from the shadows.

Lachie could see the man now, but his face was still in shadow. Lachie held up the bag. "That was bloody close that. I nearly got fecking caught!"

The man in shadow handed Lachie a card.

"What's this?" said Lachie. He read out the card, "*Mr Campbell Prebble, Carnousty Boarding House.*" Lachie coughed. "Another one? No way! Did you no hear me, I nearly got fecking caught!" said Lachie. He threw the card to the ground.

The man put his hand out to take the sack. Lachie grabbed his arm.

"I'm fed up with this cloak and dagger shite. Let's see your fecking face!" Lachie dragged the man out into the gaslight to reveal Dr Love. The doctor punched Lachie in the face. "Bastard!" shouted Lachie as he dropped the bag and clutched his nose. Dr Love grabbed the bag and scattered a bag of coins on the cobbles.

"I'll pay you double," said the doctor. He strode off up the close, disappearing under an arch.

Lachie scrambled down and picked up the coins. "You're still a fecking bastard!" shouted Lachie, as he put the card in his pocket.

***

The rain drummed down on Liz's umbrella as she navigated puddles along the street. The sound reminded her of the attic dormitory in the orphanage. The drumming of rain on the thin roof had been comforting, helping to lull her to sleep. A dog barking brought her out of her reverie.

"Miss Moliette?"

Liz turned and saw Charles with Psyche straining on a lead. "Hello Charles," she said as she bent down and patted the dog. "I was just coming to see Dr Blyth. How is he?"

"I tried to get him to rest but..." Charles shrugged.

They reached Dr Blyth's house. Charles unlocked the door as Liz gave her umbrella a shake. In the hall Charles unclipped Psyche's lead. The wee dog shot off down the wood panelled corridor to find Florian. Charles took Liz's coat while she put her umbrella in the stand.

"He's in the study," said Charles. "I'll go and make some tea."

Liz headed down the corridor. Psyche was impatiently scratching at the study door. Liz knocked.

"Come in!" said a muffled voice.

Liz opened the door. The incense smoking on the mantelpiece had a comforting menthol aroma. Florian lay on the chaise longue next to the roaring fire, sipping a port. Psyche leapt up on her lap, almost spilling her drink.

"Settle down girl" said Florian as she patted the dog. Psyche calmed down and curled up at Florian's feet.

"How are you feeling, doctor?" asked Liz.

The doctor gestured to the empty seat but Liz ignored it, went across to Florian and touched her sweating brow.

"You've got a temperature," stated Liz.

Florian shrugged, "I'll live."

"I'd better change the dressing," said Liz.

"No, Charles will do that later," said Florian.

"Are you sure you don't want me to check it?" said Liz.

Florian changed the subject. "How did you get on at the asylum?"

Liz sat down. "We think the body is Jack Fox. He's gone missing and he's an artist. The cerulean blue pastel residue under the body's fingernail matches pastels in his room."

"It could just be a coincidence. After all it's a staple colour. I'm sure I've got some lying around in a drawer somewhere," said Florian, stroking her chin.

"There was one drawing in particular, the one that I took the pastel sample from, that was interesting. It depicted a stone tunnel. Just like the Innocent Railway tunnel," said Liz excitedly.

"Ah! I see. That's sounds more promising," said Florian.

"I'm going with the Inspector back to the asylum tomorrow," said Liz.

Florian shook her head. "No need. I'll manage tomorrow."

"But doctor, you must rest. I've only one exam tomorrow afternoon. I'll come back after that," said Liz.

There was a knock at the door and Charles entered with a tea tray and a package wrapped up in brown paper. He put the tray down on a small table between the two women and handed the package to Florian. "Dr Bell's secretary dropped this off for you sir."

Florian eagerly grabbed the package and began to open it.

"Shall I pour?" asked Charles.

"That's all right Charles. Miss Moliette will be mother," said Florian.

"Very good madam," said Charles.

As Charles left the room Liz poured the tea.

"I cabled Bell for his notes on the French sailor case. Found beheaded in Leith last year. I do remember him telling me something about it now," said Florian. Liz passed her a cup of tea. "Thanks."

"You think it's the same killer?" asked Liz.

"Possibly." Florian put on glasses and skimmed through the notes.

"You'd have thought Inspector MacLeod would have remembered it?" said Liz.

Florian shrugged. "He probably wouldn't have known about it. The Inspector's only been here six months. He was transferred here, I gather, after having a breakdown when his wife disappeared."

"Oh that's awful. What happened?" asked Liz.

"I really don't know more than that. He never mentions it," said Florian.

***

A sweet pork-like smell hung in the air of Dr Love's cellar. Pickle was curled up on an empty hessian sack lying on the wooden table. Dr Love used a pair of forceps to remove Gabriel Aird's skull from a bubbling pan of liquid. He placed the skull onto a metal tray, carried it across to the sink and drained the water off. He rubbed the skull dry with a cloth. He smiled as he touched the slight bump above the left temple. He placed the skull on the table.

Pickle stirred awake and stretched out luxuriously. Dr Love patted the cat as he leaned over, pulled open a drawer from under the table and got out his sketch book. He took a pencil from his shirt pocket and began to draw the skull. Pickle got up and rubbed his cheek against Dr Love's hand. The cat sat down between Dr Love and the skull. The doctor carried on drawing, twisting round past the cat to see the skull properly.

After a few minutes Dr Love was satisfied with the sketch. Pickle lay stretched out between him and the skull. He looked up at the box shelves of skulls. There were three spaces left. He placed the skull into one of the compartments. Pickle jumped up and settled into one of the remaining spaces.

"That's not for you Pickle darling. That's for a certain type of gentleman," said Dr Love. Pickle stared at the doctor and strolled out of the compartment, as if he understood. Dr Love picked up the cat and cuddled it as he stared at another empty compartment. Pickle purred. "That one's for the perfect mixed race female. A benchmark to compare with others."

Pickle miaowed.

"Oh? I think I have a candidate," said Dr Love.

***

It was raining heavily. PC Urquhart held up a large golfing umbrella, as Inspector MacLeod brandished an oil lamp, over the beheaded body covered in green burrs.

"Move it over here!" said the Inspector, as he expanded the search out from the body. He noticed something sticking out from under a bush. He nudged it out with his foot. A muddy bowler hat covered in flowers. He picked it up.

"Right you stay here and guard the body. I'll send someone up to help you transport it. I'm going to interview the family," said the Inspector. He handed the bowler hat to PC Urquhart.

"What was his name and address?"

PC Urquhart put down the bowler hat and took out his notebook. "Gabriel Aird. His sons Bruce and Douglas were with him. Let's see where is it?Ah yes. 12 The Vennel."

The Inspector ran off down through the park to the road. He was soaked to the skin by the time he reached the Aird house, a two-storied whitewashed cottage on the hill above the village. He knocked on the door and Douglas Aird answered it.

"Inspector MacLeod. Are you Mr Aird's son?"

"Yes. I'm Douglas."

"I'd like to ask you some questions."

Douglas nodded and moved to let the Inspector in. "Through here."

The Inspector followed Douglas into a small sitting room with a spectacular evening view across the Firth of Forth. Mrs Aird was sitting on a couch, sobbing into a handkerchief. Bruce sat next to her, staring into a glass of whisky.

"Can I get you a drink? Tea, whisky?" asked Douglas.

"No thank you," said the Inspector.

Douglas pulled a chair out from a dining table against the wall and offered it to the Inspector. "I'm rather wet. I'd better not," said the Inspector.

"It doesn't matter," said Douglas. "Sit down! I'll get you a towel." Douglas went off out of the room.

Inspector Macleod sat down. "I'm very sorry about your husband Mrs Aird. Do you know of anyone who'd want to harm him?"

Mrs Aird shook her head. She got up and said, "I need to wash the dishes," She staggered from the room, sobbing.

Douglas came back in and handed a towel to the Inspector.

"Thank you." The Inspector mopped his face. Douglas went and sat in the place that his mother had vacated. "Who knew that the Burry Man was your father this year?" asked the Inspector.

"It's an open secret. He's done it the past three years," said Douglas.

"Do either of you know of anyone who had it in for your father?" asked the Inspector. Both brothers shook their heads.

"So who discovered your father's body?" asked the Inspector.

"I did," said Douglas.

"What did you do next?"

"I heard someone running through the bushes so I ran in the direction of the sound," said Douglas. "I saw a man climbing over the high stone wall at the back. I clambered up the wall, but by the time I got over he'd gone."

"So what did this man look like? Can you describe him?" asked Inspector MacLeod.

"Not really. He must have been fit as he got over that wall real fast. I didn't see his face."

"How about height? Hair colour?"

"He had a cap on. Black or dark brown. Don't know about height. Roughly my height I suppose," said Douglas. "Maybe a bit shorter."

"And you? Bruce is it?" said the Inspector. Bruce nodded.

"I didn't see him. I heard Douglas shouting so I ran up to the bushes. Then I saw father. Lying there. Like that." Bruce poured himself another whisky with a shaky hand.

"What happened next?" asked Inspector MacLeod.

"Douglas came back. He said the murderer had got away." Bruce frowned. "Why in god's name would they take his head? You need to catch the fiend that did this!"

"I assure you that we will do our utmost to catch this killer," said the Inspector. "Can you think of anything else that might help?"

Bruce looked up at Douglas and shook his head.

"The photographer took a picture," said Bruce. "He said he was a police photographer."

"Yes, that would be Mr Porter," said the Inspector. "I'll get a statement from him later."

"There was a young woman. She bent down and touched the body. Said she was a doctor or something. But that can't be right? Can it?" said Douglas.

"Who was she?" asked the Inspector.

"Didn't get her name. An Indian lady. Pretty. She was with that reporter chap from *The Reekie*. The photographer took a picture of her with my brother and me," said Douglas.

The Inspector got up. "I'll look into it. Well, you've all been most helpful. Thank you."

"What's going to happen to father's body? I mean, when can we bury him? Have the funeral?" asked Douglas, as he showed the Inspector to the door.

"We need to take the body to Edinburgh for some tests. I'll let you know as soon as possible."

Chapter 15   Autopsy

Hector sat on an uncomfortable bench in the reception of the police station. A poster on the wall above him depicted a typical sweet old lady in a hat, titled *Jessie Queen Baby Killer*, with a twenty five pounds reward. Maybe not so sweet then, thought Hector. Another old lady, Kitty Murray, with a distinctive nose and sharp intelligent eyes, sat between Hector and her wicker basket, knitting stripy blue and white socks. The needles clicked as her twin six year old grandsons Joe and Mark played with a toy wooden train on the floor.

Inspector Macleod came out of his office with Amulya Patel.

"It was like something out of a Hieronymus Bosch nightmare!" said Amulya.

"Indeed. Well I think that's all for now Miss Patel," said the Inspector.

Hector got up and went across to them. "Finished?" asked Hector.

"Yes. Let's get some lunch," smiled Amulya. Hector put out his arm and Amulya linked with him. They almost fell over when Joe pushed the train in front of them and Mark ran to catch it.

"Boys!" shouted Kitty. She put her knitting away and lifted the basket.

"Sorry!" she apologised to Hector and Amulya. They both smiled.

"You need to spend more time with your sons so that they learn to behave," said Kitty to the Inspector. He sighed. Kitty handed him a package from the basket. "I made you a mutton pie."

The Inspector took the package and said, "Thanks. I'll eat it later. Sorry I have to go, I'm busy." He quickly left the station. Kitty looked back at him and frowned.

There was another haar and the Inspector couldn't see all that well. He went through the gates of the small graveyard next door and up to the dead house. He hated the place. It gave him the creeps.

Gabriel Aird's naked body lay out on one of the tables. His Burry Man costume was in a heap on a small table next to the wall. Florian was examining the neck as the Inspector entered.

Florian looked up. "Good morning Inspector."

"Morning. How are you?" said the Inspector.

"Much better, thank you," said Florian. "Liz. Come over here and see what do you think."

Liz crossed the room and examined the neck of the victim. "The same knife?"

"Yes!" said Florian.

Florian picked up some notes and held them out to the Inspector.

"You asked about a beheading in Leith. Here's Dr Bell's notes on a case last year. Henri Blanc, a French sailor found minus his head, in Leith," said Florian.

"Can you connect the crimes?" asked the Inspector, as he quickly looked through the notes.

"The head was never recovered, but look see here!" Florian pointed to a sentence in the notes.

"The neck had been removed with a large knife. Possibly a nick in the knife three quarters down the blade from the hilt!" exclaimed Florian.

"So the same killer?" said the Inspector.

"The same knife anyway. Dr Bell always taught me to look out for the nick in the knife!" grinned Florian.

"Impressive work!" The Inspector smiled. "I have to go back to the asylum. Make sure that Jack Fox hasn't turned up. Can you come along?"

"I think that I should start on the autopsy," said Florian. She nodded towards Liz.

"I could accompany you as long as I'm back for my anatomy class at two," suggested Liz.

"Fine, come along," said Inspector MacLeod. Liz followed him as he left the dead house.

The police carriage was waiting outside the station. The Inspector and Liz got into the carriage and they headed off. The Inspector got out his notebook and began to read through it. He jotted down some notes.

Liz said," Is the job always like this? Searching for murderers. Looking for clues?"

The Inspector closed his notebook. "Not at all. Murder is very rare." The Inspector looked out the window, lost in thought. "Well, in Edinburgh anyway. Most of my job is quite mundane, catching small-time crooks."

Liz nodded. "So why did you want to join the police force?"

"My father!" said Inspector MacLeod.

"Oh, was he in the force?" asked Liz.

"On the contrary he was a cockney crook. A forger. He wasn't even a good one and he was caught. Died in prison. I didn't want my family to be brought up like I was," said the Inspector.

"Oh I'm sorry," said Liz. "So you've got a family?"

"I've two sons. Twins," said the Inspector.

"Oh how old are they?" asked Liz.

"Six years old. They're getting to be a bit of a handful now," sighed the Inspector. "Their grandmother tries her best but they're a bit boisterous and tire her out," said the Inspector.

"I see," said Liz.

The Inspector looked out of the window. "My wife disappeared three years ago."

"Oh I'm sorry," said Liz. She touched the Inspector's shoulder. He turned round.

"What happened?"

"She'd been to visit her parents in Shetland. She got on the ferry at Lerwick but didn't appear in Aberdeen. People seem to think that she committed suicide but she wouldn't have done that. Anna did have bouts of depression but we were very happy together. She loved the children," said the Inspector. He turned away and looked out the window.

"Perhaps she fell overboard. An accident?" said Liz.

"No she was used to boats all her life being brought up in a fishing port. I think she was abducted and murdered. Otherwise she'd have gotten in touch."

Liz said, "Is there no hope. Do you have proof that she is dead?"

"No. There's no body. No witnesses. God knows I've tried."

"But why?" asked Liz.

"Revenge. You make a lot of enemies when you're an inspector,"

"That's awful," said Liz.

"How about you? Do you have family?" asked the Inspector.

Liz shook her head. "I'm an orphan."

"Did something happen?" said the Inspector. "Sorry I shouldn't pry."

"It's fine. There's not much to tell. I was left at the doorstep of the orphanage as a new born. No note or anything. That's all I know," said Liz.

"It must be difficult. Not knowing. Wondering where you came from," said the Inspector.

"Oh I made up all sorts of romantic stories to myself. My mother was an African princess who died in childbirth and my father, the prince, was so sad that he gave me away. All that rubbish! I'm more likely to be the offspring of some poor beggar who was knocked up by a sailor," said Liz, laughing.

The Inspector shook his head and said, "We are what we make of ourselves."

"I agree but I'd still like to be part of a family," said Liz.

"I'm sure that one day you'll have your own family," said the Inspector. Liz sighed and looked out of the window. The haar was lifting. The Inspector took out the package from his pocket and unwrapped it. Kitty's mutton pie. He offered it to Liz.

"They are rather good."

"No thanks," said Liz. They sat in silence as the Inspector ate his pie. Liz pointed to a wee bit that had stuck in his beard.

"Sorry!" Inspector MacLeod rubbed his beard. Liz nodded and smiled.

The Inspector looked out of the window. "Here we are!"

The carriage drove through the tall iron gates of the asylum and up to the main entrance. Liz and the Inspector got out. They went up the steps to the main door and knocked.

A burly orderly with a pock-marked face opened the door.

"Inspector MacLeod and Miss Moliette to see Dr Emrie," said the Inspector.

"Oh he's engaged," said the orderly. "Can I help?"

"It is most urgent that we speak to him," said the Inspector.

"Then I suppose you'd better come in," said the orderly.

They followed the orderly down the corridor. The place seemed very quiet compared to last time. Perhaps they're all at lunch, thought Liz.

There was a slapping sound coming from Dr Emrie's office. The orderly knocked on Dr Emrie's door.

"Dr Emrie?" said the orderly. He tried to open the door but it was locked. "An Inspector MacLeod and Miss Moliette to see you."

"Just a minute!" shouted Mr Emrie. There was a scuffling sound and eventually the door was unlocked and opened. Dr Emrie stood in the doorway, holding up a rolled up newspaper. His shirt was hanging out of his trousers and his bald head was covered in sweat.

"Sorry I was chasing a damn wasp!" he gasped. "Come in." He left the door open and went and sat behind his desk.

"I'll leave you to it. I'd better get back to work," said the orderly. He nodded and walked off.

Liz and Inspector MacLeod sat down opposite Dr Emrie.

"It's unusual that Jack Fox would stay away so long. Do you really think it could be him?" asked Dr Emrie, wiping sweat off his brow.

"We think so," said the Inspector.

Liz nodded. "The pastel residue on the body matches the drawing in Jack Fox's room."

The Inspector leaned forward. "It's still not conclusive though. Did Mr Fox have any enemies?"

The doctor stroked his chin. "Plenty of imagined enemies, but as to real ones, I couldn't say."

"Then who were his friends?" asked the Inspector.

"He didn't interact with many people except for his sister Victoria. She visited regularly. I've got her details here somewhere." The doctor raked through a drawer and pulled out an address book. He flipped through it. "Somewhere in Portobello. Ah yes!" He passed the address book to the Inspector.

"*Mrs Victoria Massey. Archaeologist?*" asked the Inspector, reading the card.

"More of an Egyptologist I think is the proper term," said the doctor. "She's a widow. Charming woman."

Inspector MacLeod took out his notebook and copied the address down. "Could we see his room again?"

"Certainly," said Dr Emrie. He pulled on a bell rope. "I'll get someone to accompany you. I'm sorry I'm a bit busy at the moment."

The doctor took out a ledger and started to write in it. The Inspector smiled at the doctor and then glanced over at the window. He saw a pair of nurse's shoes sticking out from under the curtains. Obviously someone was hiding there. Randy bastard, he thought as he looked at the doctor. He glanced at Liz, but she hadn't noticed. He got up and was about to cross over to the window, when the doctor quickly slammed the ledger shut, stood up and blocked the Inspector's path.

"Can I help?" asked the doctor.

There was a knock at the door. Relieved, the doctor said, "Come in!"

A young slightly built nurse popped her head round the door.

"Nurse Cadell. Please show Inspector MacLeod and his assistant to Mr Fox's room," said Dr Emrie.

The nurse nodded, "Yes doctor." She smiled at the Inspector and Liz. "Follow me please."

They left Dr Emrie's office and followed Nurse Cadell, down the corridor to the large hallway with the grand painting above the staircase. As she climbed the stairs the nurse turned and frowned. "That painting always gives me the boak! It's about cannibalism." Liz and MacLeod nodded.

They got to the landing and went down the corridor to Fox's room. The nurse opened the door but didn't go in.

"I'll just stay here. Mr Fox has a pet rat and I'm not keen on the creatures," she apologised.

The Inspector and Liz looked around the room as the nurse waited at the doorway. The Inspector looked through the sketches on the walls. He came across a sketch of a man with a prominent bump on his forehead. He brought it up to Nurse Cadell.

"Who's this?" asked the Inspector.

The nurse studied the sketch. "That's a self-portrait of Jack. Quite a good likeness of him actually!"

"Could I borrow this?" asked the Inspector.

"Take what you want," said Nurse Cadell. "Just sign for it before you leave."

***

Liz climbed into the carriage.

The Inspector looked up at the driver and said, "Marlborough Street, Portobello, please." He climbed in next to Liz and they set off.

The Inspector unrolled the sketch and stared at it. "Perhaps the sister can provide us with some answers."

The Portobello Egyptologist. © David Hutchison.

Chapter 16   Portobello Egyptologist

The haar was disappearing and it was starting to become a fine day. They made good time and in an hour they'd arrived at Victoria Massey's house in Portobello. Just off the promenade, it was a lovely town house with a clean white façade and a manicured garden of unusual shrubbery.

A cheerful maid showed them into the cinnamon-smelling parlour which was covered from floor to the high ceiling in paintings of cats. There were several statues of the Egyptian cat god Bast on a dresser. Two tall cat mummies flanked the doorway. Victoria Massey, an elegant woman in her early thirties, hair cut in a Cleopatra style, sashayed into the room. She wore a sleeveless orange tunic with hieroglyphs embroidered in gold. Liz was quite impressed by her look.

"Mrs Massey? I'm Inspector MacLeod and this is my assistant Miss Moliette."

"It's Jack isn't it? Something's happened? What's he done this time?" asked Victoria.

"You'd better sit down," said the Inspector.

Victoria shook her head. "Tell it to me straight!"

"We've found a body wearing the clothes of an inmate of the Edinburgh Lunatic Asylum," said the Inspector.

"What?" asked Victoria.

"The body is missing its head," said the Inspector.

"Oh my god! It can't be Jack!" wailed Victoria.

The Inspector unrolled Jack's self-portrait. "There was blue pastel residue on the hands. The same as Jack used to draw this with," said the Inspector.

Victoria wiped her eyes. "Lots of people use pastels."

"I know. That's why we are here. Did he have any distinguishing marks?" said the Inspector.

Victoria pointed to Jack's forehead in the sketch. "That bump on his head. He's always had it."

"Anything else. Birth marks?" asked Liz.

"No birth marks. But there is something a bit stupid. Orion's Belt," replied Victoria.

"The constellation?" asked Liz.

Victoria nodded.

"What do you mean?" asked the Inspector.

"He has three freckles in a line on his left arm. Like the constellation. The pyramids at Giza are laid out in a similar fashion. As do our own islands here in the Forth; Fidra, Lamb and Craigleith."

"Would you be able to come with us and identify the body?" asked the Inspector.

Victoria sighed, then nodded. "I'll come along but I don't know if I'll be able you know..."

***

Inspector MacLeod and Liz entered the dead house, followed by an apprehensive Victoria. The beheaded bodies were covered with sheets. The smell was worse than before. Victoria clutched a handkerchief to her nose.

"This one over here," said the Inspector.

"Which arm?" asked Liz.

Victoria sniffed back a sob. "The left one."

Liz removed the sheet covering the left arm and moved out of the way. Victoria came closer and looked down at the arm. She burst into tears, turned and clung onto Inspector MacLeod. Obviously embarrassed, the Inspector did his best to comfort her.

He patted her back and said, "There, there dear. It was over quickly. He wouldn't have suffered." That seemed to make Victoria worse and she heaved with sobs.

Liz felt a bit awkward leaving Victoria and the Inspector like this, but it was getting late, so she said, "Sorry, I have to go. I have my anatomy class." The Inspector nodded as Liz picked up her umbrella and dashed out of the room.

"Let's get out of here. I think you could do with a cup of tea," said the Inspector to Victoria. He handed her a handkerchief.

"Thanks." She wiped her eyes.

The Inspector and Victoria left the dead house, through the graveyard and into the street. They entered the station. Kitty was waiting for him with her basket.

"Frazer, here's another pie for you." Kitty took a wrapped pie from her basket and thrust it into the Inspector's hands. She noticed that Victoria was upset. "What's the matter dear? Would you like a pie?"

Victoria shook her head. Kitty touched Victoria's arm. "It's Mrs Massey isn't it? Didn't I see you at Mrs Carnousty's a few months ago?"

"Yes. I... " began Victoria. She began to sob. Kitty put her arm around Victoria and guided her to a bench.

"Mrs Massey has just identified her brother's body," said the Inspector to Kitty.

"Oh how awful. You poor dear," said Kitty.

"I'm alright," said Victoria. She wiped her eyes and looked up at Inspector MacLeod. "Inspector, will you help me?"

"Yes certainly. If I can. What do you want me to do?" said the Inspector.

"I want to find out who killed Jack," said Victoria.

The Inspector nodded. "Yes, we all do."

"I had a pact with Jack. Whoever died first would try and contact the other. I'm sure he'll try and send me a sign. Would you accompany me to see Mrs Carnousty this evening?" asked Victoria.

"Who is Mrs Carnousty?" asked the Inspector.

"She's a medium," said Victoria.

"The best in Edinburgh," said Kitty.

"Well, I don't think that would be..." started Inspector MacLeod.

He was cut off by Kitty, who said, "Of course he'll come, dear. I will too if you like?"

Victoria squeezed Kitty's hand. "Oh that would be nice of you. It's Mrs Murray isn't it? I do remember you now."

"Yes. Frazer here, I mean Inspector MacLeod is my son-in-law, so we'll both come. Won't we, Frazer!" The Inspector nodded but didn't look very happy at the prospect.

"I'll go and get the tea," he said.

Chapter 17 White Hat

Archie was in his dark room working on the plates from the Burry Man shoot. He'd already spent forty minutes fixing them, washing off the excess gelatin and emulsion. Now he was enlarging the last print. When he was finished he examined all the prints laid out together. He was quite pleased with the result.

The one with the Burry Man and his two assistants with the Forth in the background would be his choice for *The Reekie*, but he knew that his boss Bridgewater would go for the other one with the villagers in the background. The beheaded image of the Burry Man was striking but no way would that one be ever used. That would have to go straight to the police as evidence of the scene of the crime. He put it in an envelope.

He admired the picture of Amulya and the Burry Man's two assistants, standing at the park entrance. She had a nice smile. He looked closer at the photograph. There was something white in the background. Darn it! Perhaps some of the emulsion had lifted off during the development. He picked up his magnifying glass and peered at the white blur. He noticed that it was attached to a body. It was someone wearing a white hat moving from behind a tree towards the bushes where the Burry Man had been murdered.

"Holy Moses!" exclaimed Archie.

***

Archie watched as the Inspector spread the photographs out across his desk. The Inspector picked up the photograph of the beheaded Burry Man. He took his reading glasses from his pocket and examined the photograph.

"Yes very good. Sharp. Unfortunately it doesn't tell us anything new but handy to keep for our records," said the Inspector. "Did you take any of footprints? Near the wall. The lane behind?"

Archie shook his head. "No sorry. It started to pour down and I couldn't see. But here, look at this!" He tapped on the one with Amulya.

"A nice photograph of Miss Patel and the Aird sons, but I fail to see why it is relevant?" said the Inspector.

"Gabriel Aird was killed around the time that this was taken. Look in the background!" Archie leaned forward and pointed, "Top right. Next to the bushes."

"It's a blur. A person moving?" asked the Inspector.

"Someone coming out of the bushes where a murder has just taken place," stated Archie.

"All I can see is a blurred white streak," said the Inspector.

Archie pushed forward the photograph of the Burry Man and his assistants with the crowd behind them. He pointed to Hector in his white hat.

"Hector Findlay left us for a few minutes. He said he was going to the inn to collect something he'd left there." Archie pointed to the blurred white streak on Amulya's portrait. "But this tells a different story!"

***

The manager's office of *The Reekie* was a grandiose room with a sweeping panorama of North Bridge. Reginald Bridgewater, the stout middle-aged manager with a huge grey moustache, sweated profusely as he skimmed over Hector's article. Sitting opposite him, Hector fidgeted with his collar as Reginald crossed out several sentences with his fountain pen. Reginald handed the article back to Hector.

"I think we can salvage this dog's dinner. Cut out these bits here and here!" Reginald flourished his pen across several paragraphs. Hector stared at the green ink lines crossed through his work.

"But sir, these things did happen!" complained Hector.

"Look here! I'm running a quality newspaper. Not one of your Penny Dreadfuls. Is that clear?" grunted Reginald.

"Yes but..." There was a knock at the door and a secretary entered. "The police, sir."

Inspector MacLeod and PC Urquhart strode into the office.

"What's all this?" asked Reginald.

"Sorry sir. It's not you we've come to see," said the Inspector. He turned to Hector, who stood up. "Yes! What is it? What do you want?" asked Hector.

"We'd like you to come down to the station," said the Inspector.

"But I gave you my statement!" said Hector.

"We have new evidence that'd we'd like to show you and to ask you some further questions" said the Inspector.

"Do you need him now?" asked Reginald. "We've a story to finish."

The Inspector gave Reginald a stare.

"Oh alright. I suppose I can finish this off by myself," shrugged Reginald. "Report back as soon as you've finished, Hector!"

"I will do. It's obviously some sort of mistake," said Hector.

***

PC Urquhart stood guard at the door of Inspector MacLeod's office. A tired Hector sat opposite the Inspector. The photographs were spread out on the desk between them.

"Why did you kill him?" said the Inspector.

Hector sighed in exasperation. "How many times do I have to say it? I didn't kill him!"

The Inspector pointed to the white blur in the background of the photograph with Amulya.

"So we're to believe you just went into the bushes to relieve yourself?" said the Inspector.

"Yes!"

"A witness said that you lied. Said that you said that you were going back to the inn," stated the Inspector.

"I told you already. I said that just to be polite in front of Miss Patel."

The Inspector rubbed his beard. "Tell me again why you went into the bushes?"

"I just told you. To relieve myself. To take a fucking piss!"

"Come now Mr Findlay, no need to swear is there," said the Inspector. Hector sighed.

The Inspector looked through his notes. "Mr Findlay, what size of shoe do you take?"

"Nine. Or sometimes ten. Why?" asked Hector.

The Inspector took a photograph of a muddy footprint out of an envelope and passed it to Hector.

"Size ten tackety boots. You have a pair?" asked the Inspector.

"Of course not!" said Hector.

Molly. © David Hutchison.

Chapter 18   Molly

Campbell stood with Amulya on the opposite side of the street from Surgeons' Hall. Today, at least, there were no protestors at the gates.

"I'm glad it's quiet," said Amulya.

"Wilton and his chums seem to have gotten the message," said Campbell.

Amulya looked up and down the street. "Where is she? It's nearly time."

"You should go in, "said Campbell. "I'll come to the door just in case. Are you ready?"

Amulya nodded. She and Campbell crossed the street and passed through the gates without incident.

"It looks clear. I'm off to the library then," said Campbell.

Amulya said, "Thanks."

"I'll catch you later," said Campbell. He waved and went back towards the gates.

Amulya went through the door, to a small round hall leading to a large staircase. She climbed up the staircase and entered the Playfair Hall, where the anatomy class was set up. There was a foul smell in the air. The ornate round window in the ceiling was lit up. A body was covered in a sheet, on a trolley in the centre of the room.

Lecturer Dr Nicolson, a frail sixty year old, got up from a chair as Amulya entered.   "Were there not meant to be two of you?" asked the doctor. "I can only do this class once."

"Miss Moliette will be with us presently," said Amulya.

Dr Nicolson glanced at the wall clock. Five minutes to two. He raised a bushy eyebrow. "Let us hope so."

***

Liz walked briskly out of the graveyard and up the High Street. In a few minutes she reached South Bridge. She stopped briefly opposite the Tron Kirk to get her breath back. She turned onto Nicolson Street and shortly arrived at Surgeons' Hall. She rushed up the stairs and into the anatomy class just as the clock struck two. She ran across the room and sat down next to Amulya. Dr Nicolson was standing in front of the trolley.

"Ladies. Let us begin, "said the doctor. The doctor folded the sheet down from the top half of the cadaver. The rib cage had already been removed. "You'd better come closer."

***

Wilton looked around the Surgeons' Hall garden. All clear. He opened the door and waved the piece of bread at the university mascot; Molly, a fluffy Cheviot sheep. Molly trotted forward. Wilton slowly walked backwards into the corridor. Molly stopped. Wilton waved the bread again. He tempted Molly forward, down the corridor towards the wide staircase. Wilton slowly moved up the staircase. Molly didn't seem to want to climb the stairs.

Wilton slowly descended a few steps and held out the bread. Molly climbed a few steps. Wilton gently coaxed the sheep up the staircase to the top. He moved towards the main door of the Playfair Hall. At the door he dropped the bread. He opened the door very slowly and left it open a tiny fraction. He edged slowly down the corridor past Molly. She was nervous of him but she really wanted the bread. She moved past him and went for the bread. Wilton crept back to the top of the staircase. Suddenly he rushed towards the sheep with his arms outstretched and thumped his shoes on the floor. Molly panicked and ran forward. She shot out of the corridor, knocking the door wide open, and into the large hall.

She rushed across the room knocking into chairs and sending them flying. Liz and Amulya were shocked by Molly's sudden appearance, but managed to move out of the sheep's path. Dr Nicolson wasn't so lucky. He staggered out of the way and fell awkwardly onto the floor. He screamed as his arm snapped. Molly bolted across the room.

Liz and Amulya rushed over to the doctor. "Let me see!" said Liz. She crouched down and tried to roll up the doctor's sleeve. He winced in pain.

"I think it's broken!" said Dr Nicolson.

"Have you got scissors?" asked Liz.

"In the drawer over there!" said Dr Nicolson.

"Amulya!" commanded Liz. Amulya raked through the drawer and brought back a pair of scissors. Liz quickly cut up the sleeve to the elbow revealing the white shirt underneath.

"No blood. That's good," said Liz. She carefully cut through the shirt sleeve. The doctor grimaced in pain. "Oh my god!" shouted the doctor as Liz examined the bruised area.

"I think the ulna is fractured. Displaced. Amulya?" said Liz.

Amulya inspected the doctor's arm. She nodded to Liz. "At least it's not an open fracture."

"Oh god! The bone will have to be realigned," exclaimed the doctor.

"We can go and find a doctor," said Liz.

"There's a better chance of reducing any complications if we do this right now," said Dr Nicolson.

"I don't know if ..." said Liz.

"Do it!" said Dr Nicolson.

Liz said, "Amulya can you find something to use as a splint?"

Amulya ran across to some cupboards and rummaged through them. She found a couple of wooden rulers and a dusting cloth. She rushed back with them. Liz placed one of the rulers along the underside of the doctor's arm. Liz readied herself.

"Perhaps we should wait?" asked Liz.

Dr Nicholson fainted.

"He's out. Let's do it now!" said Liz. She quickly felt along the arm for the fracture. She found it and moved the two bones back into alignment. Liz put the other ruler along the top of his arm. Meanwhile Amulya ripped the cloth into shreds. She wound the strips around the rulers, strutting Dr Nicholson's arm, binding the makeshift splints together. Dr Nicolson groaned and came to.

Liz said, "All done. I'll fetch Dr Blyth. You'll need something for the pain."

"Thank you!" The doctor grimaced.

Liz got up. She picked up her umbrella and moved towards Molly. The frightened sheep shat on the floor.

"Here, girl. No one's going to hurt you," soothed Liz. She slowly moved closer to Molly.

"Amulya, open the door!" said Liz. Amulya left the doctor, opened the door and stood back.

Liz gently hooked Molly's neck with the handle of the umbrella. She led Molly to the door and into the corridor. She closed the door behind her and unhooked the sheep.

She manoeuvred the sheep towards the staircase. Molly started to go down the stairs. Liz made sure to keep back and not hurry the sheep. Once Molly had reached the bottom of the stairs Liz edged past her and went down to the end of the corridor. She tried to open the main door. It seemed stuck. She pulled on it harder. Suddenly the door gave way. Liz stumbled and fell. Standing laughing in the doorway was Wilton. He'd obviously been holding onto the door. At that second Amulya came down the stairs. Molly panicked and bolted down the corridor past Liz and to the main door. She butted Wilton out of the way as she shot out the door.

116

Wilton screamed, "Arrggh!" as he crouched over, doubled up in pain, clutching his groin.

"Serves you right!" laughed Liz.

Molly came to a stop in the garden and began to graze on the lawn. Amulya came to the main door and joined in laughing with Liz. Wilton scowled at the women and slinked off with a staggering gait, obviously still suffering.

Liz went off to Florian's office, where she found the doctor writing up notes. Liz noticed that Florian was sweating heavily.

Liz said, "Are you alright, doctor?"

Florian fanned her face with a sheet of paper. "It's bit too hot in here. That's all."

"Dr Nicolson has been injured. We've patched him up as best we could. Could you check up on him?" asked Liz.

"Yes of course. What happened to him?" asked Florian.

"He's broken his arm," said Liz. "Can you bring something for the pain?"

Florian nodded and went over to a cabinet. She packed a few items into her medical bag.

"Let's go!"

A few minutes later Liz entered the exam hall with Florian. Amulya was relieved to see them. Dr Nicolson was sitting at his desk, in a lot of pain.

"I've tried to make him comfortable," said Amulya. "I hope we set it properly."

Florian studied the impromptu splint on Dr Nicholson's arm.

"It looks alright but I'll just need to check it. Sorry Dr Nicholson," said Florian untying the duster rag. She gently removed the splints and felt along the bone.

"Arrggh!" cried Dr Nicolson. "Sorry," said Florian, as she replaced the rulers with two lengths of thick leather, bandaged them along the arm and added a sling.

Florian nodded to Liz. "Well done! The bone has been correctly set. You'll make a fine doctor yet!"

Liz said, "Actually it was a joint effort. Amulya helped me."

Amulya smirked. "We make a good team."

"I'm sorry to interrupt but I could do with something for the pain, now!" said Dr Nicolson.

"Yes, sorry," apologised Florian. She rummaged in her bag and pulled out a bottle of laudanum.

The door burst open and Sally the maid rushed in. She thrust a note into Amulya's hand.

"Oh miss. It's Master Findlay. He's been arrested!"

"What?" asked Amulya. She frowned as she read though the note. "It must be a mistake! It doesn't make sense. I'd better go to him." Amulya and Sally rushed out the door and nearly knocked down Professor Atticus as he entered.

"Excuse me!" shouted the professor. He had the usual wide eyes. Another experiment with poison. The professor noticed that Dr Nicolson's arm was in a splint. "Are you alright Dr Nicolson?" asked the professor.

"I am, thanks to the ladies. They patched my arm up pretty good," replied Dr Nicolson.

"Wait. Did I hear correctly? The ladies patched your arm up?" asked the professor.

Florian nodded to Liz. "Liz?"

Liz nodded and said, "A clean fracture of the arm. I realigned it. We made a makeshift splint."

"We?" asked the professor.

"Miss Patel and I," said Liz.

The professor frowned. "Unqualified females cannot do that!" he barked.

"It seems that they can," quipped Florian.

"Dr Blyth please do keep your students under control!" said the professor.

"They are not my students and I think it is you that appears to be out of control," snapped Florian.

"Pah!" said the professor. He turned to Dr Nicolson. "Sir. I do most assuredly apologize. I hope that you will not sue the school if you lose your arm through these ladies' audacity!"

"I think I'm in safe hands. However I would like to make a complaint about Wilton Grimes," said Dr Nicolson.

The professor stared back, his pupils so enlarged that this irises were almost non-existent. "Why? Master Grimes is one of our top scholars. In fact he's just won the Hope Prize."

Dr Nicolson flinched as he leaned forward. "He let Molly loose. That's what caused this!"

"So you actually saw Wilton... Master Grimes doing this?" said the professor.

"I didn't see him do it exactly. Although I did wonder why he was in the garden feeding Molly earlier as I went to open up the exam hall," replied Dr Nicolson.

Liz raised her eyebrows to Florian at that. She said, "We know that he did it. He was waiting behind the door."

"That's libel!" screeched the professor.

Liz was about to reply and then decided not to. She thought she might get too carried away. The professor seemed annoyed that he hadn't goaded her enough.

"Well, all I can say is that the sooner female students are banned the better."

The professor produced a paper from his pocket and held it out. It was his petition against the women students and it was now full of signatures.

"See!" Professor Atticus grinned.

"That's really unfair!" snapped Liz.

"I must protest!" expressed Florian. She gasped and collapsed onto the floor. Liz rushed over to her.

"Dr Blyth?" asked Liz.

"Out of the way woman!" commanded the professor. He nudged past Liz and bent down. He put his ear to Florian's chest. He shook his head and began to unbutton Florian's shirt. Florian stirred and waved the professor's hands off.

"I need to get home," said Florian. "Liz help me!"

Liz helped the doctor to stand up

"Will you help me to flag down a carriage?" asked Florian.

"Of course, doctor," said Liz. She helped the doctor out of the room. The professor scowled as he watched them leave.

Chapter 19   Hector

It was a bare white cell. Just a single bed and a tin bucket in a corner. A hint of urine in the air. Hector sat on the bed, depressed and angry, head between his hands. There was a muffled whistling, the lock clicked and the door swung open. PC Urquhart stood aside and Amulya burst into the room.

"Oh Hector!" gasped Amulya. She rushed across and hugged him. "This is awful. We need to get you out of here. What happened?"

Hector did a sarcastic chuckle. "I've been charged with the murder of Gabriel Aird. The Burry Man."

"But that's ridiculous! I was there," said Amulya. "We gave statements!"

"I know. But if you remember I went off for a short while," said Hector.

"Yes. I remember you went back to the Hawes Inn," replied Amulya.

Hector shook his head. "That's the trouble. I didn't."

Amulya frowned. "What do you mean?"

Hector shrugged. "It's a bit embarrassing really. I actually double-backed and went into the bushes. I was desperate to relieve myself."

Amulya stood up and paced the room. "Did you tell the police?"

Hector nodded. "Yes. But you can see how it looks. They don't believe me."

Amulya sat down deflated.

"But didn't someone see you. Saw that you didn't, you know?"

Hector said, "They showed me that photograph of you and the Aird sons that Archie took. I'm blurred in the background. It's easy enough to make out my damn hat though." He picked up the white bowler on the edge of the bed with his right hand and gave it a filthy look. He made as if to punch the hat with his left hand.

Amulya closed her hand over his left hand. "You're left-handed, aren't you?"

"Yes, why?" asked Hector.

Amulya had a faraway look in her eyes, as if she was trying to remember something. She smiled. "Only three percent of the population is left-hand." She raised his hand.

"So?" shrugged Hector.

Amulya let go of his hand. "We need to examine the body."

"What good will that do?" asked Hector.

"From the wound you can tell whether the killer was left or right-handed," said Amulya.

"Really?" said Hector.

"Liz knows more about it than me. I'll go and see her right now," said Amulya. She got up and banged on the door. The wee hatch slid open and PC Urquhart looked through. He whistled, closed the hatch and unlocked the door.

Amulya turned back to Hector. "Don't worry. I'll get you out of this!"

Hector gave Amulya a weak smile.

***

Liz looked out the carriage window. They had turned up into Causewayside. Florian leaned against her shoulder, drifting in and out of consciousness. The carriage swerved to avoid an old man crossing the road. The sudden movement woke Florian up. "Charles dear?" asked Florian. Her eyes fluttered and she fell back into unconsciousness.

The carriage came to a stop outside Florian's townhouse. The driver got down and helped Liz take the semi-awake Florian out of the carriage. Charles must have been on the lookout from a window, as the front door immediately opened and he ran down the steps, followed by a barking Psyche. He helped Liz manoeuvre Florian up the steps and into the house.

"My stays!" gasped Liz as she got back her breath. She dropped her umbrella on the hallway floor.

"Don't worry, miss. I can manage," said Charles. He held onto Florian as Liz flopped down into a chair. Charles lifted Florian over his shoulder and carried her up the stairs. Psyche raced ahead.

Liz got her breath back and followed them. Charles pushed open a bedroom door and laid Florian out on the double bed. Psyche barked and jumped up on the bed.

Liz touched Florian's brow and frowned. "Have you any salicylic acid?"

Charles replied, "I'll go and look. Psyche get down!" Charles rushed out of the room followed by Psyche. Liz poured some water from the ewer on the dresser into a bowl. She dipped the edge of a towel into it and went across to Florian and mopped her brow. Liz started to unbutton Florian's jacket. She frowned as she felt some sort of binding under the shirt. Psyche jumped up on the bed as Charles entered.

"I couldn't find salicylic acid. Will willow bark do?" said Charles. He noticed that Liz was removing Florian's jacket. "I'll do that! You can leave now!"

Liz was annoyed. "But I need to check his wound."

Charles shook his head. "I know what to do."

"But you don't have any medical training!" said Liz.

Charles ushered Liz out of the room and locked the door. Liz stood in the corridor, fuming. How dare he! She calmed herself down and knocked on the door.

"Charles. I should really check his wound."

"I'm handling it," shouted Charles. Liz raised her fist to bang on the door, then decided against it.

"Wash the wound and apply clean bandages," she called through the door. "Call me if he gets worse."

"I will," said Charles.

Liz went down the stairs. She thought the situation most peculiar. She picked up her umbrella and left. It was raining. Again! Liz put up her umbrella and walked along the street. She wondered why Charles was so protective of Dr Blyth. Surely she had much more medical knowledge than a servant. But he didn't always act like a servant. Then she stopped and the idea hit her full on. Of course! There had been a few of the boys back in the orphanage that had been that way. You took love wherever you could find it in that place, although some treated it as a business and managed to make a fair bit of extra money from it. She remembered one boy called Peter. She'd been quite friendly with him. The warden had caught him doing it with an older gentleman in the alley at the back of the orphanage, more than once. He'd eventually been thrown out and he'd moved into a molly house down the street. Peter had smiled at her when she'd gone past a few times and had given her a swig of his gin. Dr Blyth and Charles; madge culls. She couldn't believe that she'd not noticed before. Suddenly there was a hand waving in front of her face. Liz came out of her reverie. Amulya stood in her path.

"Liz! Thank god I've found you," said Amulya. "I need your help."

"You've seen Hector?" asked Liz.

"Yes. I've just come from him. They've put him in an awful cell. They think he killed the Burry Man," said Amuyla.

"Why?" asked Liz.

"He was relieving himself near the place he was killed. Archie got him in a photograph," said Amuyla.

"But that doesn't prove anything," said Liz.

"I think I know how to get him out," said Amulya.

"How?" asked Liz.

"Hector is left-handed. If we can prove the murderer was right-handed they'll have to let Hector go," said Amulya.

Liz nodded. "Yes of course! We should be able to tell from the angle of the cut whether the killer was right or left-handed."

"And the height of the killer," said Amulya.

"Well if they were taller or shorter than the victim if it was a stabbing but not with a beheading," said Liz.

"Come on! We must go to see Inspector MacLeod and examine the bodies at the dead house," said Amulya. She linked arms with Liz as they turned down the High Street.

***

Jack Fox and Gabriel Aird, both covered in sheets, were laid out on tables in the dead house. Several incense sticks were scattered around the room in a feeble attempt to mask the putrid smell. Inspector Macleod and PC Urquhart watched as Liz and Amulya examined Aird's neck. Liz made a quick sketch of the wound. She showed the sketch to the Inspector.

"The initial cut was made from left to right therefore it was most likely made with a right-handed person," stated Liz.

"Hector is left handed! Inspector Macleod will you release Hector now?" asked Amulya.

The Inspector rubbed his beard. "Hold on! If the killer grabbed his victim from behind and slashed the front of the throat wouldn't it be the other way round?"

Liz shook her head. "Decapitation would be much easier and quicker to do from the front."

She went over to a wooden bench where the Burry Man's suit was laid out. She beckoned to the Inspector. "Look at this!" She pointed to an area of the suit where the burrs had been partly plucked off and a bloody mark was visible. "I think that this mark is the palm of the right hand where the body was held firmly during the cutting between vertebrae."

Amulya said, "Please let him go sir."

The Inspector sighed and said, "Alright. Urquhart, release the prisoner."

Amulya beamed and said, "Thank you." She turned and followed PC Urquhart out of the room.

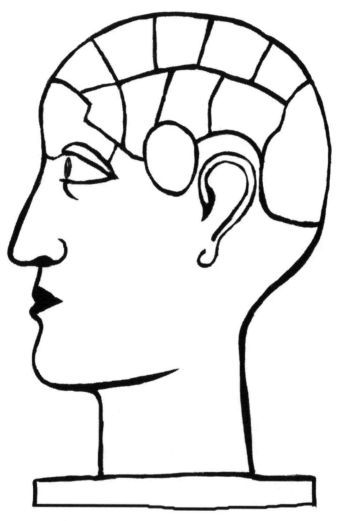

Phrenology Head. © David Hutchison.

Chapter 20   Phrenology

"So how is he choosing his victims?" said the Inspector.

Liz tapped her umbrella. "He? It could be a woman."

The Inspector sighed. "No. Gabriel Aird's son said it was a man." He took out his notebook and checked Douglas Aird's statement. "A fit man, around my height or shorter."

"Anything else?" Liz felt slightly annoyed that the Inspector had not given her that information sooner.

"He didn't see his face. He wore a brown or black cap. That's it." The Inspector put his notebook back in his pocket.

"Footprints. Tackety boots?" said Liz.

The Inspector shook his head. "No. Archie said that there was too much rain later to get footprints." He pulled the sheet over Gabriel Aird's neck. "Let's get out of here."

They left the dead house, walked through the graveyard and out of the gates. The Inspector bought some of his favourite German biscuits from a young girl vendor in the street. They went into the station. The Inspector walked up to the main desk.

"Wills, any new developments?"

"No sir," yawned Sergeant Wills, as he looked up from his paper.

"Get Urquhart to make a pot of tea for us please," said the Inspector.

Liz followed the Inspector into his office. The Inspector pulled out a chair and Liz sat down.

The Inspector paced the room. "But why keep the head?"

Liz said, "Some sort of trophy? Like big games hunters do?"

"That's possible but I think it's more than that. What did the victims have in common?" The Inspector leaned against the small fireplace. "Gabriel Aird was a fisherman. Jack Fox was an artist. I can't see the connection."

Liz said, "Artists paint fishermen. Perhaps Aird sat for Fox?"

The Inspector shook her head. "I don't think he painted fishermen. It was cats, well before he went to the asylum. Remember his sister's house?"

"All those cat paintings," nodded Liz.

"But you're right. We should ask Victoria to make sure." The Inspector jotted down a note then looked up. "An exhibition then. They met at an exhibition. Are we looking for a murderous art collector?" The Inspector removed Jack's self-portrait from a drawer.

There was a knock at the door and PC Urquhart came in with a pot of tea and cups on a tray.

"Just Assam, sir. The Earl Grey's finished. I think Wills used it all, again," said Urquhart. The Inspector frowned. "Anyway let's see what we have here." He unrolled the drawing and laid it out on the table. He placed an inkwell at one end and a metal whistle at the other to stop the paper rolling back up.

Liz poured the tea out as the Inspector and PC Urquhart puzzled over the self-portrait.

The Inspector stroked his beard in thought. "When an artist dies doesn't the price of their art go up? Perhaps all those cat paintings are worth a fortune?"

"Maybe they are. But that doesn't explain why Gabriel Aird was beheaded," said Liz.

The Inspector put the portrait down on his desk. Liz leaned forward and picked it up. She analysed the face staring out at her. A rather bland face. No particular etched lines. The eyes were small and quite close together. Bald head. Her eyes wandered to the small lump on Jack's left temple. She remembered that Victoria had mentioned it when they had asked her about any distinguishing marks. They had dismissed it as it hadn't seemed relevant at the time when trying to identify a body lacking a head. Liz had a flash of inspiration.

"I wonder...phrenology?" whispered Liz.

"What's that?" asked the Inspector, halfway through chomping on another sumptuous German biscuit.

"Phrenology. See the lump on his head. There." said Liz as she pointed to Jack's temple.

"Phrenologists believe that you can tell a person's character by the shape of their skull. It's all hokum of course."

The Inspector scratched his head and looked puzzled.

"Did Gabriel Aird have anything unusual about his head?" asked Liz.

"Urquhart. I want you to go and see the family. Find out if there was anything unusual about his head. Get a photograph, drawing, whatever, if you can," said the Inspector.

"Yes sir," said PC Urquhart. He quickly left the room. Liz could hear him whistling as he went down the corridor.

The Inspector searched through his drawers.

"What are you looking for Inspector?" asked Liz.

"I'm..." The Inspector pulled out a folder. "Here it is!" He opened the folder. "The notes on Henri Blanc. The French sailor found beheaded in Leith. Along with the ones Dr Blyth dropped in."

The Inspector skimmed through the notes.

"The crew were interviewed. Oh where is it?" He flipped over some pages. "Ah here it is! Henri Blanc had the nickname of Bosse."

Liz said, "So?" The Inspector grinned. "At first I thought it meant that the man was a bossy character but that's not it at all. Bosse is French for bump."

"Oh of course! That must be where the word emboss comes from," said Liz. "Wait... that means..."

The Inspector cut in, "Do you know of any phrenologists in Edinburgh?"

Liz put her elbows on the desk and thought. "I heard that Professor Atticus used to teach it years ago. It was a big craze in the forties."

"I can't see a professor going round cutting people's heads off," said the Inspector.

Liz shrugged. "It's an open secret that the professor has a long history of experimenting on himself with different poisons. You must see his eyes; black and soulless. Perhaps it's addled his brain and he's gone too far. Turned into a killer?"

"So how old is this professor?" asked the Inspector.

"I don't know. Mid-sixties, perhaps seventy?" suggested Liz.

"Sounds unlikely that he would have the strength to kill and behead the victims. They were both grown men," said the Inspector.

"He could have knocked them out first. Caught them unawares. Dr Blyth did look for poison in the autopsy but there are ones that don't show up and if anyone is going to know about all the different poisons it would be the professor," said Liz.

"But then we have the testimony of Aird's son. He said that the killer scrambled over a high stone wall. Can you see your professor doing that?" asked the Inspector.

"He's definitely not my professor! He's trying to stop women from doing medicine," said Liz.

"Oh?" asked the Inspector.

"The professor's star pupil Wilton Grimes attacked me when I was trying to attend an exam."

"I'd advise you to try to be impartial even though they do sound like a pair of idiots," said the Inspector.

"I suppose that you're right. No matter how much I'd like him to be the killer he's just too feeble," said Liz. "Even if he took some kind of enhancement drug."

"He could have an accomplice," said the Inspector.

"Do you really think so?" asked Liz.

"How about that star pupil of his?" asked the Inspector.

"No. I don't see it. Grimes is a coward," said Liz.

"So where can I find this professor?" asked Inspector MacLeod.

"He's got an office at the Medical School," said Liz. "If he's not there they can give you his home address I'm sure. I believe it's somewhere in the New Town."

***

The Inspector had had no luck tracking the professor down at the Medical School but a pettifogging receptionist had grudgingly given him the professor's home address in the New Town.

After a brisk walk across the North Bridge and stopping on Princes Street to wolf down a tasty Scotch pie from a street vendor, the Inspector headed downhill to the professor's house on Heriot Row. The Inspector climbed the steps and pulled on the doorbell. As he waited he looked across the street overlooking Queen Street Gardens. Very nice, he thought.

The door opened slowly.

"Yes, can I help you?" asked the maid Daphne.

"Inspector Macleod to see Professor Atticus. Is he at home?"

"He is, but I don't know if he is receiving visitors at this time. You'd better come in and wait while I see," Daphne smiled nervously and ushered the Inspector into a wide hall.

"If you could wait here please sir. I'll go and check," said Daphne. She rushed off down a corridor. The Inspector looked around the hall. On one wall was a large oil painting of a curling match on Duddingston Loch. In a few minutes Daphne returned.

"The professor will see you. Please come with me, sir."

The Inspector followed her down a long corridor. Daphne showed Inspector MacLeod into Professor Atticus's study.

"He'll be down shortly, sir," said Daphne. She smiled and left the room.

The Inspector took in the study. He noticed a white ceramic head on a desk. He crossed the room and observed the different sections painted on the head. Within each section were words such as: *hope, caution, self-esteem, intention, colour, intellect*, etc. How odd, he thought, that the word *language* would be between the left eye and cheekbone. No more so than the word *individuality* followed the bridge of the nose. The Inspector flicked a bit of dust from the middle of the forehead.

"Ah! The organ of foresight and intuition," said Professor Atticus as he closed the door behind him.

"Sorry?" said the Inspector.

The professor came over and tapped the bust in the middle of the forehead.

"According to phrenology anyway. What can I do for you Inspector?" said the professor, his pupils like wide black pits.

"Actually it's phrenology that I came to see you about. I've been told that you teach it," said the Inspector.

The professor sighed. "Eons ago. Gall did have some interesting theories but I've not taught it since the Fowler brothers made it into a carnivalesque sideshow."

The professor sat down at his desk and indicated a chair to the Inspector.

The Inspector nodded and sat down. "So you don't practise it now?"

Professor Atticus shook his head. "What's your interest in it?"

"I'm sorry I cannot divulge that information," said the Inspector.

"Oh?" said the professor.

"Do you know of any phrenologists in Edinburgh?" asked the Inspector.

The professor shrugged. "The Combe brothers are long gone. Chambers and Nicol more recently. There's Brown I suppose, but he's in Dumfries and he's not done much since his accident. No academics that I know of consider it a serious science anymore."

Inspector MacLeod patted the bust. "Yet here we are."

The professor raised his eyebrows. "It only has sentimental value. A gift."

"Where were you yesterday evening?" asked the Inspector.

"Why Inspector? Do you suspect me of something?" grinned the professor.

"Please just answer the question," said the Inspector.

The professor leaned to the side and pulled on a velvet bell rope. He leaned back and smiled.

Daphne rushed into the room.

"Yes sir?"

"Daphne where was I last night?" asked the professor.

"Begging your pardon sir. What do you mean?" asked Daphne.

"It's a simple question. The Inspector here would like to know where I was last night," said the professor.

Daphne blushed, nodded at the Inspector and then back to the professor, "Where you always is every evening. Sitting there writing. I brought your meal at seven. Boiled herring and tatties, sir. Then bread and butter pudding. I collected your tray at seven thirty. Brought your cocoa at nine. You retired with a glass of port at ten."

The professor leaned back and gestured outwards to the Inspector. "There you have it."

"Well, thank you for your time professor. If you do think of anyone you've forgotten please let me know."

"You could always enquire at the Edinburgh Phrenological Society. The meetings stopped years ago but I believe they still keep it open as a museum. It's on Chambers Street."

"Thank you," said the Inspector as he stood up. He touched the phrenology head. "A gift you said?"

The professor nodded, "Yes."

"From whom?" asked the Inspector.

The professor shook his head. "I can't remember. It was so long ago."

The Inspector smiled. "Perhaps if you came down to the station it would help to jog your memory?"

The professor frowned and said, "Oh yes I remember now. Dr Emrie it was."

"The alienist at the asylum?" asked the Inspector.

"I believe that he works there now although I've not seen him for many moons. Not since I used to go to the meetings on Chambers Street."

The Inspector smiled. "Thank you again for your help professor."

"Yes, yes. Inspector. Daphne please show the Inspector out!"

***

Twenty minutes later the Inspector was walking down Chambers Street when he came across four windows with a portrait bust above each. This was the place. He rang the bell. He waited for a long while and was just about to leave when the door was slowly opened by a short old man.

"The collection is closed. Come back another time," said the man. He started to close the door.

"Not so fast!" said the Inspector. He pushed past the man and into the front hall.

"I say!" said the old man.

"I'm Inspector MacLeod. I need to ask you a few questions."

"Oh very well. Come through here," said the old man. He hobbled down the hall and through a doorway on the left. The Inspector followed him into a large room with a bay window overlooking the street. The walls were covered in shelves of plaster heads. The old man sat in a comfy chair next to a desk, with a pot of tea.

"Would you like a cup?" he asked.

"No thank you," said the Inspector. "So are you a phrenologist?"

Wilson took a sip of his tea and shook his head. "Good lord no. I just look after the place. I'm Wilson, the caretaker."

The Inspector sat down. "I'm investigating several murders and have reason to believe that phrenology is connected to it in some way."

Wilson spluttered on his tea. "Oh my!"

The Inspector took out a notebook. "Do you know any phrenologists here in Edinburgh?"

Wilson shook his head. "Not any more. This place would have been shut down but for the Henderson Trust's head collection. We have the death mask of William Burke and the life mask of William Hare too. That's what people come to see."

"So you don't know any phrenologists?" asked the Inspector.

Wilson said, "No. Everyone's either dead or abandoned it as far as I know. You could ask that professor, pompous fellow, what's his name? Atticus! He used to be a member."

"How about Dr Emrie?" asked the Inspector.

"Oh yes. I forgot about him. He used to come to come along with Atticus, but they don't have the meetings here anymore," said Wilson.

"Oh well thank you anyway," said the Inspector.

"Oh there was a man here a few times, very interested, but I never got his name. Think he was studying to be a doctor. Said something about Charles Darwin wouldn't have developed his theories on natural selection if it hadn't been for phrenology. So he said anyway. I don't see how but I'm not a scholar."

"Could you describe him?"

"Edinburgh accent, quite posh," said Wilson.

"Age?" asked the Inspector.

"He sounded young," shrugged Wilson.

"What did he look like?" asked the Inspector.

"I'm afraid I'm quite blind Inspector!" said Wilson.

The Inspector leaned forward and waved a hand in front of Wilson's eyes. The old man didn't blink but frowned.

"I said I was blind, not stupid. I felt your hand moving the air in front of me."

"Sorry. " The Inspector got up. "Thank you. I'll show myself out."

Chapter 21 The Royal Infirmary

It was a fine sunny morning as Liz and Amulya walked along Infirmary Street.

"I'm looking forward to getting some hospital experience," said Amulya.

"Yes although I do enjoy our anatomy classes I'm getting fed up just working with dead bodies," replied Liz as they passed through the gates of the Royal Infirmary.

They went up to the main entrance and entered the building. There was a strong smell of carbolic soap in the foyer.

An old man in overalls came through a door. As he passed them Liz stopped him.

"Excuse me. Where do we report to?" asked Liz.

"Who are you?" asked the man.

"We're the student doctors," said Liz.

The man looked rather taken aback. "Oh!" he exclaimed. He pointed down a long corridor. "Try Dr Green's office. Down there. First on the right."

"Thank you," said Liz.

The man went out the main door. Liz and Amulya went down the corridor and came to Dr Green's office. Amulya knocked on the door. There was no reply. Amulya shrugged. Liz knocked on the door. Still no reply. Liz tried the door. It was locked.

"Let's see if we can find someone else to ask," said Liz. Amulya nodded. They carried on down the corridor. A young nurse came out from a set of swinging doors. She was wearing a cloth mask over her nose and mouth.

"Can you help us? We're the new student doctors. Dr Green was meant to meet us," said Liz.

The nurse pulled down her mask. "Oh, he's doing the rounds at the moment. He's in the Infectious Diseases Ward." She turned and pointed back to the doors that she had just exited. "Through that doors and to the right."

"Thanks," said Liz and Amulya, in unison.

"You'll need to put on masks if you're going to go in there!" said the nurse.

"Where do we get them?" asked Amulya.

"Hold on a minute. I'll see if I can find some for you. Wait here!" said the nurse. She went back through the doors.

"I wonder why we need masks?" asked Amulya.

"It's the ward of infectious diseases!" said Liz.

"I thought that they'd discovered that diseases weren't airborne," replied Amulya. "Isn't all that stuff about miasma debunked now?"

"Better safe than sorry," said Liz.

"I suppose so," agreed Amulya.

The nurse came back through the door carrying a couple of cloth masks. She handed them out to Liz and Amulya.

"Thank you," said Liz.

"We're most grateful," said Amulya.

"I thought that the university had chased off all the female medical students," said the nurse.

"They can't get rid of us that easily," grinned Liz.

The nurse smiled. "Good on yourselves!" She gave a wee wave and hurried off down the corridor.

"She was nice," said Amulya. Liz nodded and tied her mask on.

Amulya struggled to put her mask on.

"Here let me help you," said Liz. She helped Amulya to tie on her mask.

"Come on!" said Liz. She pushed through the swinging doors. Amulya followed her down the corridor and to another door on the right. A large sign above the door read *Infectious Diseases*.

"Oh well, here goes," said Liz and opened the door.

They walked into a long room. The smell hit them like being plunged headfirst into a barrel of excrement and vomit.

"Oh!" cried out Amulya as she tried not to gag. "Couldn't they open the windows? Didn't Florence Nightingale say that fresh air is healthy?"

"Heaven preserve us!" gasped Liz as she looked around the ward. She had never seen such a sight. It was a male only ward although some of them had skin so blotchy with open sores dripping pus that they hardly looked human. As they passed one of the beds a man with swollen milky white eyes reached out with a hand covered in cracked yellow scabs. Liz shuddered and clutched onto Amulya.

She whispered, "Have we walked into hell?"

"I've seen worse on the streets of Calcutta," whispered Amulya.

At the end of the ward a short bald man, presumably Dr Green, was checking a chart on a patient's bed. The women went up to him.

"Dr Green?" asked Liz.

The man turned round. His extremely hairy black mono-brow almost made up for the lack of hair on his head.

"Yes?" he said in a wheezing tone.

"We're the new medical students. We were told to report to you," said Liz.

The doctor frowned. His monobrow reminded Liz of a hairy caterpillar she'd once seen on the orphanage's yearly picnic at Hampstead Heath.

"I'm sorry. There must have been some mix up. I was told that the board had decided not to allow female medical students access," said the doctor.

"Oh? We weren't informed of that," snapped Liz.

"How are we to gain clinical experience if the infirmary will not let us in?" asked Amulya.

"I'm sorry. It wasn't up to me. I'm all for women doctors. We need all the help that we can get," replied Dr Green.

"It was Professor Atticus again. Wasn't it?" said Liz.

Dr Green nodded. "He certainly did come round and tried to get me to sign another of his petitions, but I told him where to go. Obnoxious man."

"Well, thanks for that anyway," said Liz.

"Look, I need to get back to my patients," said the doctor.

Liz nodded.

"Come on Amulya," said Liz.

The two woman walked back down the corridor and out through the door.

"What are we going to do now?" asked Amulya as she pulled off her mask.

Liz tore off her mask. "We're women so we'll ask women!"

"What do you mean?" asked Amulya.

"First of all we need to find out who signed that damned petition! Who objected to us," replied Liz.

"So how are we going to do that?" asked Amulya.

"Our maid Sally. I overheard her asking our landlady for a job for her cousin Daphne," smiled Liz.

"So how does that help us?" said Amulya.

"Daphne is Professor Atticus's maid. That's why," said Liz.

"Ah! So we persuade Mrs Randers to give Daphne a job and she gets us a copy of the petition!" exclaimed Amulya.

"Exactly!" said Liz.

They went through the swinging doors and into the main foyer.

"What if he doesn't keep a copy?" asked Amulya.

"Not keep a copy! He'll have a copy somewhere so that he can keep tabs on his supporters. Believe me, his type keeps notes on everything. It's a compulsion," stated Liz.

"So then we target the wives of the said doctors," said Amulya, warming to the notion.

"Yes! You're getting it. The wives, or if they're not married, then the fiancèes, sisters, mothers, aunts, whichever," declared Liz.

"That's a good plan," said Amulya.

They went out the main door and started to walk along Infirmary Street.

"But how are we going to convince them?" said Amulya.

"If I was needing a medical condition checked, especially if it was in an embarrassing place, I know that I'd much rather a woman to look over me than a man. Wouldn't you?" said Liz.

"Yes. I see your point. There must be so many diseases that women suffer needlessly, or leave too late to have checked out because of their misplaced self-consciousness," agreed Amulya.

***

Daphne knocked on the door to Professor Atticus's study. There was no answer. She opened the door and looked around the room. There wasn't any sign of the professor. She entered and went across to his desk. She tried to open the main drawer but it was locked. She tried the other drawers but they mostly contained small glass bottles labelled with different poisons.

"Damn!" cursed Daphne. "Where is it?"

She rummaged through some ornate wooden boxes on the desk. Suddenly she heard a rasping cough coming from the corridor. Daphne scanned the room. She quickly ran to the bay window and hid behind a curtain.

The door opened and in came the professor. He clutched at his throat as he coughed and went straight across to a cabinet to the right of the fireplace. He opened it and took out a green bottle. He unscrewed the stopper, poured out some vile-looking concoction into a glass, and downed it.

"Ahhh!" he gasped. He replaced the stopper on the bottle and put it back into the cabinet. He went across to his desk and sat down. He took a bunch of keys from his pocket, opened the main drawer and took out a leather-bound ledger. He opened it up to where a silk ribbon held the place. He took a folded note from his waistcoat and flattened it out next to a blank page on the ledger, He picked up a fountain pen and began to transcribe the note into the ledger.

Daphne stood stock still. She'd skipped on lunch and she suddenly felt her stomach rumble. The professor looked up from the ledger. He stared around the room. He shrugged and went back to writing. The ink ran out. The professor opened a brass ink well on the desk.

"Oh bother!" he said.

He pulled a drawer open and searched in it for more ink.

"Where is it," he sighed. He got up and went towards the window.

Daphne pressed further back against the glass. The professor reached out and yanked on the bell pull. He went back to his desk. He coughed and patted his chest. He impatiently tapped the desk with the end of the pen.

"Where is that lazy girl?" He got up, went back towards the window and gave the bell pull a hard tug. Daphne wondered that the whole contraption didn't come falling down.

The professor went and sat on the side of the desk. He tapped the desk with his pen and waited. He sighed, got up, and marched off out of the study into the corridor.

Daphne quickly crept out from behind the curtain and up to the desk. She picked up the note, scanned it and placed it back down on the desk. She flicked through the ledger, looking for anything to do with the Royal Infirmary.

"Ah!" gasped Daphne. She found a page with the title *Royal Infirmary Petition*. There were eight names. She tried to memorise them. She muttered under her breath, "Dr Sam, Dr Wood, Dr Nairn, Dr Dore, Dr Grant..." She shut her eyes and said, "Dr Sam, Dr Wood...damn!" She sighed and opened her eyes. She knew that she'd never remember them. She ripped the page out of the ledger and stuffed it down her cleavage. She flicked the ledger back to the blank page and scurried out of the room.

After a few minutes the professor came back into the study with a new bottle of ink. He sat down and filled the fountain pen. He began writing where he had left off.

There was a knock on the door.

The professor sighed and put down his pen. "Come in!"

Daphne came in with a bowl of soup.

"I've brought you some soup," said Daphne.

"Isn't it a bit early for lunch?" said the professor.

"Yes sir but I can't do it later as I need to go out and buy groceries. Last time I left it too late and the smoked salmon was finished and I know how much you like your smoked salmon," said Daphne.

"Oh very well," tutted the professor and he leaned back as Daphne brought the soup around. She "accidently" spilled the soup all over the ledger.

"You   bloody   idiot!"   shouted   the   professor. "Oh my. I'm so sorry sir!" gasped Daphne. "Here, I'll clean it."

She grabbed the ledger and rushed out of the room. The professor watched her leave, too shocked to say anything.

Daphne went to the kitchen and wiped down the book. She picked up a clean cloth and went back to the study. The professor was pouring himself a drink from the cabinet. She put the ledger down on an edge of the desk that was clear of soup spill. She wiped the table. The professor downed his drink, came across the room, picked up the ledger and looked through it.

He held up the place where Daphne had torn the page out.

"What's happened here?" he asked.

"Oh that page was too wet, sir. It was seeping into the rest. I tore it out," said Daphne.

"I hope that you kept it. I can dry it out. There was important information on that page. Where is it?" said the professor.

"Oh sorry sir. I threw it in the range. It was no use to man or beast," said Daphne.

"I've a good mind to fire you," said the professor. "But I'm not an unreasonable man and it was an accident, so I'll just take the cost of a new ledger off your wages."

"Of course sir. I'm so sorry," said Daphne.

Daphne scurried out of the study, trying not to laugh.

***

Liz and Amulya were drinking tea in the sitting room of Buccleuch Place. The door opened and in came Sally with a huge grin on her face.

"She did it. Here you are!" said Sally. She unfolded a note and handed it to Liz.

"Well done Sally. We'll make sure that Mrs Randers knows that Daphne would be an asset here," said Liz.

As Liz read the note Amulya got up and peered over her shoulder.

"It looks like we only need to convince four of them to change their minds and the petition will be repealed," said Liz.

She carried on reading down the list.

"Dr Sam. I know his wife, Faith. Oh and Dr Paycock's sister Miranda too. Hector introduced me to them at a reading at the galleries last week," said Amulya.

"I know Charlotte, Dr Wood's sister," said Liz. "Campbell introduced me to her last year. She asked to do my portrait but I didn't fancy stripping off for that kind of thing."

"I'd have done it if she'd asked me," said Amuyla.

"I'll suggest you to her then. Who else?" Liz scanned the list.

"I've met Dr Listern's mother," said Liz.

"How?" said Amuyla.

"Campbell introduced me to her at that Charles Darwin lecture a few weeks ago," said Liz.

"Yes. I wished I could have gone to that but I wasn't feeling well that day," said Amulya.

"Anyway. That's it. The four we need!" exclaimed Liz.

"If we can convince them all," said Amulya.

"Let's get to it then," said Liz. "I should be able to see Charlotte and Mrs Listern later today if they're not busy."

"Well I was going to see the new McTaggart show at the Scottish National Gallery with Miranda tomorrow. I'll see if she's free today," beamed Amulya.

***

The Dragonfly Tea Room was packed out as usual. Liz made her way past the queue that stretched from out of the building into the street, getting some disapproving looks as she passed some of the waiting customers. A skinny young waitress with a frown popped out in front of her.

"I've a table booked. The name's Moliette," said Liz.

The waitress brightened up. "Oh with Miss Wood?"

Liz nodded.

"She's waiting for you. Over by the window, behind the pillar," smiled the waitress. "I'll let you settle down and bring your order across shortly."

Liz smiled and headed past the Shakespeare mural to the main part of the café where large windows gave a panoramic view of Edinburgh Castle.

Charlotte Wood, a striking woman with blonde hair and a prominent nose, saw Liz and waved her over.

Charlotte got up and grasped Liz's hands. "Oh Liz, how are you?"

"Quite well thank you. And yourself. How are you? How's the art coming on?" said Liz.

Charlotte sat down. "Wonderful actually. I'm just back from Paris. Bursting with new ideas of colour and light. I should have gone years ago. I'm going to try out a new style called impressionism."

"What's that?" asked Liz.

138

"It's all about being in the moment. Quick brush strokes with raw paint. None of your blended colours!" gasped Charlotte.

"It sounds like you've been inspired," said Liz.

"I've got a new show coming up in Glasgow in a few months," said Charlotte.

"That's wonderful," said Liz.

"Indeed," said Charlotte. "So what's so urgent that it couldn't wait until tomorrow?"

Just at that moment the waitress appeared with two pots of tea.

"The chamomile's for me and the Earl Grey's for Miss Moliette," said Charlotte.

The waitress put the pots down on the table.

Charlotte upturned her cup and poured out her tea.

"It's all going to be nude men," laughed Charlotte.

"All in the name of art of course," grinned Liz.

"Have you changed your mind about sitting for me? It would be wonderful not to paint the same skin tones again and again, do something different," said Charlotte.

"I actually have a friend, Amuyla, an Indian woman, who'd love you to paint her," said Liz.

"Well, do introduce me," said Charlotte.

"But that's not what I was going to talk to you about. I wanted to..." Liz broke off as the waitress returned with a towering display of sandwiches, biscuits and cakes.

"Thank you," said Liz and Charlotte together.

"So what is it then?" asked Charlotte.

"It's your brother. I need you to get him to change his mind," said Liz.

Charlotte picked on a cucumber and pickle sandwich.

"What's he done now? That good for nothing scoundrel. He's not got you, you know?"

"No. Nothing like that," said Liz, blushing.

She selected a fruit scone, sliced it open and spread butter and apricot jam on it.

"The scones are excellent here, aren't they," said Charlotte.

Liz nodded, her mouth full.

"I feel sorry for that poor dear wife of his. She hasn't a clue," said Charlotte. She picked a piece of shortbread, took a bite, screwed up her face. "Too smooth. Cook always adds a touch of semolina to the flour for that extra crunchiness. What was I saying?"

"Mmmmh. Something about Walter's wife?"

"Oh yes. Arabella. She doesn't know about his mistress. Why were you asking about him?" said Charlotte.

"He's signed this petition so that women can't train at the Royal Infirmary. I need to do clinical training if I'm to get my degree," said Liz.

"I'm surprised. I didn't think Walter would sign something like that!" exclaimed Charlotte.

"Well, Professor Atticus can be quite persuasive," said Liz.

"That explains it," said Charlotte. "Atticus. What a creep! Seemingly he cured Walter of the clap. Walter took him along to my opening last year. The fairy paintings. Remember, the one you didn't come to?"

"I was studying," said Liz.

Charlotte tutted. "He went into some tirade about how there were no relevant women artists in the history of art. I had to remind him the famous portrait of Marie Antoinette was created by Élisabeth Louise Vigée-Le Brun. Of course I didn't tell him that I never liked her work. Anyway he walked off in the huff."

Charlotte picked up a brandy snap filled with cream. She bit into it. "Yum, you must try one of these!"

"So can you have a talk with him. See if he'll change his mind. Withdraw his signature from the petition?"

Charlotte wolfed down the rest of the brandy snap.

"Of course. Consider it done," said Charlotte.

"Are you sure he'll listen to you?" asked Liz.

"Yes. Otherwise I'll threaten to tell Arabella about his little extramarital affair," beamed Charlotte. She grabbed an angel cake. "Come on Liz. Eat up or I'll have to eat them all by myself!"

***

Liz checked the address on her piece of paper and knocked on the door of the grand house on Inverleith Row.

After a long wait an elderly butler opened the door. "Yes?"

"I'm Liz Moliette. I would like to speak with Mrs Listern," said Liz.

"I see. Wait here," said the butler. He closed the door. After another long wait the door opened again.

"I'm sorry but Mrs Listern is not receiving visitors," said the butler.

"But it's very important that I talk..." The door was shut in her face.

Liz started down the steps when she heard the sound of a window opening.

"Miss Moliette! Miss Moliette!" shouted two children.

Liz looked up. Milton and Tabitha were waving from the window.

"What are you doing here? Are you coming back to be our governess?" shouted Milton.

"Hello children. How are you?" asked Liz.

"Papa's dead!" shouted Tabitha.

"Come away from the window!" said a woman. She looked out the window. It was Mrs Helena Hughson. "Oh Liz it's you. Hold on."

Mrs Hughson herded her children away from the window and closed it. Liz wasn't sure what was happening but then the front door opened.

The butler appeared. "Please come in miss."

"Thanks," said Liz and entered.

Milton and Tabitha ran down the staircase. They came up and hugged Liz. Mrs Hughson came down the stairs.

"I'm sorry to hear about your husband," said Liz.

"I wish I could truthfully say I am," said Mrs Hughson and gave a little smile. "Edgar had a heart attack. Very sudden. How are your medical studies going?"

"That's why I'm here to see Mrs Listern. I'm hoping that she can persuade her son to help me continue with my studies," said Liz.

"My aunt isn't well. Come through here," said Mrs Hughson. Liz followed her into a large sitting room and they sat down. Liz recognised the style of a couple of tapestries on the walls.

"Please come back and stay with us. The new governess is really mean," said Milton.

"Yes, she smells," said Tabitha.

"Children, go out and play!" said Mrs Hughson.

"Alright mother," said Milton. The children ran off out of the room.

"How's your baby?" asked Liz.

"She's a little angel. Miss Downie, that's the new governess, is looking after her," said Mrs Hughson. "So what do you want to persuade my aunt to do again? Maybe I can help?"

"Her son, Dr Listern, has signed a petition put out by Professor Atticus which basically prevents us women from getting our clinical training at the Infirmary," said Liz.

"He has, has he? We'll soon see about that," said Mrs Hughson. "That's the least that I can do."

"Oh thank you," said Liz. "You don't know how much this means to me."

***

An hour later Liz arrived back at Buccleuch Place. Sally opened the door.

"How did it go miss?" asked Sally.

"Very well I think," said Liz.

"I'm glad. Miss Patel is back too. She thinks her meeting went well. She's already gone and seen Mrs Randers and has given Daphne a glowing reference. It would be wonderful if you could too?" said Sally.

"Of course I will," agreed Liz.

"It would make me so happy if Daphne were to come and work here with me. Do you want something to eat now?" said Sally.

"Oh no thanks Sally. I've already had a big lunch. Any more and I'll burst my corset!" said Liz. "Anyway I need to quickly change. I'm going down to Leith and help out at Dr Love's surgery."

Sally was about to head downstairs and then stopped and turned round. "Oh I forgot. Mrs Randers said that you can have your old room back now that she's found out that you're working for Dr Blyth."

Liz grinned. "Wonderful!"

Sally nodded. "Seemingly she's a big fan of the doctor. He helped her daughter to have one of those ceaser things when she was having a difficult birth," said Sally.

"Do you mean a caesarean?" said Liz.

"Yes that's it!" grinned Sally.

"Anyway that's good news," said Liz. "I'll go and move my stuff now."

"I've done it already," said Sally.

Amuyla opened her door as Liz came to the top of the stairs.

"How did you get on with Dr Wood's sister, what's her name?" asked Amuyla.

"Charlotte!" answered Liz.

"Yes, Charlotte," said Amulya.

"She's definitely going to get her brother to change his mind," said Liz.

"That's wonderful!" exclaimed Amulya.

"She wants to meet you too. Maybe paint your portrait," said Liz.

"Me. A model! How exciting," laughed Amuyla.

"I also went to see Dr Listern's mother. I didn't actually see her as she's not well, but Mrs Hughson was there. Helena Hughson. She's Mrs Listern's niece."

Amulya shook her head. "Really!"

"The husband's dead. Heart attack," said Liz.

"He's no loss," said Amulya.

Liz nodded. "She and the children seem fine. Anyway she said that she'll sort her cousin out. What about you?"

"I saw Donaldina; Dr Blackfoot's wife, and then Faith; Dr Sam's daughter. They're both on board!" said Amulya.

"Great. If they all work out we'll succeed," said Liz. "The board meet again next week so we should know by then."

Chapter 22 Leith Surgery

Liz alighted from the horse-drawn tram at Bernard Street. The port of Leith was a bustling hub of activity as stevedores shifted cargo from ship to shore and vice versa. She walked across the bridge over the Water of Leith and onto Commercial Street, then down the lane behind the classically influenced customs house.

The salty air was fresher than in the city and Liz took a few deep breaths before heading into the rather run down seamen's mission.

She tapped the appropriate ship's anchor styled knocker. A young man leaning on a crutch opened the door.

"I'm here to assist Dr Love," smiled Liz.

The young man nodded and let her in. She followed him as he hopped, surprisingly fast, through a large smoky room where the smell of stale sweat was overpowering. The walls were covered in paintings of ships and framed sea charts. Several rows of what looked like salvaged church pews were filled with not just seamen but people from all walks of life and ages, waiting to be seen by the free doctor. A dog was barking at scruffy children playing hide and seek under the pews.

The young man stopped at a door and knocked on it. "Your assistant is here doctor!"

"Come in!" was the muffled response from behind the door.

The young man nodded to Liz. She smiled back and opened the door. The examination room was cramped. A man in his sixties with massive white sideburns was sitting in a chair, stripped to the waist. Dr Love was kneeling in front of him holding a stethoscope. He turned and smiled at Liz.

"I'll catch up with you in a minute." He turned back to his patient.

"And again!" said Dr Love. The patient coughed and spluttered. The doctor handed him a handkerchief. The patient wiped his mouth and made to hand the handkerchief back.

"Keep it. It's nothing serious. I'll give you something for your cough," said Dr Love. He took a small bottle and passed it to the man. "No more than four drops a day. Best taking it just before meals."

"But I have no money to pay you sir," said the man

"That's alright. It's paid for by charity," said Dr Love.

"Oh thank you sir. God bless you!" said the man and got up. He gave Liz a toothless grin as he passed her. He went to open the door and turned back. "Will I send the next one in?"

Dr Love shook his head. "No. but thank you." The patient nodded and left.

"Liz, so good of you to come."

"It looks like you've got a full house, Paul," said Liz.

"It's been very busy this morning," agreed Dr Love.

"Well we best get cracking on with it," said Liz. "Unless you need a rest?"

"No. I'm fine."

"What would you like me to do first?" asked Liz.

"If you could bring in Mrs Coley and her daughter in?"

Liz nodded and went off to the waiting room.

"Mrs Coley?" shouted Liz.

It turned out that one of the children playing hide and seek was Mrs Coley's daughter. Over the next few hours Liz took notes and consulted with the doctor on patients with a great variety of ailments. The crowded waiting room gradually emptied until there were only a few left. After helping the doctor, to treat a particularly nasty rash on a sailor's back, Liz went through to the waiting room. There was only one patient left, Bridy, who reeked of drink. Liz took her through to the doctor.

"And what can I do for you mistress?" asked Dr Love.

"It's Miss. Bridy Scott. It's my ear, doctor," she said.

The doctor beckoned to the chair. Bridy sat down, removed her hat and pulled aside her long red curls to reveal an ear that was purple and swollen. The doctor examined her ear with a magnifying glass. He touched the ear.

"Ouch!"

"Sorry. How did you get that?" asked Dr Love.

"My man Lachie. I think you know him," said Bridy.

The doctor shook his head. "I don't think so."

"Well he knows you anyways. Said you are a head specialist!" grinned Bridy.

Dr Love stood up.

"I don't think I can do anything for you! Miss Moliette, can you show this woman out," said the doctor.

"Certainly doctor."

Liz thought to herself that Paul was being a bit abrupt and noticed that Bridy winked at him as she stood up. Liz ushered her out into the waiting room.

Bridy turned to Liz. "Oh I forgot. I'd be obliged if you'd give this to the doctor." She handed a folded piece of paper to Liz. With that she strutted off out of the waiting room. Liz went back into the examination room.

"That woman, Miss Scott. She forgot to give you this." Liz handed the note to Dr Love.

The doctor read the note and frowned.

"Paul. What was that all about?" asked Liz.

"Oh nothing. Just a prescription," said Dr Love. He put the note in his pocket.

"Oh?" said Liz.

"I need to order some more laudanum. See you shortly." As the doctor left the room Liz noticed that the note had fallen from his pocket onto the floor. She picked it up and read it. "16 West Port 7p.m. Bring the money!" Liz folded up the note and put it on the table. She sat down and wondered what it meant. In a few minutes the doctor returned.

"You dropped that," said Liz, pointing to the note on the desk.

"Oh? Thank you," said Dr Love. He pocketed the note. The doctor patted her on the arm. "You did an excellent job today."

"Thanks, I enjoyed it," replied Liz.

"I'm sorry but I'm very busy tonight. A lot of work piling up. Would it be possible to put off dinner until tomorrow night? Same time. Eight o'clock?"

"Oh yes that's fine," said Liz, "I don't know your address though."

"Oh how silly of me," said Dr Love. He handed Liz a card.

"There should be a tram leaving Bernard Street in a few minutes so I'm going to head off. Unless there's more to be done?" asked Liz.

"No. That's it. I just need to stay a while and finish off the paperwork."

146

Séance. © David Hutchison.

Chapter 23 Séance

Kitty and Inspector MacLeod sat opposite each other in the carriage. Kitty put her knitting down and grabbed his hand. "Honestly she's really good. I think that she could help you. She's one of those gifted mediums," said Kitty.

"I'm only doing this because Victoria asked me to," said the Inspector as he pulled his hand away.

"And it's time that you thought about marrying again. The children need a mother. God knows I've tried, but looking after two boys is exhausting. That Victoria. Her being a widow will help too. You've both got something in common," said Kitty.

"Dead spouses. That's not a very romantic start. That is if I was even thinking of romance. Which I'm not," said the Inspector, his face reddened.

"She is a comely creature. If only she had better dress sense, but I can help her out with that," said Kitty.

The Inspector looked at his mother-in-law's outfit and held his tongue.

The carriage came to a halt. The Inspector pulled down the window.

"Carnousty's Boarding House, Queen Street, sir," said the driver.

Kitty gathered up her ball of wool which had fallen onto the floor of the carriage. She put it in her basket. Inspector MacLeod helped Kitty down from the carriage. They went up to the front door of the elegant townhouse. Kitty pulled on the bell. The housekeeper Miss Kilpatrick, an effervescent seventy year old with protruding eyes, opened the door.

"Ah! Mrs Murray. So nice to see you again. When was it?"

"Back in the spring," said Kitty.

"Oh yes!" said Miss Kilpatrick.

Kitty smiled and said, "This is my son-in-law Frazer Macleod."

"Welcome Mr Macleod. Please do come in," said Miss Kilpatrick. She led them through the house to the parlour. Above the mantelpiece an old family portrait, of a lady in a sixteenth century wig with a cat in her arms, dominated the room. The fire was burning low. There were already three people sitting at the round table in the centre of the room, one of whom was Victoria Massey, in an exotic glittering dress. She smiled at the Inspector.

"Good evening Inspector!" said Victoria. The Inspector smiled. "Mrs Massey."

"Oh an inspector. How exciting!" said Miss Kilpatrick. "So you already know Mrs Massey then?"

The Inspector smiled and said, "Yes we've met."

Miss Kilpatrick gestured towards the man and woman in their early thirties. "Let me introduce you to Mr and Mrs Dougald Temple."

The Temples nodded solemnly. Kitty smiled and said, "Kitty Murray and this is my son-in-law Inspector Frazer MacLeod." Kitty sat down one chair away from Victoria. She put her knitting basket down on the table. The Inspector sat down between them.

Miss Kilpatrick picked up Kitty's knitting basket and said, "I'll put this over here for the meantime." She placed the basket on a small table near the window. She went across to the mantelpiece and lit the candles on a grotesque pair of candelabras; all cherubs and roses. She came back to the table with one of the candelabras and placed it in the centre.

The door opened and Lucia Carnousty entered. She was wearing a sombre black dress with jet jewellery to match. She'd also tied her hair up in a faux gypsy scarf. Lucia smiled graciously as Miss Kilpatrick introduced everyone.

"Nice to see you again Mrs Murray," said Lucia. She turned and smiled at the others. "I do hope we have a good session today." She sat down between Kitty and Dougald.

"Miss Kilpatrick, the shutters!"

Miss Kilpatrick closed the wooden shutters on the two large windows and the room darkened. She sat down between Lucia and Victoria.

Lucia said," "Now ladies and gentlemen. We shall begin. Please join hands!"

Kitty took the Inspector's right hand. He gave an embarrassed smile as Victoria grabbed his left hand.

"Shouldn't we have a crystal ball or something?" whispered the Inspector to Victoria.

"Shhh!" whispered Victoria.

Miss Kilpatrick overheard and said, "Now, now Mr MacLeod. Mrs Carnousty is not a fortune teller so we have no need of crystal balls or ouija boards or any such gimmicks."

"Sorry," said the Inspector.

"Now that we've got that out of the way let's begin," said Miss Kilpatrick. "Lucia, are you ready?"

Lucia nodded. She bowed her head. After a few moments she said slowly, "Lady Anne. Give me the power to connect with the spirit world!"

The Inspector looked up to the mantelpiece. The painting of the lady in the wig, presumably Lady Anne, flickered in the candlelight.

"Lady Anne. Are you here?" said Lucia. There was a long silence. Lucia tried again. "Lady Anne?"

The candles on the mantelpiece flared up and Lady Anne seemed to glow for a moment then the candles dwindled down.

Miss Kilpatrick whispered, "She's made contact."

Lucia looked up and around at the faces at the table. Then she focused her gaze on the painting of Lady Anne.

"Do you have a message for anyone?"

A long silence.

Lucia tried again. "Lady Anne?"

The candles flickered up again. Lucia bent her head. She made a low whimpering sound. Then she spoke in a little girl's voice.

"Mama."

Mrs Dougald Temple gave out a sob. "Eunice?"

"Mama?"

"Eunice dear it's mother," said Mrs Dougald Temple.

"Mama. I'm playing with the fishes."

Mr Dougald Temple looked around the room. "Our daughter drowned. It's her!"

"Mother and father miss you dreadfully," sobbed Mrs Dougald Temple.

"Yes we do my sweet," said Mr Dougald Temple.

"Papa. It's so nice to play with the fishes. Where's mama?"

"We're here darling!" said Mrs Dougald Temple.

"They're coming for me. Mama? Papa?"

The table suddenly shook then abruptly stopped.

"She's gone," whispered Miss Kilpatrick.

The Inspector made to get up. Victoria held him back down and whispered into his ear, "We're not finished yet."

"Sorry," said the Inspector.

After several seconds Lucia's eyes opened wide. Her voice went lower and the accent was different when she spoke a single word.

"Vicky?"

Victoria gasped. "That's Jack's voice! Jack is that you?"

"Vicky."

"Oh Jack. Is it really you?" exclaimed Victoria. "Tell me about..."

"It's peaceful here."

"I miss you so much," said Victoria.

"So peaceful..."

"Jack?" asked Victoria, "What happened? Who killed you?"

"I..."

Lucia seemed to shudder. Her eyes shut.

"Are you there? Jack?" asked Victoria.

Lucia slumped forwards.

Miss Kilpatrick said, "She's channelling someone else."

"Can't you get him back?" asked Victoria. Miss Kilpatrick shook her head.

The table started shaking. Lucia's head flipped up, eyes wide open. Her voice became higher in tone.

"Frazer?"

"It's Anna!" said Kitty. The Inspector shook his head. Kitty frowned at him.

"Frazer?"

"Anna darling, it's me, your mother," said Kitty.

"Frazer?"

"Answer her!" whispered Kitty to the Inspector.

The Inspector sighed and said, "Yes. Who is this?"

"Beware!"

"What?" asked the Inspector.

"Beware!"

Lucia blinked and suddenly came out of her trance-like channelling state.

"Beware? That could mean anything!" grumbled the Inspector.

Lucia's voice was back to normal when she asked, "Did we contact anyone?"

"The Temple child, Mrs Massey's brother and Mrs Murray's daughter," said Miss Kilpatrick. She looked at the Inspector and said, "She never remembers."

"It was Anna's voice!" said Kitty. "I'm sure it was. Didn't you think so Frazer?"

The inspector shook his head and let go of Victoria and Kitty's hands.

Mr Dougald Temple asked, "Can we try again?"

Lucia clutched her head and sighed.

Miss Kilpatrick said, "I'm afraid Mrs Carnousty is exhausted."

Miss Kilpatrick patted Lucia on the back. She went across the room and opened the shutters. The light flooded in. She brought Kitty her basket and said, "If you could all make your way to the front hall please. Mrs Carnousty needs to gather herself together."

Everyone, apart from Lucia, rose. Inspector MacLeod went up to the mantelpiece. He drew his finger across a small hole in the wall, next to the candelabra. Ah! That's where the draft flickered the candles. Deliberate or chance, thought the Inspector. He turned round and caught Lucia watching him between her fingers.

Miss Kilpatrick ushered everyone into the hallway and opened the front door. Mr and Miss Temple were first out. Mr Temple handed a generous wad of bank notes to Miss Kilpatrick. She said, "Thank you. Perhaps we'll have another message for you next time."

Mrs Dougald Temple said, "I do hope so. We miss Eunice so much."

Her husband nodded and said, "It's such a comfort to be able to contact her if even only so briefly."

The Temples nodded to the others and left.

Victoria handed money to Miss Kilpatrick and said, "I wish I could have asked him more."

"Well perhaps next time," said Miss Kilpatrick.

Victoria turned to Kitty and the Inspector. "I've a carriage waiting. Could I give you a lift?"

"Yes, that would be nice," said Kitty.

"I'll wait for you outside," said Victoria. She went out the door.

Kitty paid Miss Kilpatrick. "Please do come again," said Miss Kilpatrick.

"Oh yes we will. Won't we Frazer?" said Kitty.

The Inspector replied, "I'm afraid I'm a tad busy at the moment."

Miss Kilpatrick replied, "Oh well perhaps another time Inspector. Goodbye."

Kitty and the Inspector left the house and went down the steps to Victoria's waiting carriage. The Inspector helped Kitty up into the carriage. He got in, pulled the door closed and sat next to Victoria.

"I've told the driver to go via the police station," said Victoria.

"Thank you," said the Inspector.

Victoria said, "So Inspector, do you believe in spiritualism?" The Inspector shrugged. Kitty said, "He doesn't. I believe for him."

"So who's Anna?" asked Victoria.

"Anna was my wife," said the Inspector.

"Oh!" said Victoria.

There was an awkward silence for a while.

"And you my dear, what do you believe?" asked Kitty.

"She has to believe. It's her profession. Egyptology is based on the afterlife," said the Inspector.

"It did sound like Jack's voice," said Victoria. "But he didn't mention Freddy. So I'm not sure."

"What do you mean?" asked the Inspector.

"Freddy was our pet cat when we were children. A beautiful ginger tom. We always said that whoever died first would contact the other through a medium. The code word to make sure it was one of us was Freddy. He didn't use it."

"Maybe things get mixed up when you're dead," said Kitty.

A few tears streamed down Victoria's face. "Yes, I'm sure that's it." She wiped her eyes.

"I forgot! I need to do some shopping. Can you let me out here?" said Kitty.

"Of course," said Victoria. She pulled down the window and asked the driver to stop. Meanwhile Kitty winked at the Inspector.

Kitty got out of the carriage. "Hopefully I'll see you again soon," said Kitty to Victoria. She waved and went off down the street.

Victoria and the Inspector sat in silence for a while.

Victoria said, " I..." at the same time as the Inspector said, "Why don't..."

They both laughed.

"You first Inspector!" said Victoria.

"You can call me Frazer," said the Inspector.

"Yes Frazer. Then call me Victoria," smiled Victoria.

"If it's not too presumptuous of me I'd like to ask you out to dinner," said the Inspector.

"Oh that would be wonderful," gasped Victoria.

"Next week sometime?" asked the Inspector.

"I look forward to it," said Victoria.

The carriage stopped. "The police station, madam," said the driver.

The Inspector got out. Victoria pulled down the window and looked out at him. The Inspector leaned forward and kissed her firmly on the mouth.

"See you next week," said Victoria to the Inspector. She looked up to the driver. "Ok driver. Portobello!" She waved to the Inspector and the carriage sped off.

***

Later that afternoon PC Urquhart returned to the High Street Police Station. He went in to see Inspector MacLeod, clutching an envelope.

"Sir," said PC Urquhart. He handed over the envelope. "I promised Mrs Aird that we'd get it back to her."

The Inspector impatiently opened the envelope and withdrew a wedding photograph of Mr and Mrs Aird. She was sitting on a chair in her best day dress. Gabriel was standing behind her with his hand leaning on her shoulder. Both looked straight ahead with slight smiles on their faces. The Inspector pulled a magnifying glass from a drawer and examined Gabriel's head. He had a small lump protruding from his forehead.

"Well done Urquhart. That confirms it!" said the Inspector.

"What?" asked PC Urquhart.

"We're looking for a phrenologist," replied the Inspector.

PC Urquhart whistled.

The inspector nodded. "A killer phrenologist."

Hector and Campbell. © David Hutchison.

Chapter 24   Calton Hill

A full moon shone down on Calton Hill, highlighting the National Monument, also known as *Edinburgh's Disgrace,* so-called as there wasn't enough money raised to complete this copy of the Greek Parthenon, built to commemorate the fallen of the Napoleonic Wars and one of the reasons that Edinburgh is sometimes referred to as *The Athens of the North.* Campbell and Hector sat together on one of the steps of this unfinished edifice.

Campbell shivered. "It's a bit cold for summer," he said.

Hector took off his jacket. "Here you go. I'm quite warm," said Hector.

"Oh, thank you," said Campbell. He pulled on Hector's jacket. It was a bit large for him but it was nice and warm.

"So what have you dragged me up here to tell me then?" asked Campbell.

Hector looked around to make sure that no one was around. He had no idea that they were being watched by Lachie Merry, who had positioned himself in some nearby bushes.

Hector grabbed Campbell's hand.

"You know that I can't stop thinking of you," said Hector.

"And I you," said Campbell.

Hector sighed. "It's just that... I have to marry or I'll be cut off from my inheritance."

Campbell replied, "But you'll be an editor soon. Then you won't need your father's money!"

Hector said, "It's not just the money. Father has many influential clients that he could send my way."

Campbell frowned. "Don't you want to be your own man? Make your own mark?"

Hector nodded. "Yes but... I thought Amulya might..."

Campbell pulled his hand back and shook his head.

"But we can still see each other. You know when..." said Hector.

"When your future wife is away?" snapped Campbell. "Fit me in just when you feel like it?"

"I have to get married. Father keeps asking and I do like Amulya," said Hector.

"You don't. Not like me!" moaned Campbell. He stood up.

Hector stared up at Campbell. "I'm sorry. There's no future for us. Maybe one day..."

Campbell jumped down the monument steps. Hector got up and rushed after Campbell. He grabbed Campbell's arm.

"Just leave me alone!" shouted Campbell as he swiped Hector's hand from him. Hector stood still and watched as Campbell made for the path leading down the hill towards Greenside Parish Church. Campbell stomped down the steep path in a bad mood. After the first set of steps he stopped and took off Hector's jacket. He threw it to the ground. He ran down the steps, almost knocking over tramp Rab Souter.

"Hey!" shouted Rab. Campbell ignored him and carried on running. Rab swayed and righted himself. He noticed the jacket lying on the path and picked it up. He tried it on. A good fit. He felt in the pockets. He grinned, "Ahh!" and pulled out the silver pocket watch with the tartan ribbon that Campbell had lent to Hector. He'd get enough money for that wee beauty to keep him in whisky for a few weeks. Feeling pleased with himself, Rab buttoned up the braw jacket.

Lachie watched as Hector went back up and sat on the steps of the monument. Lachie darted across the grass and down the path where he'd seen Campbell heading. He saw what looked like Campbell, standing still, half way down the path. He supposed that Campbell was relieving himself. Lachie quickly sneaked down the steps. He grabbed Rab from behind and dragged him into the bushes. The tramp put up a fight but Lachie was getting very experienced at this burking now. Or so he thought. Rab bit Lachie's hand.

"Bastard!" shouted Lachie.

Rab screamed. Lachie twisted the man's neck and there was a horrible snapping sound.

Hector stood up when he heard the blood-curdling scream coming from down the hill. He quickly jumped down off the steps and made for the path. He got to the top and looked down. The path was silver in the moonlight. But empty. Hector walked down quickly calling out, "Campbell?" He reached the church at Greenside without finding anyone.

Lachie waited in the bushes, with the tramp at his feet, until the sound of Hector's footsteps faded. He looked out onto the path. There was no one around. He pulled out the surgical knife from a wide pocket on the inside of his jacket. He got to work. Within a few minutes Rab's head had been removed and bagged.

Chapter 25   A Secret Revealed

Liz entered the hallway at Buccleuch Place. As she was removing her hat Sally came running up from the basement.

"Oh miss! Charles, I mean Mr Okoro, was here miss. Not half an hour ago. He asks that you go to Dr Blyth's residence as soon as you gets in. It's urgent!"

"Thank you Sally," said Liz. She quickly replaced her hat and went out. She rushed along the street and was out of breath by the time that she arrived at Dr Blyth's house. Charles must have been looking out again for her because as soon as she climbed the steps the front door opened. He looked worried.

"I didn't know what to do. She's ... you'll find out anyway. Come on!" gasped Charles. He rushed through the hallway and up the stairs. Liz followed him into Florian's bedroom. Psyche was whimpering at the bottom of the bed. Florian was lying out, unconscious.

"She's been out since this afternoon," said Charles.

Liz thought about Charles' use of the feminine personal pronoun and remembered that Peter had sometimes referred to his particularly effeminate gentleman customers as she. Liz touched Florian's forehead. It was dripping with sweat and hot. She opened Florian's shirt. There was padding around the chest, making it difficult to remove.

"What's this?" asked Liz.

"You'll see," said Charles.

Charles helped Liz to remove the shirt. Florian's whole chest was tightly bandaged. A stain seeped through on the left side.

"I think you overdid the bandaging," said Liz.

Charles shrugged. He held Florian upright as Liz unwound the bandages. As the final layers came off Liz was shocked. Florian had breasts.

"Oh my god!" gasped Liz. She quickly unwound the rest of the bandages. Just below Florian's left breast was the knife wound. It was weeping pus and the stitches had fallen apart.

"Carbolic acid. Do you have any?" asked Liz.

"I don't know. Maybe in the study?" said Charles.

Liz stood up. "I'll look. Boil some water and I'll need a sharp knife. Needle, thread."

Liz rushed out of the room and down the stairs. All the time in her mind thinking Florian's a woman! She ran down the corridor and into the study. She scanned the room. She searched through the cabinets until she found a bottle of carbolic acid. Liz ransacked cupboards and drawers and eventually discovered some clean bandages. She dashed through the corridor and back up the stairs into Florian's bedroom.

Charles came in and placed a pan of boiled water, covered with a towel, onto the dressing table. Liz poured the carbolic acid into the steaming water. She dipped one edge of the towel into the water and gave her hands a quick wipe down.

Charles handed her a sharp knife. "What are you going to do?" he asked.

She dipped the knife in the water. "I need to drain the pus out of the wound. Did you get the needle and thread?"

Charles nodded. "There's a sewing kit in the drawer of that dressing table."

"Good. I'll need tweezers too."

"I'm sure there's a set in the drawer," said Charles. He got up and raked through the drawer.

"Yes got them!" He held up a leather pouch containing a nail file and tweezers.

Liz nodded. "Dip them in the water!"

Liz bent over Florian. She quickly snipped the stitches with the knife, then made two shallow cuts across the wound. Florian twisted and moaned. Psyche yelped and jumped up onto the bed. "Down girl!" commanded Charles. He picked up the dog and went to the door. He put the dog outside and shut the door. Psyche scratched at the door and barked.

"Tweezers!" said Liz as she handed the knife back to Charles. He took the knife and passed her the tweezers. Liz unpicked the threads as the fresh blood helped to flush out the pus. Liz dipped a bandage into the sterilised water and mopped the wound. Florian stirred but did not waken.

"Can I see the sewing kit?" said Liz as she handed the tweezers back to Charles.

Charles took out a small tartan-covered box out of the drawer, opened it and held it out to Liz. There was a range of items; large curved upholstery needles, medium and small needles, pins, cotton threads of many colours, a tin needle threader with an embossed Minerva, a cloth measuring tape and a tiny pair of scissors.

"Thread that medium needle. Use the strongest thread," said Liz.

Charles picked up the needle threader and a bobbin of white cotton. He quickly threaded the needle as Liz dried the wound with a fresh piece of bandage.

"Done!" said Charles

"Dip it in the water," said Liz.

Charles did so and handed it to Liz.

Mercifully Florian did not move too much as Liz sewed up the wound.

"Will Florian be alright?" asked Charles.

Liz shrugged and sighed. "That's all we can do for now. If she... I can't believe I'm saying she... if she comes round we need to get her to drink plenty of water."

Charles said, "Thank you!"

Charles wrung out a cloth and wiped Florian's head.

Liz asked, "So why all the subterfuge?"

"Florian's life is being a doctor. Surely you can understand that," said Charles.

"Yes of course. But she could have been an example to us all. A doctress!" replied Liz.

"Remember only a few years ago who'd have thought the Medical School would have let women matriculate!" said Charles.

"Don't you think I don't know that!" said Liz. She chuckled. "Can you imagine the professor's face? He'd have a heart attack."

Charles stood up and dropped the cloth into the water. "You can't tell anyone."

"Why not?"

"Florian doesn't want anyone to know," said Charles.

"But she must make a stand for women!" snapped Liz.

Florian groaned. Charles wrung the cloth out and wiped Florian's head. "Keep in there, Florian darling."

Liz was touched by Charles' devotion to Florian.

"At least wait until she pulls through... if she does," said Charles.

"Yes of course. I'm sorry," said Liz.

Charles suddenly took Liz's hand. "I should tell you ..." Charles stared at her, his brown eyes full of emotion.

"What?" asked Liz.

He shook his head. "It's nothing. I'm sorry."

Liz awkwardly removed her hand from his. "I have to go now. I'll check back in the morning."

Liz got up. Charles made to get up.

"No. Stay with her. I'll show myself out," said Liz. Charles nodded.

Liz left the bedroom and went down the stairs. She picked up her umbrella and left the house. As she walked down the street she thought of what she'd discovered. She still couldn't quite get her head around it. How long had Florian Blyth been living as a man? Was that even her real name? Florian? She'd heard a rumour. Amulya had mentioned it after a class in the history of surgery. A surgeon called Barry. In the military. He'd done the first caesarean section in Africa and seemingly when he'd died someone said that he was actually female. Liz had always thought it was a fable, probably spread about by Florence Nightingale, who'd had a run in with him, or was it her? It was all so confusing, but thrilling! What if there was a massive undercover group of women disguised as men doing so-called men's jobs.

"Penny for luck. Miss!" An old woman hunched in a filthy shawl brought Liz out of her thoughts as she tried to pin a sprig of white heather onto Liz's jacket.

"No thank you!" said Liz. The old woman wheeched the sprig off and spat on the ground, just missing Liz's shoe.

Liz made her way down Candlemaker's Row. The Grassmarket was quietening down. Traders were packing up their stalls and selling off pies at half price. Liz was tempted but she thought she'd better save herself for dinner. She paused at Ned Holt's miniature outdoor theatre. He was packing a covered cart. She'd been intrigued by the signs advertising *The Thousand Year Old Mummy* and even more interesting *The Living Skeleton* but had never crossed the threshold. She assumed that it would be along the lines of the fake *Mermaid* she'd seen with Amuyla at the Newhaven Festival earlier in the year.

Liz walked up towards the West Port, a place made infamous as the lodgings of Burke and Hare. She counted the tenement house numbers and calculated where number fifteen was; across the street. She found a deep doorway to lean against and waited.

She had almost fallen asleep when a church bell pealed. She pulled herself up straight and peered across the road. A young girl selling watercress walked past with half-full baskets. Liz glanced down the street and then quickly pulled back into shadow. Dr Love was striding up her side of the street! She hoped that he would cross over before he came near her. Dr Love walked up almost towards her. He paused near her doorway, with his back to her. Liz tried to shrink further back into the doorway, but it wasn't possible. Luckily he didn't turn around but crossed the street to number fifteen. Liz heaved a sigh of relief. Dr Love pulled the bell and waited. A window above opened and a woman looked out. She popped her head back in before Liz could get a proper look at her. Dr Love pulled at the doorbell again. The door was opened by Lachie Merry. Liz recognised him at once. She was shocked. What was Paul doing meeting with the man who had stabbed Florian? Lachie handed a canvas sack to Dr Love. The doctor paid him, turned and stomped off back down towards the Grassmarket.

Liz slipped out of the doorway and followed Dr Love. Her head was spinning with questions but she tried to concentrate. She hadn't really analysed why she'd spied on him but now that she'd seen Florian's mugger she couldn't stop. Dr Love quickened his pace and turned off up Candlemaker Row. Liz hurried up to catch him. She rushed round the corner and straight into Dr Love, who was standing facing her as if he had been waiting for her. Liz gasped.

"Fancy bumping into you here!" smiled Dr Love.

Liz quickly regained her composure. "Oh I was visiting a friend." She looked down at the doctor's sack. He grinned and held it up.

"Rabbit. A fresh one. You do like rabbit stew?"

Liz said, "Hmm... Yes. I do."

Dr Love smiled. "Excellent. I shall expect you at eight tomorrow then. Goodbye."

"Goodbye, Paul," replied Liz.

He walked off along the Cowgate. Liz stared after him.

***

The Book of Skulls. © David Hutchison.

Dr Love put the sack down on the table next to Pickle. The cat stirred awake and stretched out. He rubbed the cat's cheek. "Who's a pretty boy?"

He lifted up a large metal pan from under the table and filled it with water from a bucket. He lit the gas stove and hiked the pan onto the burner. He noticed that Pickle was sniffing around the bag. "Hey that's not for you Pickle darling!"

The doctor shooed the cat off the table. He held the ends of the sack and pulled it away to reveal the severed head, covered in blood. He used a rag to clean the face. He frowned and threw the cloth down. "The bloody idiot!" he cursed. Pickle jumped up on the table. "Oh well it might come in handy for something. No point in wasting it," he said to the cat. Dr Love grabbed the head by the hair, dropped it into the pot and put the lid on. He checked his pocket watch, went through the corridor and up the stairs. The oak-panelled grand hall was covered in displays of taxidermy. The collection, as well as the house, had been left to him and his sister by his rich Uncle Benedict. He pulled on his outdoor coat and took his cane from the elephant foot stand below the stuffed moose.

"Is that you dear?" called a voice from above. It was Dr Love's invalid sister Odette, who lived on the first floor. She was propped up in her wheelchair at the top of the grand staircase, a magazine on her lap.

Dr Love waved up at her. "Odette. I'm going out. I may be a while. Do you need anything first?"

Odette said, "No thank you Paul dear. I'm engrossed in this story in *The Dark Blue* about a succubus."

"A succubus. That's a bit gory for you. I hope you don't have nightmares," said Dr Love.

"It's actually rather romantic," said Odette.

"Well, don't wait up for me," said Dr Love as he put on his top hat. He strode across the hall and left by the main door.

In a short while he reached the Grassmarket. There was a crowd gathered around two men fighting. He skirted past the crowd and headed up to the West Port. He pulled on the bell of Lachie's lodgings. A window opened above and Bridy Scott peered out.

"What do you fucking want at this time of night?" she shouted.

"I need to speak urgently with Lachie Merry," said Dr Love.

"Well good luck with that!" shouted Bridy.

"What do you mean?" asked Dr Love.

"He's off out on the piss, he is. That good for nothing pile of shite!" Bridy closed the window.

"Hey!" shouted Dr Love. He picked up a pebble off the street and threw it at the window.

The window opened. "What the fuck now?" shouted Bridy.

"Where does he usually go?" asked Dr Love.

"Christ's sake. Try the Green Man!" She slammed the window shut.

Dr Love made his way back down the West Port and through the Grassmarket. The men were still fighting and a couple more had joined in. He gave them a wide berth and headed down the Cowgate. He went under the George IV Bridge and arrived at the entrance of the Green Man, just as a very drunk Lachie was being frogmarched out by an irate barman.

"You can't throw me out. I fought for this country!" wailed Lachie. The barman pulled the door shut. Lachie took several steps, leant against the wall and sunk to the ground. He took a hip flask out of his pocket and took a swig. He spoke to himself, "I fought... eh?" He noticed Dr Love.

"You!" He held out the flask. He swayed as he mumbled, "Another one wanting doing sir?"

"Shhh! Pull yourself together man!" hissed Dr Love.

"No need to lose your head over it!" Lachie roared with laughter at his own joke. Dr Love smacked him across the face. The flask went flying across the pavement onto the cobbles.

"You brought the wrong head!" hissed Dr Love.

Lachie crawled over to the flask and picked it up.

"What the f'ing hell did you do that for? That was good whisky that was!" moaned Lachie. He rubbed the end of the flask with the cuff of his jacket and tried to take a drink. He held the flask up and turned it upside down. Empty.

"Did you hear me? You brought the wrong one!" shouted Dr Love.

"Away and twirl your whirly with a whin!" mumbled Lachie. He slumped over and fell asleep.

Dr Love shook him, but Lachie was out for the count. The doctor tutted and headed off down the street. As he walked he wondered what he was going to do. He desperately needed the head of an intelligent homosexual male with no obvious head deformity so that he could compare it with the one that he had already "collected" of a homosexual male with a bump indicating low intelligence. This really was pivotal for his phrenological research paper. He knew of several molly houses in Edinburgh but finding someone with the right intellect was the problem and he didn't have the time to waste. He'd just have to "collect" Campbell Prebble himself. He hurried along the street with a plan forming in his mind. It was too late to find him tonight but he had a good idea where to find Campbell in the morning.

166

Chapter 26 Gray's Anatomy

Charles folded open the wooden shutters and light flooded across the bed. Florian stirred awake. Charles touched Florian's head. Relief spread across his face.

"Good. Your fever's gone," said Charles.

Florian groaned and tried to sit up. She flopped back down.

"Easy," said Charles.

Florian sat up again. This time with success.

"How long have I been out? God I'm thirsty!" gasped Florian.

Charles filled a glass from the jug on the dressing table. "A day," said Charles. "Here!" He passed the glass to Florian, who drank it down greedily.

"I couldn't have pulled through without you," said Florian.

Charles took the glass from Florian. "Liz did it."

"Liz?" asked Florian.

"Your daughter. She pulled you through. Cleaned and sorted your wound."

Florian gasped. "But that means ..."

Charles nodded then said, "I didn't tell her the rest of it."

***

A severed arm with the skin peeled off lay on a marble slab on a bench in the lecture hall. Dr Morris, a grey-haired man in tweeds, waved a scalpel in one shaky hand and looked across the bench at Liz and Amulya. Liz wondered, if he wasn't careful he'd cut himself.

Dr Morris said, "Can you point to the capitate?"

Liz and Amulya looked at each other. Liz turned the arm slightly and pointed to an area on the hand.

"Dr Morris smiled. "Correct. And where is the metacarpal?"

Liz pointed to a length of finger where it joined the bone.

"Correct," said the doctor. He turned the arm on its side and pointed to a strip of muscle running from the side of the thumb to the wrist. "What is this called?"

Liz shrugged. "The exterior pollicis longus?"

Dr Morris shook his head. "Almost. It's the abductor pollicis longus!"

A knock on the door echoed through the hall.

"Come in!" said the doctor.

PC Urquhart entered, whistling as usual. "Excuse me but the Inspector needs Miss Moliette's help"

"Oh no! Not another one?" exclaimed Amulya. The PC nodded. Liz looked to Dr Morris, who shrugged. "Yes, off you go Miss Moliette."

Liz put her coat and hat on. She grabbed her umbrella, smiled at Amulya and headed off with PC Urquhart, out of the lecture hall.

In the street she bumped into Hector, who greeted her enthusiastically.

"Liz! They let me go, thanks to you! I was coming to see Amulya."

"That's great! Sorry I'm in a bit of a rush. I've got to go and meet the Inspector," said Liz.

Hector could sniff another story. "Another victim! That's it. Isn't it?" asked Hector. He plucked his note pad from his pocket. "Who's it this time?"

Liz shrugged. "I really don't know anything about it. I'll see you later." She hurried to catch up with PC Urquhart.

***

The sumptuous Playfair Library was deadly quiet. Campbell was reading through a medical text book and taking notes. He sat back and looked up at the neoclassical barrel-vaulted ceiling. He stretched, yawned and rubbed his eyes. He was startled when Dr Love appeared from behind him.

"Sir?" said Campbell.

"Master Prebble." Dr Love picked up the text book and read the cover. He dropped the book back on the table. "Second rate. What you need is *Gray's Anatomy*!"

"I know but all the copies are lent out," said Campbell.

"I believe I do have a copy at home. I'm just going there now if you'd like to come and borrow it?" said Dr Love.

Campbell's eyes lit up. "Really? That would be such a help!"

Dr Love beamed. "Of course. Always glad to help the prospective doctors of tomorrow. Come on then."

Campbell excitedly cleared his books away into his leather bag. He eagerly followed Dr Love down the length of the library. Wilton

169

Grimes came out of an alcove and watched as they left. He frowned and wondered what they were up to.

***

Odette wheeled her chair to the window, then back a touch. She didn't want people to think that she was a nosey neighbour. What a glorious day, she thought as she looked up at the sky, then down across the garden and into the street. Just at that moment Dr Love came down the street followed by Campbell. They turned and came through the gate. Odette thought the young man Paul was bringing home looked intriguing. She quickly patted down her hair in the mirror and made for the top of the staircase.

Dr Love unlocked the front door and ushered Campbell in.

"What a lovely house you have," said Campbell as he took in the grand hall.

"Thank you," said Dr Love. "The library is this way."

"Paul?" called Odette, from the top of the stairs.

Dr Love looked up and waved. "It's just me dear. With one of my students."

"Oh?" said Odette.

Dr Love nodded to Campbell and gestured up to Odette. "My sister, Odette. This is Campbell Prebble."

Campbell smiled up at Odette. "Good morning."

"Good morning," replied Odette.

Dr Love waved back at his sister and guided Campbell to the library and closed the door.

Odette was miffed that Paul hadn't come upstairs and properly introduced her to the young man. She wheeled her chair around and returned to her sitting room.

Campbell was impressed with Dr Love's well-stocked library and he excitedly explored the shelves. Dr Love crossed to a sideboard, put out two glasses and poured sherry into each. He checked that Campbell was engaged looking through the book titles. "I think it's on the top right shelf," said Dr Love, as he took a small ampule from his pocket and dripped a few drops of a green liquid into one of the glasses.

Campbell pulled a book down. "Found it!"

Dr Love turned and crossed the room with the drinks. "Here you go," said Dr Love. He held out a glass to Campbell. "Sherry."

"I don't usually before lunch," said Campbell.

"What? A student refusing alcohol?" exclaimed Dr Love, mock offended. Campbell grinned and took the glass.

"Sláinte!" said Dr Love and raised his glass. Campbell reciprocated and they both took a sip of sherry.

"If there are any other books that you'd like to borrow have a look," said Dr Love.

"Oh thank you!" said Campbell. He put *Gray's Anatomy* down on a table. He took another sip from his sherry and continued to look through the titles. Dr Love sat in a comfortable chair and lit his pipe. After a short while Campbell placed the empty glass on the table.

"You do have a comprehensive collection," said Campbell as he pulled out another book and began to look through the pages. Suddenly he staggered. He straightened himself. "That sherry hit the spot." Suddenly he keeled over onto the carpet.

Dr Love took a drag on his pipe. He laid the pipe on a saucer on the table. He got up and went across to Campbell. He leaned down and raised one of Campbell's eyelids. He checked Campbell's pulse. Campbell was unconscious, but breathing normally. Dr Love went to the library door and looked out. He looked up to check if his sister was near the landing. It was all clear. He thought that he'd better make certain, so he went across the hallway and climbed the grand staircase. He checked on his sister in her sitting room. She was sleeping. Her magazine *The Dark Blue* had fallen to the floor. He picked it up and placed it back on her lap. He went back downstairs.

Dr Love knelt down and tried to hoist Campbell up over his shoulder but couldn't manage. He grabbed Campbell from behind and under the arms. He dragged him out of the library and into the hallway. As Dr Love crossed the hallway one of Campbell's feet caught on the elephant foot stand and it fell over. Umbrellas and canes scattered across the stone floor.

Odette woke up and called out, "Paul?" Odette wheeled herself to the top of the stairs.

Dr Love quickly dragged Campbell across the hallway and through a doorway into a corridor. Further down the corridor was the door to the cellar.

"What was that?" Odette shouted down.

Dr Love came out of the corridor and righted the stand. "I was just showing my student to the door and I tripped up. How stupid of me."

"I would have like to have met him, Paul. Next time introduce him to me properly," said Odette. "I do get fed up here on my own with only fiction to keep me company."

"Of course dear," said Dr Love as he replaced the canes and umbrellas into the stand. "Master Campbell is rather shy of women but I'm sure that you'll meet again." Dr Love grinned.

"Oh and Paul. There's still that awful smell. What are you doing in that laboratory of yours?"

"I'm sorry about the smell but I'm at a critical stage in my research. It will be over soon I promise," said Dr Love.

"It can't be good for your health," said Odette. She shrugged and wheeled off out of sight.

Dr Love rushed into the corridor. He stepped past Campbell's inert body and opened the door to the basement. He decided not to risk damaging Campbell's fine skull by dragging him down the steps. He hoisted Campbell over his shoulder and, with some effort, carried him down the steps and along the corridor that ran the length of the house, into the cellar that he had converted into a laboratory. Dr Love gently placed Campbell on the floor. He cleared the equipment off the long wooden table. He hoisted Campbell up onto the table and bound him down with ropes.

***

Inspector MacLeod came out of the bushes as Liz and PC Urquhart came up the path. "Another one," he said. He held up a silver pocket watch dangling from a tartan ribbon. He opened up the back cover and read out the engraving," Always laugh when you can. It is cheap medicine. To Campbell Angus Prebble on his eighteenth birthday."

"No!" gasped Liz.

"Are you sure you want to see the body? We can see if Dr Blyth's well enough to..." said the Inspector, but Liz barged past him into the bushes. In the small clearing a headless body lay out on the ground. Liz thought of Campbell's smiling face. She staggered against a bush and threw up.

"Here." The Inspector passed her a handkerchief.

Liz wiped her mouth and nodded her thanks to the Inspector. She bent down to examine the body. The bushes rustled and Florian appeared, out of breath.

"Dr Blyth. You didn't have to," said the Inspector.

"Nonsense," snapped Florian. She crouched down next to Liz and inspected the severed neck. "Just like the others. Miss Moliette?"

Liz said, "The Inspector found Campbell's watch on the body but I don't think it is Campbell. Look at his clothes. The jacket is of quality, but note the holes in the trousers and shoes. Campbell wouldn't wear shoes in such a poor state of repair."

Florian nodded. She examined one of the victim's hands and commented," Chipped nails, ingrained dirt."

Liz said, "Campbell is fastidious with his nails. It can't be him!"

"I think this man was a down and out. A tramp perhaps," said Florian. "I'd guess approximately five foot seven inches in height." She wiped her forehead.

"Are you alright, doctor?" asked Liz.

"I'll be fine," said Florian.

"Then I must go and check on Campbell," said Liz.

"Where does he stay?" asked the Inspector.

"Carnousty's Boarding House on Queen Street," said Liz.

"Oh I know it. I'll come with you. I'd like to ask him some questions," said the Inspector.

"We need to get this victim to the dead house so that I can do a thorough examination," said Florian.

"Urquhart. Round up some help and get the body to the dead house," said the Inspector.

"Yes sir," said PC Urquhart.

"Then go down to the bottom of Jacob's Ladder, where most of the drunkards hang out. See if they've noticed any of the regulars have gone missing," said the Inspector.

"Right on it, sir!" said PC Urquhart.

***

Liz and Inspector MacLeod arrived at Campbell's lodgings just as Lucia was having a conversation with Hector at the top of the front steps.

"I'll tell him that you called,"said Lucia to Hector. She smiled when she saw Inspector MacLeod. "Inspector! Were you looking to book another session?"

"No. We are looking for Campbell Prebble," said the Inspector.

"He's not here. I'm not sure where he is. Try the library." said Lucia. "I have work to do so please excuse me." She smiled, went back into her house and shut the door behind her.

Hector noticed Liz's worried look. "Liz? What's up?"

The Inspector held up the pocket watch on its tartan ribbon. Hector took it. "Where did you get that?" asked Hector. "Campbell lent it to me but I thought I'd lost it."

"On the body of a beheaded man on Calton Hill," said the Inspector.

"Oh my god! Campbell? We were up there last night," exclaimed Hector.

Liz touched Hector's arm. "We don't think it is Campbell," said Liz.

"Thank god!" exclaimed Hector.

"What were you two doing on Calton Hill last night?" asked the Inspector.

Hector frowned. "Star gazing."

"Star gazing?" asked the Inspector. "Are you sure?"

"What do you mean?" asked Hector.

173

The Inspector said," It's a bit of a coincidence you turning up near a beheaded body again don't you think."

"I swear that I had nothing to do with it. Campbell, I mean Mr Prebble, can vouch for me," replied Hector.

The Inspector shrugged. "So when did you last see Mr Prebble?"

"Not since last night on the hill," said Hector.

"So where did you go after Calton Hill?" asked the Inspector.

"I went back to my lodgings. I was getting cold and I'd lent my jacket to Campbell," said Hector.

"Why did you lend your jacket to him?" asked the Inspector.

"He was colder than me and he wanted to stay out a bit longer. That was all," said Hector.

"So where is he likely to be?" asked the Inspector.

"As Mrs Carnousty said, probably at the library. I could go and look?" said Hector.

The Inspector began, "I don't think..." He was interrupted by Liz who said, "I'll go with him and we'll report back to you."

"Alright. I'll head back to the station and see if PC Urquhart or the doctor have discovered any more information," said the Inspector.

***

PC Urquhart was coming out of the gates of the dead house as the Inspector arrived at the station.

"Urquhart. Any news?" said the Inspector.

The PC whistled. He looked pleased with himself. "The dead man's Rab Souter, sir."

"Oh! That was quick. How did you find that out?" said the Inspector.

"I did what you said and I interviewed some of the drunks down Jacob's Ladder." PC Urquhart took out his notepad and looked it up. "Yes, here it is. A Bert Grant. Said his pal Rab, Rab Souter that is, went up the hill last night and has gone missing."

"That's a start but how can you be sure it's him?" said the Inspector.

"An eagle sir," smiled PC Urquhart.

"An eagle?"

"Yes sir. Tattooed on his left forearm, according to Bert Grant. So Dr Blyth's examined the body and found the same tattoo, sir, "said PC Urquhart.

"Well done Urquhart," said the Inspector. "How about bumps on the head?"

"What do you mean sir?" asked PC Urquhart.

"Did Rab, what's his name?"

"Souter sir," said PC Urquhart.

174

"Did Souter have any distinguishing marks or bumps on his head?" asked the Inspector.

"Oh I see sir. I did ask Bert Grant about that. No sir. No marks or bumps," said PC Urquhart.

"Okay that's all for now Urquhart. I'd better go and see Dr Blyth."

The Inspector went off into the dead house. The smell was even worse than last time. He held his handkerchief to his nose. The newly beheaded corpse lay on a table. Dr Blyth, at the other side of the room, was washing her hands in the sink.

"Ah Inspector!" said Florian. She dried her hands and came over as the Inspector stared at the naked corpse on the table.

"The eagle tattoo," said the Inspector. "Does it have any significance apart from identifying the victim?"

"Ah I see you've being speaking to PC Urquhart," said Florian.

The Inspector nodded. "PC Urquhart asked Souter's friends if he had any distinguishing marks or bumps on his head but they said no."

Florian went to a table and picked up a dark blue jacket. "A single breasted university style. Alongside the finding of the silver pocket watch, I have a theory."

"What is it?" asked the Inspector.

"Mistaken identity. The victim either stole or found the jacket with Campbell Prebble's watch. Campbell Prebble was the intended victim," said Florian.

"Or Hector Findlay," said the Inspector. "Hector Findlay said that he had lent his jacket to Campbell Prebble. So I reckon that somehow Rab Souter got his hands on the jacket. They're both around the same height and age."

"So it could have been either man," said Florian. The Inspector nodded. Florian frowned. "I've met both men and neither have any bumps or unusual shapes on their skulls as far as I remember. Neither men are like the other victims. Why change the modus operandi?"

The Inspector stroked his beard in thought. "Calton Hill is a known cruising ground for homosexuals."

"Campbell Prebble is certainly effeminate but that doesn't necessarily make him homosexual. I don't know about Hector Findlay, however Gabriel Aird was a family man. I don't think you've got anything there Inspector."

"Just thinking ideas out loud, doctor," said Inspector MacLeod. "I must look into all the possibilities."

"I'll check up on Aird and Fox's medical records and see if I can find anything else," said Florian.

"Alright. In the meantime I think I'll make another visit to Dr Emrie," said the Inspector.

***

Campbell was unconscious, tied down on the wooden table. Dr Love checked that the knots were still tight. Satisfied, he crossed the cellar to a small table, on which sat his leather medical bag. He opened the bag and withdrew a surgical knife. He went back across to Campbell and put the knife down on the table next to him. He examined Campbell's skull. He unbuttoned Campbell's collar. Campbell made a moaning sound. He was coming round. Dr Love thought that he should do it quickly before Campbell woke up. He grabbed the knife and held it above Campbell's neck. A bead of sweat trickled down his face and into his eye. Dr Love put down the knife and wiped his eye with his handkerchief. He picked up the knife and raised it above Campbell's neck. "I do this in the name of science so that one day Odette and others like her can be cured!" said Dr Love.

Campbell's eyes fluttered open. Dr Love put down the knife, "Fuck!" Dr Love grabbed a bottle from a shelf. He took out the stopper, put his handkerchief over it and turned the bottle upside down letting some liquid soak into it, then replaced the stopper.

Campbell mumbled, "What's ...?" Dr Love pressed the handkerchief over the struggling Campbell's nose. Campbell went limp. Dr Love picked up the knife. He tilted Campbell's head back and exposed the neck. He lined up the knife to the neck.

"I do this in the name of..." Pickle jumped up on the table. "Pickle!" shouted Dr Love.

The cat miaowed.

Exasperated, Dr Love put the knife back down on the table. He patted the cat. "Pickle darling, I'm pathetic. I can't do this. Not on a live one. Some doctor I am!"

He pulled on his outdoor coat and put his hat on. He left the house and headed down to Lachie's lodgings in the West Port. The streets were fairly quiet. On arriving he pulled the doorbell. After a short while Bridy came to the front door.

"What do you want?" asked Bridy.

"Has he sobered up?" asked Dr Love.

"What you want with him?" asked Bridy.

"I need his services. Another job," replied Dr Love.

"What's it worth?" asked Bridy.

Dr Love said, "Considering he messed up last time I shouldn't be paying him anything. However I will make it worth his while."

Bridy smiled. "He's still sleeping it off. Lazy shite. When do you want him by?"

Dr Love replied, "Nine o'clock. Tell him it's an easy double this time."

Bridy nodded. "An easy double. Nine o'clock. Where?"

Dr Love handed her a card with his home address.

***

Wilton was trying to read a book. He found it difficult to study in the Playfair Library. Too many distractions. He'd picked a quieter alcove away from his friends as he really needed to get some work done. He looked up as Hector and Liz went past. He wondered what that idiot of a reporter was doing with that Liz Moliette.

Hector and Liz came to the end of the library. "Well, he's not here," said Hector.

"Where could he have gone?" asked Liz. Hector shrugged. They went out of the library and sat down on the stone steps.

"I hope nothing's happened to him," said Liz.

"I wish I hadn't argued with him now," said Hector.

"Friends argue. Its human nature," sighed Liz. "Where else can we look?"

Wilton came out of the library. He walked past Liz and Hector, down the steps. He stopped at the bottom, turned and stared up at Liz and Hector.

"Asking lecturers to gang up on me now!" snapped Wilton.

"What do you mean?" asked Liz. She and Hector both rose.

"Don't tell me I didn't see your darling Campbell being all friendly with Dr Love," frowned Wilton.

"When was this?" asked Hector.

"In the library earlier. Left together like best friends. You can't fool me," said Wilton.

"Where are they now?" asked Liz.

"How should I know!" said Wilton. He strode off in a huff.

"Phew! That's a relief. He's safe with Dr Love," said Hector.

"I'm actually going to Paul's for dinner tonight," said Liz.

"Paul is it now? I thought you were keen on him," teased Hector.

"It's just a thank you for helping out in his surgeries," replied Liz.

"Well if Campbell's still with him ask him to go and see the Inspector," said Hector. "I'd better go. I've a load of writing to catch up on."

***

Inspector MacLeod sat down opposite Dr Emrie.

"This is getting to be a habit, Inspector," said the doctor.

"Quite so doctor. The body is Jack. His sister has confirmed it," said the Inspector.

Dr Emrie sighed. "That's a pity. He was coming on so well."   Dr Emrie started to rise. "If that's all, I've got patients to attend to."

"Tell me about phrenology. Do you practise it? Or know of anyone that does?" asked the Inspector.

Dr Emrie sat down. "It's a fascinating subject. Of course I don't hold with all the theories that have been associated with it but there is something in it."

The Inspector asked, "Hasn't it been proven to be a quack science?"

"You could say mesmerism is a quack science but it works. What is your interest in it?" said Dr Emrie.

The Inspector leaned forward. "We have three headless bodies in the dead house. Two at least we know had unusually-shaped skulls: Jack Fox and Gabriel Aird. "

Dr Emrie took off his glasses and polished them. "Obviously I'm sorry about Jack. I didn't know this, Mr Aird. What do you want of me?" asked Dr Emrie.

"Do you practise phrenology sir?" asked the Inspector.

Dr Emrie shook his head. "No. It's only of historical interest to me."

"Then, do you know of anyone that does?" asked the Inspector.

Dr Emrie frowned. "Not really. There are a few of us that share the historical interest."

"Like who?" asked the Inspector.

"Professor Atticus. He used to teach it a long time ago. Not anymore but he likes to keep up to date with the latest theories," said Dr Emrie. "We went to a few of the meeting at the Phrenological Society, but that's closed down now."

"Anyone else?" enquired the Inspector.

"Well I did lend a book to Dr Love," said Dr Emrie.

The Inspector nodded. "Dr Love?"

"Dr Paul Love. For his research. He lectures at the Medical School. Does a lot of charitable work too," said Dr Emrie.

"Do you have an address for him?" asked the Inspector.

Dr Emrie scribbled down the address on a piece of paper and handed it to the Inspector. "His home address. He lives in the old family home with his invalid sister. They have a wonderful library."

Chapter 27   Rabbit Stew

Liz held the shimmering green dress up against herself and looked into the tall mirror on the back of the door. She sighed and threw the dress on the bed. She picked up a white dress off the bed and held it out against her body. There was a knock at the door.

"It's me," said Amulya.

"Oh come in," said Liz.

Amulya entered, took in Liz and the white dress and shook her head.

Amulya picked up the green dress.

"Amulya?"

"What?"

Liz put down the white dress and took the green one from Amulya. "Don't you ever wish you were a man?" asked Liz.

"No. Of course not!" said Amulya.

"If I were a man, life would be so much easier. Just think about it. No hoops or corsets. Layers of petticoats," said Liz.

"I can deal with the conventions of dress. I like my petticoats. Mind you, I'm so relieved when I take off my corset," laughed Amulya.

"A man is given the opportunity to graduate here," said Liz. "We should not have to go abroad."

"From my perspective I am already abroad. I've more freedom here than in India," said Amuyla.

"Of course," said Liz.

"Hector's feature on the riot has helped. By our time to graduate I'm sure that they will have changed their minds," said Amulya.

"I'm beginning to doubt it. I wish I could afford to go to Paris or even Berne," sighed Liz. "Miss Jex-Blake has set up a woman's medical school in London. I heard she's trying to get the Royal Free Hospital to take on female students in the wards. It would be a good place to get some training. We could both apply."

"I've always wanted to live in London, well for a while, but my parents really want me to graduate here. The senate will cave in. They hate bad publicity," said Amulya.

"Yes they do and Hector's been such a big help," said Liz. "You're lucky to have met him."

Amulya nodded. "I know."

"How are things with you two?" asked Liz.

"I know I've only met him a few days ago but honestly it feels like it's been ages. He's not at all like any of the men I've met before," said Amulya. "Not that I've met many. Well not ones that my family hasn't arranged for me to meet that is."

"I don't think I could ever go through with an arranged marriage," said Liz.

"I used to think so, you know to keep my family happy, but since I've moved to Edinburgh I've changed my mind," said Amulya.

"Yes. I've certainly had my eyes opened since I've moved here," said Liz.

"Oh, have you got a secret? I bet it's to do with Paul!" gasped Amulya. "Go on tell me!"

"Then it wouldn't be a secret, Amulya," Liz smiled. She tried to unbutton her dress. "Can you help me out of this?" said Liz.

"Go on tell me. If it's not Paul is it something to do with your parents? Have you found out who they are?" asked Amulya.

"No, why do you say that?" asked Liz.

"If I was you I'd want to find out," said Amulya, as she unbuttoned the back of Liz's dress. She touched Liz's red hair. "With your red hair and skin colouring I'd say you were Afro Irish."

"Is that a thing?" asked Liz.

"I don't know," shrugged Amulya.

"What's important is that we are women and we are going to be doctors!" Liz stepped out of her dress.

"Yes madam!" saluted Amulya. Both women laughed.

***

The carriage drew up outside Dr Love's townhouse, a solemn classical structure on Regent Road. Liz got out and paid the driver. She didn't really have the money spare for the carriage but she didn't want the green dress to get dirty. Umbrella tucked under her arm, she went up the steps and through the tall iron gates. The garden looked unloved and slightly overgrown. She went up the short path to the front door.

Odette was lying on the chaise longue in her upstairs sitting room, reading her magazine. She drained the last of her glass and rubbed her eyes. Her eyes closed and the glass fell from her hand onto the carpet. Dr Love came into the room and picked up the empty glass. He lifted one of her eyelids and checked that she was out for the count. The doorbell went. The doctor put the glass on the sideboard and went down the stairs to the front door. He pulled the door open and smiled at Liz.

"Come on in Liz. I've given the maid the night off so it's just us," said Dr Love, as he took her hat and umbrella.

"What about your sister?" asked Liz.

"Oh Odette's not feeling well. She's lying down," replied Dr Love.

"I'd love to meet her sometime," said Liz.

"I'm sure you shall one day. One way or another," grinned Dr Love. He placed Liz's hat on a table and put the umbrella into the elephant foot stand. He caught Liz staring at it. "My uncle liked to hunt and he was also a bit of an amateur taxidermist as you can see."

Liz looked around the grand hall and the sweeping staircase. "This is a most impressive house." She looked up at the stuffed moose.

"I find it rather old-fashioned really. I'd get rid of it all but Odette won't have it. Anyway come through to the dining room. Cook's left everything out on heated trays so I should be able to manage."

Liz followed Dr Love into a sumptuous dining room. The gas lights were low and several candelabras lit up the long table. Covered dishes sat on glass candle heaters between the settings for two.

Liz noticed an unusual painting of a cat on the wall. She thought that it looked familiar in some way. She went up to it.

"Who painted this?" she asked.

"A patient of a friend of mine. Do you like it?" said Dr Love.

"I'm not sure," said Liz. "What's his name?"

"Oh I've forgotten," said Dr Love.

Liz looked around for the signature.

"I don't think he signed it. Anyway come and have this food," said Dr Love. He pulled a chair back for Liz. She came and sat down. "Thank you Paul," said Liz.

***

Even though it was summer the fire was merrily blazing in Florian's study. She was sitting at her desk, scanning through a pile of medical records. Charles popped his head around the door?

"How are you getting on?" asked Charles.

Florian sighed. "I've gone through Aird and Fox's notes. Now where did I put Dr Bell's notes? I'm sure I did get them back from the inspector."

Charles walked into the room, crossed to a cabinet and pulled a drawer open. He took out Dr Bell's notes and handed them to Florian.

"Thank you!" said Florian. She quickly flipped through the notes and smiled.

"What is it?" asked Charles.

"Dr Love. They all visited Dr Love!" said Florian. "I seem to remember something about Liz was planning to go to his for dinner. We better go past her lodgings first to check that she's not left."

Charles dashed out into the street and quickly hailed down a carriage. Florian and he climbed into the carriage. Psyche jumped in too.

"We're going to Regent Road but can you stop off first at Buccleuch Place," said Florian to the driver.

They shortly arrived at Buccleuch Place. Charles got out and ran up the steps. He rang the doorbell as Florian waited anxiously in the carriage. Sally opened the door.

"Where's Miss Moliette?" asked Charles.

"Oh she's gone to see Dr Love," said Sally. "Did you want to leave a message?"

"Sorry we don't have time. Liz is in danger!" said Charles. He rushed down the steps.

"She's already left," said Charles, as he got into the carriage.

Florian was really worried that they weren't going to get to Dr Love's in time to prevent anything happening to Liz.

"Driver. Regent Road. As fast as you can. A life depends on it!" shouted Florian.

Amulya came to the front door as Sally was closing it.

"What was that all about?" asked Amulya.

Sally shrugged. "Something about Miss Moliette being in danger."

***

Liz was surprised how good the soup was. Mock turtle.

"I hope you're not offended. I've never asked before but obviously you're mixed race?" said Dr Love.

"It's not exactly something that I can hide Paul," said Liz.

"Do you know which of your parents were black? Your mother or father?" asked Dr Love.

"Oh Paul are you doing some sort of study on me?" asked Liz.

Dr Love laughed.

"I don't know anything about my parents," said Liz.

"Are you finished?" asked Dr Love.

"What?"

"Your soup?" said Dr Love.

"Yes thanks. That was delicious," said Liz.

Dr Love cleared the soup plates away and served the stew. He opened a bottle of wine and poured some into Liz's glass.

"It's a pity that your sister isn't well enough to join us. I hope she recovers soon," said Liz.

"She has a rare bone disease. Some days she's fine but recently she's had more bad days than good," said Dr Love.

"Oh I'm sorry to hear that," said Liz.

"One day my research might help her or people like her," said Dr Love. "Enough medical talk. Let's eat." The doctor ate a mouthful of stew. "How is it?" he asked.

"Very nice thank you," said Liz.

"I do love a hearty rabbit stew," said Dr Love.

Liz wiped her mouth with a napkin. "I didn't mention it before but I did see the man who you bought the rabbit off."

"How did you..? Ah I see! You read the note," said Dr Love. He put down his fork and smiled. "Are you spying on me Liz?"

Liz laughed nervously. "Of course not!" She took a sip of her wine. "What do you know about him?"

Dr Love shrugged. "Lachie Merry is his name. A war veteran, down on his luck. I help out by buying the occasional rabbit off him. Why do you ask?"

"I'm sure it was him who stabbed Dr Blyth."

Dr Love shook his head. "Lachie? No way! He's not violent."

"If he's a war veteran surely he's trained in violence," said Liz. "Besides wasn't that his woman at the surgery? The one with the bruises."

"Domestic violence is inexcusable, but what can one do about it?" said Dr Love.

Liz rubbed her eyes. Her vision was blurred. "Paul?"

"What is it?"

"I feel strange," said Liz. "The wine couldn't have gone to my head so quickly. I've only had one glass." Liz struggled to stay awake. She shook her head and tried to sit up straight. Dr Love got up and moved behind her. He reached out and stroked her temples.

"What are you doing?" slurred Liz. She tried to stand up but couldn't move. "What's wrong with me?"

Dr Love smiled and said," Such a beautifully shaped cranium. Your sacrifice will be duly noted by science."

Liz made another effort to stand but she slumped back down into her seat and fell unconscious. Dr Love went out of the dining room into the grand hall. He went upstairs and checked that Odette was still out, which she was, and then went back down to the dining room. He hoisted Liz up into his arms and carried her out of the room and into the grand hall. He quickly carried Liz across the hall and into the corridor leading to the basement door. He put Liz down and unlocked the door. He lifted her up, carried her down the steps and along the corridor, towards the laboratory at the back of the house. He put her down and unlocked the door. He lifted her up again and moved into his laboratory. Campbell still lay unconscious, tied down to the table. Dr Love manoeuvred Liz into a wooden chair. He grabbed a coil of rope from a shelf and bound Liz to the chair. He checked the knots, then took a rag from a drawer and gagged Liz's mouth. Dr Love leaned against the table and mopped his brow. He took out his pocket watch and checked the time.

A faint ringing came from upstairs. The doorbell. Was that Lachie? Dr Love snapped his pocket watch shut. He went out of the laboratory, along the corridor and up the stairs. He made sure to lock the basement door. He went into the grand hall and across to the front door, just as the bell was pulled again.

Dr Love said, "Lachie. About time!" as he pulled the door open. It wasn't Lachie standing on the threshold but Inspector MacLeod.

"Dr Love I presume?" asked the Inspector.

Dr Love recovered his composure and nodded. "Can I help you?"

"Inspector Macleod. I'd like to ask you a few questions," said the Inspector.

"What about?"

The Inspector took his hat off. "Oh just routine. Can I come in?"

Dr Love frowned. "It's rather inconvenient. I've given my staff the evening off so I'm a bit rushed."

The Inspector smiled. "You could always accompany me down to the station."

The doctor sighed and opened the door wide. "You'd better come in then Inspector. I trust that this is not going to take too long." Inspector MacLeod was shown through to the sitting room. Dr Love crossed the room picked up the tongs and placed a few coals on the fire.

The Inspector looked through his notes and said, "So where were you on Thursday?"

"What do you mean?" asked Dr Love.

"Can you give me an account of your whereabouts on Thursday?" asked the Inspector.

"I would be doing what I usually do. Giving lectures. You can check with the university," said Dr Love.

The Inspector checked his notes. "What about Thursday evening?" asked the Inspector.

Dr Love rumbled in his desk drawer, pulled out a ticket tab and handed it to the Inspector. "I went to the Reid Concert at the Music Hall in the Assembly Rooms."

"Very good," nodded the Inspector. He jotted a note down. "And what about Friday?"

"Just the same. More lectures. I'm afraid my life is very routine," said Dr Love.

"Friday evening?" asked the Inspector.

"At home. Look what is this all about Inspector?" said Dr Love. "I am rather busy."

"Can anyone vouch for you being at home on Friday evening?" asked the Inspector.

"My sister. She lives with me," said Dr Love.

"Ah, could I then speak to your sister?" asked the Inspector.

"Yes certainly, but not at the moment. My sister is sleeping. She is an invalid and is very weak. I could get her to give a statement tomorrow if needed?"

"Fine. So tell me your movements on Saturday?" asked Inspector MacLeod.

"A surgery in Leith during the day then home," said Dr Love. "Miss Moliette can vouch for me."

"Miss Moliette. Dr Blyth's assistant?" asked the Inspector.

"She's one of my students who volunteers at the free surgeries," said the doctor.

"I know her. And Saturday evening?" asked the Inspector.

"Home. Again, my sister can confirm that," said Dr Love.

The Inspector nodded. "One other thing. Phrenology?" said the Inspector.

"Phrenology. What about it?" asked Dr Love.

"Are you interested in it?" said the Inspector.

"I have a certain curiosity, as I do with all science," said Dr Love.

"Do you practise it?" asked the Inspector.

"It is not something I teach if that's what you mean?" said Dr Love.

"Do you know any phrenologists?" asked the Inspector.

"No," replied Dr Love.

"Not even, say Dr Emrie at the asylum?" asked the Inspector.

"Dr Emrie is interested in many things. For instance he has a fine collection on witchcraft but as far as I gather he does not fly around on a broomstick and practise pagan rituals," replied Dr Love.

"I see," said the Inspector, as he scribbled in his note book.

"Are we finished? I do have to prepare for an important lecture at the Royal Society tomorrow," said Dr Love.

The Inspector put his note book in his pocket and stood up. "Thank you for your cooperation. If you could get your sister to drop into the station tomorrow."

Dr Love nodded. "Certainly. If she's feeling better I'll bring her down myself."

***

Downstairs in the cellar Pickle stirred awake. The cat crept out from his hiding place under a shelf. He leapt up onto the table and strode up and down the length of it, inspecting the still form of Campbell, tied to it. Liz made a muffled groaning sound. Pickle jumped off the table and onto Liz's lap. The cat stretched up and rubbed his cheek against Liz's chin. She stirred and woke up. She tried to scream but the gag prevented her. Pickle leapt back onto the table and observed her. Liz looked around wildly as she took in her surroundings. She saw Campbell lying on the table.

She tried to dislodge the gag by rubbing her face against her shoulder but to no avail. She struggled to untie her wrists, but it was no use. The knots were too tight. She needed something to cut the rope. She frantically scanned the basement. There was a glass bottle on a shelf a few feet away. If she could just reach it she could knock it over and maybe use a glass shard to cut the rope. Liz pushed on the stone floor and tried to move the chair. It didn't budge. She tried lifting herself up and pushing back at the same time. She managed to move a few inches. Encouraged, Liz tried again. A few more push jumps and she hit the shelf. The bottle fell over and rolled to the back of the shelf. Liz banged her chair against the shelf but the bottle didn't move. She tried again. The bottle rolled off the shelf and smashed onto the floor. Yes! Liz rocked the chair from side to side and finally the chair fell over. Liz hit her head hard on the stone floor.

***

Dr Love crossed the room and held the sitting room door open. Just as the Inspector was passing through there was a muffled sound of glass breaking. The Inspector stopped on the threshold and stood still.

"What was that? I thought you said that the staff were out?" asked the Inspector.

"Oh, it'll just be Pickle. He's so clumsy," said Dr Love.

"Pickle?"

"My cat. Always knocking over things chasing mice," grinned Dr Love.

"Shouldn't you check?" asked the Inspector.

The doorbell rang and Dr Love quickly ushered the Inspector into the hall and across to the front door. He pulled the door open. Lachie

Merry was leaning against the wall, vomiting into a flower pot. He wiped his mouth and looked up with bleary eyes.

"Sorry. The missus said you'd some work for..." He noticed the Inspector behind Dr Love. "Oh evening sir."

The Inspector nodded and moved out onto the steps. "Inspector MacLeod. And who are you?"

Merry looked confused. "An Inspector?" He suddenly bent over and wretched. Vomit landed on the step, just missing the Inspector's feet. Lachie wiped his mouth. "Sorry. I shouldn't have had those damn oysters."

Dr Love grabbed Lachie's arm and pulled him into the house. "Lachie is here to fix the boiler."

Lachie grinned, "Ah yes! The boiler. Maybe I should come back another time if you gentlemen are busy?"

Dr Love shook his head. "Nonsense. The Inspector was just leaving and I've been waiting all day for that boiler to be fixed. Goodnight Inspector." Dr Love shut the door on the Inspector.

The Inspector shrugged and walked off.

Dr Love locked the door. He turned to Lachie. "You took your time. Come on!" The doctor strode off across the hall.

***

Lying on her side, Liz managed to manoeuvre the chair along the floor towards a large piece of broken glass. She twisted around and felt about for the shard. She carefully got it between a thumb and forefinger and started to cut through the rope. It was difficult work and she cut herself several times but after a short while she had one hand free. She quickly cut the other hand free and then untied the ropes binding her ankles. She clambered up and rubbed her hands and ankles. Blood dripped from her left finger.

Liz went to Campbell and shook him. "Campbell! Campbell! Wake up!" Campbell's eyes fluttered open, but then shut. She tried to shake him again. "Campbell!" she shouted as she untied his bonds.

A key turned in the lock of the door. Liz looked around for somewhere to hide, but there was nowhere. She picked up a glass jar as Dr Love and Lachie came through the door.

Dr Love smiled. "I'm truly sorry Liz. I'll miss working with you. I promise you Lachie will make it as painless as possible." The doctor nodded to Lachie, who smiled revealing a mostly toothless grin.

"Why are you doing this Paul?" shouted Liz. "What's wrong with you?"

***

Odette was still lying in a drugged stupor on the chaise longue. Pickle came up to her and began to lick one of her hands that was hanging down. She stirred awake. "Pickle?"

She rubbed her head as she felt another headache coming on.

The cat miaowed.

"Pickle. It's not dinner time yet!" The cat disagreed.

Then she heard muffled shouting from below. She hoisted herself into her wheelchair and moved out into the hall. She wheeled herself to the top of the stairs and looked down.

"Paul? Is that you?" called Odette. She sighed and slowly dragged herself up out of the wheelchair and leaned on the oak bannister.

"Paul?"

Odette unclipped a walking stick that was attached to the back of the wheelchair. She carefully moved onto the stairs. She slowly descended, holding onto the banister with one hand and the other leaning on her walking stick.

***

Inspector MacLeod was walking along the street when he heard a dog barking. He looked up and saw a carriage flying past, with Psyche's wee head sticking out. Intrigued he turned and followed the direction of the carriage.

Several minutes later the carriage pulled up outside Dr Love's house. Florian and Charles disembarked, followed by Psyche, tail wagging. They went through the gates and up the garden path. Florian reached out to pull the bell but stopped when she heard a faint sound.

"That sounded like Liz shouting," said Florian.

Psyche dashed along a path leading around the side of the house.

"It came from round the back," said Charles. "Wait here! I'll go and look."

"Not on your life!" said Florian.

Florian and Charles followed the path Psyche had just taken. There was a window slightly open and a distant sound of something smashing came from it. Psyche tried to jump up onto the sill.

"Stay!" commanded Florian. The dog sat down. "Good girl!"

Charles pushed the window up higher. He helped Florian over the ledge and then he entered. "Stay!" Psyche gave a high whine as Florian disappeared from the dog's view.

Charles and Florian crept down the corridor to the grand hall. Florian spied Liz's umbrella in the elephant stand. She picked it up and brandished it in the air like a sword. Charles turned to see what she was doing. Florian shrugged. There was a muffled scream from the doorway at the far end of the hall.

"Come on!" whispered Charles.

***

Dr Love moved slowly towards Liz. "Why am I doing this?" said Dr Love. "Because I want to further science, to better our knowledge and understanding of phrenology. It is the key to breeding out hereditary diseases."

Liz backed behind the table. "You and Mr Prebble will be the crowning glory of my work," said Dr Love.

"You're insane Paul! You're murdering people. Don't you understand?" screamed Liz.

Campbell sat up and looked around. "What's going on?" He tried to come off the table and stumbled. Dr Love nodded to Lachie, who moved past him, towards Liz and Campbell. Liz hurled a glass jar at Lachie. It missed and hit the wall. Campbell got unsteadily to his feet. "What the hell's going on?"

"Tomorrow I will present you to the Royal Society. A new epoch of phrenology will enlighten us!" said Dr Love.

"Paul. No!" gasped Odette, standing in the doorway. Dr Love turned to see his sister clutching her chest. She collapsed, hitting her head hard on the stone floor. Dr Love rushed across to her. Odette was knocked out. A pool of blood seeped out on the floor next to her head.

"Odette!" shouted Dr Love. He held her up and stared into her blank eyes. He shouted at Lachie, "Kill them! Kill them both!"

Lachie lunged forward and grabbed Liz by the throat. She struggled to pull his hands off but he continued to strangle her. Her vision began to swirl as the air was cut off. She thought that this was it. She was going to die. Campbell was still too dazed to help.

Suddenly Charles appeared in the doorway. He rushed past Dr Love and tried to prise Lachie's hands from Liz's neck. Liz gasped down some precious breath. Charles almost succeeded but Dr Love reared up from behind and smashed a specimen jar over his head. Charles dropped to the floor, dazed.

Lachie grabbed and squeezed Liz's neck again. She tried to pull his hands off, scratching at them. All of a sudden Lachie's hands went loose. He fell down against Liz and onto the floor, Liz's umbrella was sticking from his back. Standing above was Florian.

"You okay?" asked Florian. Liz nodded.

"Charles!" Florian dropped down to check Charles. He was coming round. She helped him to stand.

"Oh my head!" groaned Charles.

Liz went to check on Odette. She looked into her eyes and tried for a pulse. "Odette?"

"Is she...?" asked Florian.

Liz said, "She has a pulse, but it's weak."

189

Florian bent down and examined Odette. "I think she's just knocked out. We'd best not move her yet. I'll just make her more comfortable." Charles took off his jacket and handed it to Florian. She propped it up under Odette's head.

Liz went to check on Campbell.

"Are you alright?" Liz asked.

Campbell said, "What happened. I was speaking to Dr Love and then..."

"Dr Love. Where's he gone?" asked Liz.

From upstairs there was a sound of a door slamming and a police whistle shrilled off.

***

Dr Love rushed down the garden path toward the gate, followed by Psyche barking at his heels. A horse-drawn carriage was speeding down the street. Dr Love rushed out of the gate and across the road. Psyche bolted out and bit the doctor's ankle. The doctor tripped and fell in front of the carriage. The driver pulled the coach to a stop, but it was too late. The crumpled figure of Dr Love lay on the ground. Psyche howled.

The driver swore, "The fucking idiot rushed out in front of me!"

Hector and Amulya disembarked from the coach. Amulya rushed down and checked the doctor. He seemed to be dead. She shook her head and stood up.

***

Florian and Charles helped Campbell up the steps and into the corridor. Liz went ahead and found Inspector MacLeod sitting on the floor in the grand hall. She helped him up. "What happened? Where is he?" asked Liz.

"He came right at me. Knocked me flying," said the Inspector.

Liz rushed out the door. She ran down the garden and met Amulya and Hector at the gate.

"Liz. Paul's dead! The carriage. He came right out at us." Amulya put her arm around Liz.

Liz shrugged it off, grabbed Amulya's hand and stared into her face. "Amulya! Paul was the killer. Well, he organised the killing anyway."

"What do you mean?" asked Amulya. "Paul. Dr Love?"

"Yes. Where is he?" asked Liz.

"Over there," said Amulya. Liz moved to the shape beside the carriage wheels. It was just a long coat, bunched up.

"Where?" asked Liz. Amulya came over.

"He was here. Just here. He was dead." The Inspector came up and looked around. "He can't have got far," said the Inspector, and ran off down the street.

190

Hector noticed Campbell being helped by Florian and Charles down the garden path.

"Campbell!" Hector ran up the path and took over from Florian and Charles, who continued out of the gate and into the street.

"Sir down here!" said Hector. He manoeuvred Campbell to a garden seat behind a high bush.

"Campbell are you alright?" asked Hector.

"Luckily just a throbbing headache," smiled Campbell.

"I was really worried about you," said Hector. "I don't know what I'd do if something happened to you." He grabbed Campbell's hand and stared at him earnestly. Hector took Campbell in his arms and they kissed passionately. Just at that moment Amulya popped her head around the bushes and saw the two men kissing.

"Oh sorry!" said Amulya, as she staggered back in shock.

Hector abruptly pulled away from Campbell and got up. "It's not what you think!"

"I don't think anything!" said Amulya. She turned and went down the garden path, tears brimming in her eyes.

"Amulya!" shouted Hector.

"Leave her be," said Campbell. "She'll get over it."

"But what if she tells someone?" said Hector.

"She won't," said Campbell.

Amulya wiped her eyes as she went back out of the gate. She caught up with Liz. Florian was crouching on the road, inspecting the bloody stain.

"Not much blood," said Florian.

"He must have been pretending to have been injured," said Amulya. "There's been a lot of pretending going on. Nothing is ever as it seems."

Liz stared at Amulya. "Are you alright?"

"Yes. I'm tickety-boo. I think I will apply to go to London with you after all, if you're still thinking of going?" said Amulya.

"That would be wonderful," said Liz. "I needed something to cheer me up after all this."

***

Odette woke up and found herself on the cold stone floor of Paul's basement laboratory. She was horrified as the images of what had happened came flooding back to her. What had Paul been up to? He had looked as if he was possessed. She'd never seen him like that before. Was it all a bad dream? She touched her head where she had fallen. "Arrggh!" It was very painful.

She sat up and then she saw it. The body of a man, in a pool of blood, partly hidden by the long table. Odette reached out, grasped the end of her walking stick and pulled it toward her. With an effort she hauled herself up off the floor. She leaned against the table for support as she made her way round it towards the body. He was lying on his front and his face was to the side, his dead eyes wide open in shock. Odette gasped. She remembered that he had been trying to strangle a woman and then she couldn't remember what had happened next. She looked around the room. At the far end rows and rows of skulls were displayed on wooden shelves. All very bizarre. And Paul. Where was he?

She turned and made for the door. There was a miaowing sound and Pickle appeared in the doorway.

"Oh puss. Where's Paul gone?" The cat turned and rushed off down the corridor. She followed it. The cat stopped at the bottom of the steps. As Odette caught up the cat rushed up the steps and disappeared. Odette clambered up the stairs slowly. She came out into the corridor and made her way to the grand hall. The door lay wide open. The cat stood in the doorway.

"Paul! Where are you?" shouted Odette.

She staggered across the grand hall to the door. The cat rushed out down the steps and into the garden. Odette hobbled to the door and leaned against the doorframe.

She suddenly felt dizzy and fell to the floor, hitting her already injured head again.

"Paul!" shouted Odette.

Hector and Campbell were kissing on the garden seat, screened from the doorway by the bushes. Hector pulled away from Campbell's kisses.

"Did you hear that?" said Hector. He stood up.

"What?" said Campbell.

Hector went to the garden path and headed back to the house. He saw Odette lying on the floor.

He rushed up to her. "Are you alright?"

"I...who are you? Where's Paul?" murmured Odette. Hector helped her to sit up.

"It looks like you've had a bad fall. I'll get my friend. He's medically trained. Oh wait, here he is!" said Hector as Campbell came up the path.

When Campbell saw Odette he rushed up and bent down beside her.

"My God! Are you alright?" said Campbell.

Odette slumped over and seemed to lose consciousness for a few seconds then she came too.

"Try and stay awake!" said Campbell.

She murmured something unintelligible. Campbell held up three fingers.

"How many fingers can you see?" he asked.

Odette tried to concentrate. "Mmmh. Three?"

"Good! Come on let's get you somewhere more comfortable." He looked across at Hector. "Help me lift her!"

The two men carried Odette across the grand hall into the sitting room. They carefully laid her down on a chaise longue.

"Go and fetch Dr Blyth!" said Campbell. Hector rushed out of the room.

"Where's Paul? I want to see him," said Odette.

"Don't worry about that now," said Campbell. "Let's see that head injury of yours." He scrutinized her skull. He could see that there had been some damage. Odette reached up with her hand to touch it.

"No! Leave it alone!" said Campbell.

At that moment Dr Blyth and Liz ran into the sitting room.

"I was coming back to check on you!" exclaimed Florian at Odette. She and Liz went up to Odette. "I'm sorry. I should have left someone with you."

"She's suffering from concussion and a possible fracture,"said Campbell.

Florian examined the injury on Odette's head. "It's worse than I thought, or you've hit your head in the same place again?"

Odette nodded.

"She was lying beside the front door," said Campbell.

Florian nodded. "Yes. I think you have a fracture." Odette struggled to move. "Please keep still miss," said Florian. "You've had a bad fall but you'll be okay."

"I don't understand. Where's Paul?" asked Odette.

"Shhhhh! Calm down," said Florian.

The Inspector came into the room and saw Odette. He asked, "Is she fit to be questioned?"

Florian replied, "Not really. Just be quick."

"Miss Love. Do you have any idea where your brother would have gone?" asked the Inspector.

"Paul? I don't know. I was looking for him. I ..." Odette sighed.

"That's enough. She's not fit!" said Florian.

"Okay. I'm going back to the station to raise the alarm. I'll send PC Urquhart back to keep an eye on the place. Do you need me to send a carriage to take this lady to the hospital?" said the Inspector.

"No. No hospital," cried Odette. "Please don't take me there. Paul says hospitals are dangerous." She grabbed Florian's arm. "Promise you won't!"

"Okay I promise. Just try to relax," said Florian. She looked around the room. "Hector and Campbell can you boil a pan of water and find some clean towels? Dish towels would do."

"Come on Hector! We'll try the kitchen," said Campbell.

"Through there and to your right," said Odette.

The men went to find the kitchen. They went into the grand hall and saw the door leading off to the right. They went through the door and down a corridor which opened out to a large kitchen at the back of the house. Hector found a large iron pan hanging from a rack, He took it down and filled it up with water at the sink. Meanwhile Campbell searched through drawers in a sideboard and eventually found some cotton dish towels. Hector put the pan on the gas cooker. He searched around and found matches on a shelf. He lit the gas ring and set the pan to boil.

Back in the sitting room Florian examined Odette's skull again. She checked Odette's eyes. "I think the swelling is too much. Liz, see the left eye? The pupil is fixed and dilated." Liz nodded.

Florian continued, "Blood is building up below the dura mater causing an epidural hematoma. Try lifting your right hand!"

"I can't," said Odette. "I've got a terrible headache!"

I'll need to relieve the pressure quickly," said Florian.

"How can you do that, doctor? Trepanning a burr hole?" asked Liz.

"Yes," sighed Florian. "It's risky but what else can I do."

"See if Dr Love has left his medical bag around. I'll need a cranial drill."

"A drill?" asked Odette. "Oh my god!"

"If I don't do it you'll die," said Florian. "It won't hurt too much. Where does Dr Love keep his medical things?"

"He keeps everything in that damn basement of his," said Odette.

"I'll go and look for it," said Liz. She got up and ran out of the room. She went across the hall and through the door to the narrow corridor to the door to the basement. She rushed down the stairs, nearly tripping over Pickle, who was lying on the stairs.

Liz ran down the corridor and into the basement laboratory. She saw Lachie's body lying on the floor and moved around past it. She looked all around the room but couldn't see anything that looked like a cranial drill. Under the table she found Paul's black leather medical bag. She lifted it up and emptied the contents out onto the table. She opened up a promising looking box but it only contained syringes. She turned and opened up a cabinet but it was only full of glass bottles. She stared at the rows of skulls in the wooden case that covered the whole of the end wall. Where would he have kept it? She noticed several drawers below the bottom row of skulls. She pulled a drawer open. It contained a large leather-bound book with the image of a skull on the cover. She lifted the book out and read the title: *The Book of Skulls* by Dr P Love.

Oh my god! she thought. Paul's opus! She put the book down on the table and searched the second drawer, where she had more luck. She pulled out a wooden case and opened it. Inside was a cranial drill and several extra parts. She shut the case and put it into Paul's medical bag. Liz chose a small glass bottle of carbolic acid from the pile on the table and added it to the bag. She grabbed the bag and dashed out the door, down the corridor and up the stairs. Luckily Pickle had moved out of the way. By the time she came back into the sitting room Odette was unconscious.

"Hurry. Give me it!" said Florian. Liz fumbled in the bag, took out the wooden box and handed it to Florian. At the same time Campbell came back into the room with dish towels, followed by Hector carrying a pan of steaming water.

"Where will I put this?" asked Hector.

"On the floor over there next to the fireplace," said Florian. Hector carefully put the pan down.

"What about the towels?" asked Campbell.

"Tear them into strips .We'll need them as bandages," said Florian.

"Right you are," said Campbell. He began to tear up the towels.

"I forgot to ask you to find some carbolic acid," said Florian to Liz.

"It's okay,doctor. I picked some up," said Liz. She brought the bottle out of the bag.

"Great! Put some into the water," said Florian.

She picked out the drill handle from the box and attached a sharp drill bit to it. She handed it to Liz. "Dip this in too and bring a damp towel."

Liz quickly dipped the end of the cranial drill into the water. Campbell handed her a strip of towel. She ran back to Florian with the towel and drill.

"Thank heaven for small mercies she's out. We won't need to use the chloroform," sighed Florian. She wiped her hands with an edge of the towel, then with another edge gently wiped the side of Odette's skull.

"Liz can you hold her head steady in this position," said Florian. Liz moved round behind Odette and held her head tightly. Florian positioned herself above and to the left side of Odette's head. She braced herself.

"I've never done this before. If I go too far I could cause irreparable brain damage," said Florian,

"But what happens if you don't do anything?" asked Liz.

Florian sighed, "She'll most likely die."

"You can do it!" said Hector.

"Yes. If anyone can, it's you," said Campbell.

"Let's hope so. Here goes!" Florian guided the drill head to an area an inch from the fracture. She turned the drill slowly, using all her might to keep it straight and down. After several short twists she eased off.

"That's it!" said Florian. "You can let her go gently." Liz carefully let Odette's head rest on the upper part of the chaise longue. Florian handed the drill to Hector, who went and put it in the pan of water.

"More towels!" said Florian.

Campbell handed Florian some dry strips of towel. She used one of them to carefully soak up the extra blood that rose from the burr hole. She used the wet towel again to clean away the last of the blood. She took the remaining dry towel strips and used them to tightly bandage Odette's head.

"That's all I can do. We'll have to just hope that she pulls through," said Florian. She stood up and went and washed her hands in the pan. She dried them on a towel that Campbell handed to her.

"I need a drink!" said Florian.

"We all could do with one. I don't think she'll mind," said Hector as he looked across at Odette sleeping with the bandage around her head. He went up to the sideboard and found some glasses and a bottle of tawny port in the cupboard below. He poured out a generous measure into each of the four glasses and handed them around. "Here's hoping the operation is a success!" he toasted.

Everyone clinked glasses.

Chapter 28   The Book of Skulls

I t took several days to search the house properly but nothing of importance was found. Dr Love was still at large and no sightings had been made of him.

PC Urquhart whistled as he gently packed a skull into a wooden crate. The Inspector came in. "How are you getting on?" asked the Inspector.

"That's the last of the ones you asked me to pack," said Urquhart. He handed the Inspector an envelope of receipts. "I've checked them against these."

The Inspector quickly looked through the receipts. "Fine." He put them back in the envelope and dropped it into the box of skulls.

PC Urquhart looked across at the almost empty compartments on the shelves where there were only six skulls left. "What about those ones?"

"Leave them there for the moment," said the Inspector. "I'll see if the doctor can help us to identify them."

He picked up a large leather-bound tome, *The Book of Skulls*, off the table.

"What about this sir. Shall I pack it away?" asked Urquhart.

"No. I'll take that," said the Inspector. "I've a use for it."

"Oh sir! You think he'll come back for it?" asked Urquhart.

"I'm betting on it," said the Inspector. "Have you locked the back door and made sure all the windows are locked?"

"Yes, sir," said Urquhart.

The inspector picked up the book and flicked through it. The drawings were amateurish but they did have character. He closed the book.

"What about the spare back door key. Was it where Miss Love said it would be?"

"Yes sir! Under an old cauldron near the door. I left it just as you said to," replied Urquhart.

"Good work Urquhart," nodded the Inspector. He left the laboratory with the book under his arm.

***

Odette put down the magazine and felt her bandaged head. Her headache had improved but she couldn't really concentrate on anything. She wheeled across to the bay window. Arthur's Seat was basked in a gorgeous orange, the reflection of the setting sun.

There was a knock at the door.

"Come in," said Odette.

Inspector MacLeod entered with Liz and Florian.

"How are you feeling?" asked Liz.

"My head still hurts. But it's not too bad," said Odette.

"I'm just going to check your bandages," said Florian, as she went round the back of the wheelchair. She examined Odette's head.

"Everything looks okay," said Florian.

"How long will I have to wear this?" asked Odette.

"We'll have a proper look in a week," said Florian, as she came back round to face Odette.

"Inspector MacLeod. Is there any news of Paul yet?" asked Odette. The Inspector shook his head. "I'm afraid not."

"I still find it hard to believe that Paul had those people killed," sighed Odette. "I suppose when he was doing those evil things he must have thought that the end justifies the means. You know he's always been a gentle person. He wouldn't even go fly fishing with me because he couldn't bear to let a brown trout suffer."

Liz nodded. "I would have found it hard to believe too, if he'd not drugged me, tied me up and then got his lackey to try and kill me!"

Odette said, "It's all my fault. If I didn't have this disability he wouldn't have tried so hard to find a cure."

Liz took Odette's hand. "Nonsense! If it hadn't been you he would have found something else to concentrate on that would have tipped him over the edge."

"Knowing that doesn't help," said Odette. She pulled her hand away. She looked up at the Inspector. "What's happening with all those ... skulls in the basement?"

The Inspector said, "We're still going through your brother's surgery records and matching them up with anyone who has been killed or disappeared. We've found receipts from private collectors for thirteen of the skulls. PC Urquhart is sorting them out at the moment. We'll leave them in a crate."

"I don't want them or have anything to do with them!" said Odette.

"You can dispose of them as you wish. Perhaps the Medical School will want them," replied the Inspector.

Odette shrugged.

"I'm sure that Surgeon's Hall would be happy to acquire them for their collection if the university doesn't. I could enquire at both places if you like?" said Florian.

"Yes, please do," said Odette.

The Inspector rubbed his beard thoughtfully. "But that still leaves six skulls without provenances. We know that three of them belong to recent victims." The Inspector counted them off on his fingers. "Jack Fox, Gabriel Aird and Rab Souter."

"How about the French sailor?" asked Florian. "Henri Blanc?"

"Sorry yes I was coming to him. He was fairly recent. That still leaves two unaccounted for," said the Inspector. "Dr Blyth. Would you be able to identify the skulls?"

Florian sighed. "Let's have a look. Liz, you come too!"

"Perhaps you could ask Merry's partner. She might have some information?" suggested Liz.

"I went to her lodgings. A neighbour saw her leaving with her bags very early this morning. I've put a call out to look for her," said the Inspector. He moved forward and placed *The Book of Skulls* on the table.

"I'm sure that he will return for this. It's his life's work."

Florian opened up the book. There was a short foreword dedicating the book to Odette. There were many detailed drawings of skulls, mostly all with slight deformations. There were reams of tables of measurements, and many chapters on brain functions.

Florian looked up at the others. "I do think that mental functions are stored in certain areas of the brain. I'll give him that." She quickly flipped through the book. "Some of the connections and theories that he is coming out with here are rather outlandish." Florian scanned through a series of conclusions towards the end. The last few pages were still blank. She closed the book and handed it to the Inspector. "Let's see those skulls."

Florian and Liz followed the Inspector down to the laboratory in the basement. Florian looked at the row of six skulls lined up on the table. "I would need to refer to my and Dr Bell's notes to make a better judgement but by just looking at these I can make some suggestions," said Florian.

Florian picked up two skulls and put them to the left side of the table. She turned to Liz. "Do you notice anything different between these two here and these four there?"

Liz looked back and fore between the two sets of skulls.

"Those two look more delicate than the others?" suggested Liz.

Florian nodded. She lifted up one of the skulls from the set of two. She put it back down and picked up a skull from the bigger pile. "Males tend to have thicker, heavier skulls than females. So very roughly these two skulls on the left are probably female and this one and the other three are male. Remember very roughly. Anything else?"

"I can't see any difference really, doctor," said Liz. "Perhaps these two have a very slightly darker patina but that could just be my imagination."

"These skulls would have started off all the same colour but see here," said Florian. She scratched the surface of one of the set of two skulls with her finger to show a lighter patch underneath. "It's just a thin layer of grime. What does that tell us?"

Liz shrugged. "He should have kept them under glass to keep them cleaner?"

"Perhaps," said Florian. "And?"

"That they are older?" asked the Inspector. " I mean not that the people they belong to were older, I wouldn't have a clue how to determine that, but that those skulls were processed probably a few years before that four there."

"Yes! Inspector, "said Florian. "Assuming that the same process was used and afterwards that they were stored in the same place, with the same amount of light."

She turned back to Liz. "Now as far as we know all the recent victims were men, so let's try and see if we can better confirm the sex of each of these skulls." Florian picked up the first of the group of four skulls. She pointed to slight ridges above each eye socket. "These ridges here and here are the supercillary arches, colloquially known as the monkey brow. It is much more defined in males than females. Also notice the orbit." Florian rubbed her finger over the top edge of an eye socket. "Men tend to have squarer orbits with blunter upper eye margins. See how this one is quite blunt." She held the skull out to Liz who touched along the outer ridge of the socket with her finger. "Compare it with this one," said Florian as she picked up one of the skulls from the left.

"Yes doctor. I can feel the difference," said Liz.

"Also there is another ridge that is often more pronounced in the male. The temporal line. It's where the muscle attaches to the parietal bone. It goes all the way down to the mandible," said Florian.

"I'm not noticing much difference between the two here," said Liz as she touched both skulls.

"Well, it is very slight," said Florian. "Never mind. The jaw line is a better indicator. It's much broader and squarer in a male and more pointed in a female. The line between the outer edge of the jaw and ear is vertical, whereas in females the slope is much gentler. So what do you think Liz?"

Liz pointed to the first of the four skulls. "I think that one is male."

"I agree," said Florian. "Going by my rather crude method I would say that the four skulls on the right are male and the two on the left are female."

The inspector flipped through the doctor's book and then placed it on the table in front of the skulls.

"The last three entries in Dr Love's book are of Caucasian males, but of course he may not have written it in order. There were over forty entries and we've only recovered nineteen skulls in total," said the Inspector.

"He could have copied them from other collections," said Liz.

Florian nodded. "Apart from the Medical School and Surgeon's Hall there are many private collections in Edinburgh alone. I myself have a human skull in my bone collection."

"You do?" said the Inspector.

"It was a graduation present, and no I'm not a phrenologist," said Florian.

The Inspector sighed.

"Are you able to do any further identification?" asked the Inspector.

"As you can see there are slight bumps on each of these skulls. If I remember from Dr Bell's notes, Henri Blanc had a bump on his front left temple." She picked up a skull and pointed to a small bump on it. "So I would assume that this is Henri Blanc." She looked at the teeth. "Of course we would need his dental records to confirm." She put the skull down to one side.

"You would have to look up your notes on the family's description of each relative," said Florian.

"Urquhart. Have you the notes?" said the Inspector.

"Yes sir," said PC Urquhart. He took out his notebook and flicked through it. "Gabriel Aird had a lump on his forehead, in the middle."

Florian picked out a skull with a slight bump on the forehead and placed it to the side.

"And now Jack Fox?" asked Florian.

PC Urquhart looked through his notes again. "Where is it? " He began to whistle.

"Urquhart!" said the Inspector. "I believe I have that note." The Inspector took out his notebook and flicked through it. "Jack Fox had a lump also on the forehead but to the left side."

Florian picked up the skull with the bump on the left of the forehead and put it with the others. "As I said you should check with the dental records to corroborate these findings."

"I'll arrange to get the dental records sent to me," said the Inspector.

Florian picked up the last male skull." No obvious unusual bumps on this skull. You can see quite a few have teeth missing and one of the skulls has a silver filling."

"I'm guessing that is probably Rab Soutar," said the Inspector. "What about these two?" He pointed to the two skulls on the left.

Florian picked up one of the female skulls. "Slight bump on the back of the head. Some wisdom teeth so at least over eighteen years of age. Quite a few missing and the remaining ones are worn down so I would say that this one belongs to an older woman."

"Race?" asked the Inspector.

"Possibly European but I really couldn't say for sure. The nasal aperture is usually narrower in Europeans compared to Africans, and Asians have a more heart-shaped nasal aperture. The orbits of African skulls are more rectangular than either European or Asians, but that's as far as my knowledge extends," said Florian. She picked up the last skull and looked all around it. "There doesn't seem to be any bumps." She touched the nasal aperture. "Fairly narrow nasal aperture so probably European. " She examined the teeth. "She has all her wisdom teeth, so over eighteen years of age. The teeth aren't so worn down as with the other skull so probably a younger female but I can't be more specific than that."

"Thank you doctor," said the Inspector. He jotted down a few notes in his book. "So we're still looking for the decapitated bodies of two women." He put his notebook away. "Urquhart if I could get you to label each skull with the doctor's notes," said the Inspector.

PC Urquhart nodded, "Yes sir."

"Then pack them up and we'll take them back to the station," said the Inspector.

"What about the larger crate. Will I take that too sir?" asked PC Urquhart.

"No we'll leave them here for now," said the Inspector.

***

Paul tried moving his legs. He was getting cramp sitting in an awkward position inside the rhododendron bush. He peered through a gap in the leaves, across the park and the road, to his mansion. The carriage was still parked there, with the driver waiting, smoking a pipe.　　　The main door was hidden by the overgrown bushes in the garden, but after a few minutes PC Urquhart came out the gate, carrying a crate.　It was too wide to fit in the door so the driver got down and helped PC Urquhart to secure the crate to the back of the carriage.　The carriage moved off. The PC stood guard at the gate.

Paul wondered what was in that crate. His collection, probably. They were invaluable to him but it was the book that he really needed to retrieve.　He looked up at the window on the first floor.　There was someone sitting at the window, looking out. He gasped. It was Odette. She was alive!　He almost fell out of the bushes.　His elated mind rushed with ideas. He would have to see her. Explain why he had done those things. They were for her. He would make her understand. But what if she didn't? The research was the main thing. He couldn't get distracted by personal things. He must get the book back and secure it in a safe place, then he would seek her out.

He carefully crept down through the bush. He peered out and scanned the park.　There didn't seem to be anyone around. He'd have to be careful of the policeman across the road at his front gate though. He followed the right path along the small park, keeping to the bushes.

　　　Suddenly he heard laughing and saw a man opening the gate for a woman, at the Regent Road entrance. At that end of the park there was a long open stretch of lawn, clear of bushes.　Paul moved further back into the foliage as the couple walked, arm in arm, slowly down the path.　They stopped and kissed, just a few yards from him. The man grabbed the woman's hand and tried to coax her into the bushes.

"Please darling. Just a quick one!" said the man.

"Not here!"　The woman laughed. "I've got my good dress on."

The couple kissed again.

"We'll soon have that dress off," said the man.

"You're a right Prince Charming you are!" laughed the woman. "Besides didn't you notice the policeman at the top of the road?" The man shrugged.　PC Urquhart had crossed the road and was staring down into the park.

"Come on!" said the woman to the man.　The couple carried on down the path that linked to Abbey Mount. PC Urquhart whistled, turned and walked back across the road to his stance at the gate to Dr Love's mansion.

Paul scanned the long stretch without bush cover. How was he going to get past without the policeman seeing him?　He heard the sound of horses' hooves on the cobbles coming closer from the left. He waited until the carriage was going past. Now was his chance!　He rushed out from the bushes and reached the gate. He ran beside the carriage as it turned up the hill on Carlton Terrace Brae, always keeping the carriage between him and the sight of the policeman.

The driver looked down at him and gave him a strange look. "I'm not for hire sir!" Paul ignored him and cut off along another path, hidden by a high hedge, running parallel to Royal Terrace. He stopped behind the hedge and got his breath back. After a minute he was recovered. He moved along the path until he reached Greenside Parish Church at the end of the terrace.

He waited until two carriages went past, then rushed across the street to the steps at the bottom of Calton Hill. He was almost halfway up the steps when someone came down them. He thought about ducking into the bushes but the person had seen him and it would probably look strange. Paul slowed down as he walked up the steps, keeping close to the wall, his head down.

As the person got closer Paul realised from his gait that it was another man. The man stopped a few yards up the path and leaned against the wall. His face was in shadow. Paul slowed down and wondered what the man was up to. Then he remembered. Of course. This was a known homosexual meeting place. He quickened his pace and strode up past the man.

"You got a light?" asked the man in a familiar voice.

"No!" murmured Paul.

"It's you! Sir!" The man moved out from the shadows. It was Wilton Grimes.

"Oh my god!" shouted Wilton. Paul grabbed Wilton by the head. He banged his head with all his might against the stone wall. "Arrgh!" shouted Wilton.

Paul banged him again against the wall again and Wilton was knocked out. Paul let him go. Wilton collapsed to the ground. Paul looked quickly around. He grabbed Wilton around the waist and dragged him into the bushes. He checked Wilton's pulse in his neck. He was still alive but he'd be out for a while though.

Paul made his way back through the bushes then he suddenly stopped. He remembered Wilton winning the Hope Prize. He'd never thought of Wilton as much of a student, but he must be, if he'd won that prize. A replacement for Campbell Prebble. It was too good a chance to miss. He had to do it by himself. There was no Lachie to help him now. He went back into the bushes. He took his surgical knife, wrapped up in a small sack, from his coat pocket. With no protesting Pickle getting in the way it was easier to do the deed.

A few minutes later he came back out of the bushes and checked that the steps were clear. He felt strangely detached, as if in someone else's body. He dashed out and up the steps, to the top on the hill. On his right was the National Monument of Scotland, glowing in the setting sun. He ran along the path until he came to a clump of gorse bushes. He remembered this spot was near to the foot bridge in Regent Gardens and should be quieter than the area near the tennis court. There was a door in the wall further down but he didn't have his gardens key on him. He looked both ways. It was all clear. He scrambled up the stone wall. It was difficult, and carrying the small sack too, but he managed to haul himself onto the top of the wall. He looked into the private gardens below. There didn't seem to be anyone around. He carefully lowered himself down from the wall and dropped to the ground. He fell over as he landed and bruised his side.

"Damn!" he cursed under his breath. He already had bruises from being knocked by the carriage but luckily so far he'd not broken any bones.

He crossed the foot bridge and headed north east towards the gates at Regent Terrace Lane. He ducked behind a tree when he saw a couple walking a dog near the water pump. He waited until they moved off, ran across Regent Gardens, skirting the back of the mews and reached the gate. He scaled the wall. From the top of the wall he looked down the lane. All clear. Paul dropped down and quickly crossed the lane towards the back of his mansion. He climbed over the wall next to the back garden gate. He crept through the unruly garden towards the back of the mansion. He peered into the kitchen window. It was dark but a light shone from the hallway. Paul tried the kitchen door. It was locked. He turned and looked around the garden. The key was in its usual place; under the old cauldron potted up with nasturtiums. He went back to the door and unlocked it. He quietly pushed the door open and crept into the kitchen.

He stopped to listen out for any sound. All good. He put the sack in a corner and made his way to the corridor. He looked out across the grand hall. It seemed quiet enough. Paul quickly crossed the hall towards the corridor leading to the basement. All at once there was the sound of footsteps. Paul moved further down the corridor and knelt behind a cupboard. The footsteps crossed the hall and up the stairs. It must be the maid, he thought.

He waited until her footsteps faded away upstairs and then he headed to the basement door. He opened the door and waited at the top of the steps, listening out for any sound. Satisfied that it was all clear he descended the steps and went along the corridor to his laboratory. He pulled the door open but it was too dark to see anything. He felt for the candlestick and box of matches that he always kept handy on a wee shelf beside the door. He found the matches and lit the candle. He held up the candlestick and was horrified to see that his shelf of specimens was empty. Where were all the skulls? He noticed a crate in a corner. He rushed over to it and opened it. He looked through it. There were all of the skulls that he had bought off collectors, but none of the ones that he had personally ordered. It couldn't be helped. He could always replace his collection but his book of research, his *Book of Skulls* was what was really important. He crossed over to the table and pulled the drawer open. The book was gone! Where was his life's work? He looked round the room. He went back over to the crate of skulls. He took all the skulls out and checked the bottom of the box. Nothing! He looked on and under the shelves. Perhaps Odette or the maid had found it and moved it for safe-keeping? He thought that it was more likely that the police had taken it away, but he must go and look. There was always a chance that it was still here and he wanted to see Odette anyway.

He took the candlestick with him as he went back along the corridor and up the stairs. He looked out onto the grand hall. It was quiet. He quickly moved across the hall and reached the large staircase. He stopped again to listen. Satisfied, he climbed the stairs and headed to Odette's sitting room. He gently opened the door and went into the room. It was empty. The fire was almost out. He went across to Odette's rosewood writing desk. If she was going to store anything that would be the place. He put down the candlestick and looked through the side drawers. Lots of letters. Why did she write so many letters and never post them? The main drawer was locked. He looked through the various ornaments on the desk, a Toby Jug full of hat pins and other junk. Nothing. He picked a letter opener out of her beloved coco de mer vase and forced it between the lock and the top of the desk. The letter opener bent but the drawer opened. He pulled the drawer open and looked inside. Just a couple of issues of Odette's favourite magazine *The Dark Blue*. "Damn!"

He went to the window and checked below. The policeman was still on guard at the front gate. Paul picked up the candlestick, went to the door and looked out across the landing to the two doors opposite. The nearest was Odette's bedroom and the one next to it was the maid's, who also acted as a nurse to Odette. The landing was clear. Paul crept out and went to Odette's door. He carefully turned the knob and slipped into the room.

"Odette!" whispered Paul.

He could see that someone was sleeping in the bed, the covers pulled over their head. He crept up to the bed. "Don't worry. It's only me." He bent over and touched what he thought was Odette's shoulder. All at once the blankets were thrown back and Inspector MacLeod sat up in the bed. He pointed a pistol at Paul.

"Ah! Dr Love. How nice of you to visit," said the Inspector.

Paul threw the candle at the inspector and rushed to the door. Inspector Macleod fired. It missed and shattered a vase on a stand next to the door. Paul dashed out of the room and leapt down the main staircase, taking several steps at a time.

The Inspector blew his whistle and tapped on the window. Below in the garden PC Urquhart saluted and ran through the gate towards the front door. Paul ran across the grand hall to the front door. He wrenched it open but the entrance was blocked by PC Urquhart brandishing a baton. Paul turned and ran down the corridor into the kitchen. He pulled the door shut and pushed the kitchen table against it. He rushed to the back door, opened it and locked it behind him. He ran into the garden.

The Inspector met PC Urquhart at the kitchen door. They tried to push the door open.

"I'm going round the back. Make sure he doesn't come back this way!" said the Inspector. He dashed down the corridor and out the front door. He ran down the garden path into the street. He turned to his right, ran along the street and took another right into the lane. He ran up the lane and climbed the wall of the back garden. It was quite dark so he couldn't see if Dr Love was hiding there.

The maid's room opened and Liz stood aside as Odette wheeled herself out. They went to the top of the stairs.

"What happened? Is Paul hurt?" shouted Odette down the stairs.

"I'll go and look," said Liz. She went down the stairs towards the banging sound coming from the kitchen. There in the corridor she came across PC Urquhart, just as he'd managed to push the kitchen door wide enough to get through.

"We heard a gunshot. Did he get away?" asked Liz.

"He ran through here, miss. The inspector's gone round the back. Best if you stay back," said Urquhart.

Liz harrumphed. She attempted to squeeze through the doorway. "Bloody bustle!" she moaned. She was stuck. PC Urquhart heaved on the door and the table was forced back. Liz wriggled through the doorway and into the kitchen. PC Urquhart followed her into the kitchen, just as the back door opened and Inspector MacLeod appeared at the doorway.

"I need lights! He might be hiding in the garden," said the Inspector. He turned and peered out into the garden. The gaslight from the kitchen only stretched a few yards into the overgrown garden. Liz went over to the table and found an oil lamp. She lit it and brought it over to the inspector.

"Thanks." He took the key out of the lock and handed it to Liz. "Lock the door behind us so that he can't come back this way. Urquhart, come with me!"

Urquhart followed the Inspector into the garden and Liz locked the door behind them. She went to the window and watched as the two men went through the garden with the lamp.

After several minutes the Inspector came back and tapped on the window.

"He's gone."

Liz unlocked the back door and the Inspector came back in followed by Urquhart.

PC Urquhart whistled.

They all went out into the corridor and to the grand hall. Odette was waiting at the top of the staircase.

"What happened, was it my brother?" asked Odette.

"Yes," said the Inspector. He climbed the stairs.

"You didn't hurt him, did you?" asked Odette.

"I missed," said the Inspector. "He got away."

"Thank God!" exclaimed Odette. "Well I mean thank God you didn't hurt him but I know that he should be caught."

"I smashed one of your vases, sorry," said the Inspector.

"That's the least of my worries, Inspector," shrugged Odette.

"What now?" asked Liz.

"I'll put out a message to watch all the ports. If he tries to leave the country hopefully we'll catch him then," said the Inspector.

"He might come back and try and find his book again," said Liz.

"Well, it's locked up in my office down at the station so good luck with that," said the Inspector. "Urquhart, you stay and guard the entrance. I'll send someone over to relieve you in a few hours."

"Do you think that is still necessary?" asked Odette.

"Well, he might try again. He doesn't know that the book is at the station does he?" said the Inspector. Odette shrugged.

Liz sighed, "If no one needs me I think I'll head back to my lodgings. I've got to start work at the Royal Hospital tomorrow."

"You're welcome to stay. The maid won't be back until tomorrow night," said Odette. "It would be reassuring to have your company."

Liz said, "Yes of course. I can stay tonight." Odette clutched her hand and smiled.

"Well, I'd best be off," said the Inspector. He tipped his hat to the ladies, walked down the stairs and left by the main door.

"Would you like a night cap before you retire?" asked Odette. "I need something to soothe my nerves after all this."

"Alright, just a small one," said Liz.   She followed Odette to her sitting room. Odette wheeled herself over to a cupboard and brought out some glasses and a bottle of sherry. Liz went to the window and looked out. She saw PC Urquhart speaking to the Inspector at the gate below.

"I don't know if I did the right thing. If I'd had Paul to myself I think that I could have persuaded him to turn himself in," said Odette, as she poured out the sherry.

Liz came across the room. "I think he's way past persuading now. He's obsessed."

Odette nodded. "You're probably right."   She handed a glass to Liz. "Here you go!" They clinked glasses. "Sláinte!" said Odette.

"Your health!" said Liz. She sipped a drop. "Mmmh, this is much nicer than the stuff Amulya buys."

Suddenly there was a thumping noise from downstairs.

"What was that?" asked Odette.

"I don't know. I'll go and look," said Liz.

"Will I call down to the constable?" asked Odette.

"No. Not yet," said Liz. She drained her glass. Odette did too. Liz made her way to the top of the stairs, followed by Odette.

"Stay here and keep a look out for me," whispered Liz. Odette nodded. Liz quietly descended the staircase. She paused at the foot of the staircase and scanned the main hall.   She looked back up to Odette, who pointed down to the corridor leading to the kitchen.

"I think it came from there," Odette mouthed silently.

Liz made her way across the hall and into the corridor. She pushed the kitchen door open. The oil lamp was still lit on the table, but there were plenty of shadows. She heard a slight noise and turned. At the far end of the table was a metal bucket lying on its side in a pool of water. Pickle was lapping up some of the water. Liz chuckled to herself. Scared by a cat indeed! Pickle looked up and miaowed. She bent down to pat it, but the cat strode off to a pantry cupboard.

"What is it puss. Are you hungry? Did they forget to feed you?" The cat miaowed and scratched against the cupboard door. "Ah! So that's where they keep your food, puss," said Liz. She pulled the door open.

All at once Paul rushed out of the cupboard. He spun Liz around, clamped a hand over her mouth and held a surgical knife up to her throat.

He whispered, "Make a sound and I'll kill you. Do understand?"

Liz nodded.

"Now I'm going to take my hand away and you're going to be sensible and do what I say. Got that?" whispered Paul.

"Paul. Give yourself up. It's not too late," whispered Liz.

Paul chuckled. "I overheard the inspector saying that my book is at the police station. I need you to go and collect it. Bring it back to me."

"What if I don't? I don't think you'll kill me. Not without Lachie to do your dirty work for you!" said Liz.

"I tell you, if you don't fetch my book I'll have to kill Odette," said Paul.

"You wouldn't" said Liz.

"Are you sure about that? If you don't believe me have a look in that sack on the shelf," said Paul.

Liz looked behind Paul. A jute sack was wedged between bags of flour.

"What's in it?" asked Liz.

"Let's say that I've got a substitute for Master Prebble. An intelligent homosexual. Have a look."

Liz didn't want to look, but she wasn't sure if Paul was capable of murder by his own hand. She had to look. She picked up the sack. It was heavy. She brought it over to the lamp on the table. She shook the sack open. Wilton's head rolled out onto the table. Liz gasped.

"Is everything alright?" shouted Odette, from the stairs.

"Tell her that everything is fine. You just have to go out for a while but you'll be back soon," said Paul. "Then leave and bring back my book. I'll give you..."

"Liz?" shouted Odette.

"I'll give you an hour. If you're not back by then she gets it," whispered Paul.

Liz nodded. She left the kitchen and went to the main hall. Odette was starting to come down the steps.

"Don't!" said Liz.

"Phew. I thought that something had happened to you," said Odette. "What was the noise?"

"It was only your cat. It knocked over a bucket," said Liz.

"Oh the poor dear. I forgot to feed him," said Odette.

"I have to go out but I'll be back within an hour," said Liz.

"Oh what for?" asked Odette.

"Just some exam revision stuff that I need to pick up from my lodgings," said Liz.

"Can't it wait until tomorrow?" asked Odette.

"I won't be long. Don't worry. PC Urquhart is standing guard," said Liz, as she crossed the hall towards the front door. "I'll see you in an hour." She opened the door.

"Alright," said Odette. She moved from the bannister and into her wheelchair.

Liz looked back towards the corridor leading to the kitchen. Paul, hidden from Odette, was watching Liz. She quickly went out the front door. She shut the door behind her, leaned against it and tried to calm down. After what seemed like ages, but in reality was only a few seconds, she straightened up and went down the steps. She marched down the path to the gate, where PC Urquhart was whistling something tuneless. He turned as she opened the gate.

He said, "Oh miss. I thought you were staying in for the evening?"

"I was, but then I remembered I've stuff to pick up for exam revision. I should be back in an hour," said Liz.

"Very good miss."

Liz went off down the street. She thought it would be quicker to get a carriage and opened her purse. Damn! She didn't have enough money. She quickened her pace and made for Jacob's Ladder; a set of steps cut into the side of Calton Hill and a shortcut to the High Street. Not a great idea to go down these steps at this time of night, especially a woman on her own, but she'd already been faced with death twice over the past twenty four hours, so what the heck! She rushed down the steps.

About halfway down a drunk lying in a corner lunged up at her but she easily dodged him and carried on down to the bottom of the steps. She crossed the street, up the hill and turned onto the Canongate. She wondered how she was going to get her hands on Paul's book. It wasn't as if she could just walk into the station and take it. Or could she? She tried to think of a plan as she got nearer to the station. She felt a few drops of rain. She was about to put up her umbrella when an idea hit her.

A crow perched on the gaslight over the station entrance cawed down at Liz as she passed underneath. Sergeant Wills looked up from the counter as Liz entered.

"Hello miss," said Wills.

"I'm sorry. It's so stupid of me but I seem to have misplaced my brolly. I had it last night in the Inspector's office, I think," said Liz.

"He's no here. Couldn't you come back tomorrow?" asked Wills.

"Well it's raining now and I don't want to make a fuss but it's a special umbrella. A present when I left the orphanage," said Liz.

Sergeant Wills shrugged. "Och I suppose it'll be alright since you work with the inspector anyway." He turned to the wall where sets of keys hung from hooks. He picked out a set and went to open the hatch on the counter.

"Oh I'll go and see if it's there. Don't want you leaving the desk unmanned," said Liz.

Sergeant Wills smiled and handed the keys to Liz. "Well you know where it is. Don't go breaking open the safe," he laughed.

"Thank you," said Liz, her heart thumping as she tried to return the laugh. She marched off to the Inspector's office.

"Oh wait!" shouted Wills.

Liz turned. Wills lit a candle in a brass candlestick and held it out.

Liz went back and took the candlestick. "Thank you." She went down the corridor, put the candlestick on a side table and unlocked the office. She picked up the light, went in and closed the door behind her. She put the candlestick down on the desk. She stared across at the safe. She hoped that he'd not stored the book in there. She opened the main drawer of the desk. Just police reports. A tin of tobacco. She looked in the side drawers, all empty apart from one bottom one. A newspaper was folded in it. She pulled the newspaper out and underneath was the *Book of Skulls*. "Thank God!" sighed Liz. She picked up the book and wondered how to hide it. She opened up the newspaper and folded it around the book. She carried the book and the candlestick out into the corridor and put them on the side table. She locked the door, picked up the book and put it under her arm. She picked up the candlestick just as Sergeant Wills came down the corridor.

"You were taking a long time. Did you find it?" asked Wills.

Liz shook her head. "Unfortunately not. I must have left it in the Green Man."

The sergeant noticed the newspaper under Liz's arm.

"Oh I saw it on the table. I didn't think that the inspector would mind. Odette asked me to bring her something to read," said Liz.

"Oh yes. I heard that you were staying over there tonight. It's a sad business with her brother. We'll catch him. Don't worry." As they walked into the reception Kitty was waiting at the desk.

"Good evening. Sergeant. Miss Moliette isn't it? How are you?"

"I'm fine thank you," smiled Liz.

"I was coming to pick up the twins. Frazer is going for dinner with Victoria so I said I'd look after the boys," said Kitty.

Sergeant Wills said, "Oh he said that the plans have changed. He's running late and to just go over to his house. My daughter Eilidh is there now looking after them until you arrive."

Kitty tutted. "He could have sent word earlier so I wouldn't have needed to come past here."

"I'm sure Eilidh will be happy to look after them for the rest of the evening," said Wills.

"Oh no need. I don't want to put her out. The twins always look forward to seeing their grandmother," said Kitty.

"Well I must be off. Goodbye," said Liz and quickly went off out. She ran down the Canongate and turned left down a street. She leant against a wall and got her breath back.

***

"She was rather abrupt. Rude I thought," said Kitty. "Why was she here? Was she looking for my Frazer?" asked Kitty.

Wills shrugged. "She said she was looking for her umbrella. Thought she'd left it in the inspector's office."

"And why did she have that newspaper?" asked Kitty.

"What do you mean?" asked Wills.

"I recognised the picture. My daughter. How could I ever forget it! It's the article from when my poor Anna disappeared, from the face of this Earth," said Kitty.

"She probably didn't realise. I'll go and get it back from her!" said Wills. He dashed off out of the station. He looked up and down the street but there was no sight of Liz. He went back into the station.

"No sign of her," said Wills.

"Strange! Well I'd best go and see the boys," said Kitty. "By the way do you know which restaurant Frazer was going to?"

"Nannie Dee's, on Causewayside," said Wills.

"Thanks. Goodnight," said Kitty.

***

Nannie Dee's was heaving. Victoria took a sip of her wine and smiled at Inspector Frazer MacLeod. He had hardly touched his venison and was looking at a painting on the wall; a depiction of Tam O'Shanter trying to cross a bridge on horseback, with a witch straddling the bridge, grabbing onto the horse's tail, trying to pull them back.

A waiter came up to the table.

"Are you finished sir?" asked the waiter.

"Frazer!" said Victoria.

The Inspector snapped out of it. "Sorry?"

"Are you finished sir?" asked the waiter.

"Yes sorry. I'm not that hungry," said the Inspector.

The waiter gathered up their plates and went off.

Inspector Frazer MacLeod rubbed his beard. "I'm finding it difficult to stop going over it. We nearly caught him."

Victoria took his hand. "You know who he is now. He won't be able to hide forever. My brother will be avenged."

The Inspector nodded. "You're right."

"We need to move on. We have our lives to live," said Victoria.

213

"I know. This is the first time I've been out since Anna disappeared. Sometimes I think it would have been easier if I knew for sure that she's dead."

Victoria patted his hand. "You still have two lovely boys."

The Inspector cleared his throat and topped up Victoria's glass.

"Frazer!"

The Inspector turned round.

Kitty came rushing through the restaurant, nearly knocking over a waiter carrying a tureen. "Excuse me!" she said to the waiter and came up to their table.

"What's wrong?" asked the Inspector.

"Sorry to bother you, having your first date and all that, but I've just been down to the station and that assistant of Dr Blyth's was acting all funny."

"Liz?"

"Yes that's her. She had something wrapped up in that newspaper. You know the one with Anna's picture on the front, and then she disappeared," gasped Kitty, trying to catch her breath back.

"That's odd. Why would she do that? She was meant to be staying over at Odette Love's tonight. Was she looking for me?" asked the Inspector.

"No. She said that she was looking for her umbrella," said Kitty.

"There's something wrong. I'll pick up Dr Blyth and get over there right now!" The Inspector pulled some money out of his wallet and put it on the table. "Sorry Victoria." He leaned over and gave her a quick kiss.

"Kitty, you can keep Victoria company."

"Well, I..?" said Victoria.

The Inspector hurried out of the restaurant. Kitty sat down in the Inspector's seat.

"I wonder why she had that newspaper. Is she looking into my daughter's case?" said Kitty.

A waiter appeared, holding out two plates. "Meringue roulade?"

***

Liz searched in the hedge where she'd hidden her umbrella earlier. Luckily it was still there. She opened it up and quickly headed for Jacob's Ladder. The rain had driven off the drunken man she'd met earlier on the steps. Liz reached the top of the steps without incident. She paused to catch her breath and not for the first time did she wonder why women were supposed to wear corsets. She made her way along Regent Road. PC Urquhart was still whistling as he stood guard at the gate to Dr Love's mansion.

"Hello miss," said PC Urquhart as he opened the gate for her.

"Thank you," said Liz. "Nothing's happened since I've been away?"

"No. It's been quiet as the grave," said PC Urquhart. Liz nodded. She made her way up the garden path to the front door.

"It's only me," shouted Liz as she entered. Odette was waiting at the top of the staircase.

"Did you get your exam revision things?" asked Odette.

"Yes. I'll be up shortly," said Liz. She noticed Paul beckoning to her from the corridor to the kitchen. "I'm going to make a cup of tea first. Do you want one?"

"Please. There's a Dundee cake in the pantry. Blue tin," said Odette. She turned and wheeled herself off to her sitting room.

Liz crossed the hall and into the corridor towards the kitchen. Paul went into the kitchen and waited until she came in. He closed the door.

"Did you get it?" he demanded.

Liz placed the folded newspaper on the table.

"What's this?" asked Paul. He rushed over and picked it up. "Her?" He opened the newspaper. "Ah!"

He picked up the book and held it to his chest. He grinned. "I have everything I need now. Except for one thing."

He gently put his book down on the table and removed his surgical knife from his waistcoat.

"What do you mean, can't you just leave now?" pleaded Liz. Paul shook his head.

"Go now! I'll give you until tomorrow before I tell the police," said Liz.

Paul moved round the table towards Liz. She edged away from him.

"I'm afraid there's an essential item still missing from my collection," sighed Paul.

"You should leave while you can," said Liz. She brandished her umbrella, the shining tip glinted in the lamplight. Paul laughed and lunged forward. Liz dodged to the side. Paul lunged again. Liz ran across to the pantry. Paul chased after her. She twisted out of the way as he slashed out with his knife, cutting through sacks of flour. Liz edged backward and fell over the bucket on the floor. Paul grinned as he raised the knife, ready to strike. Suddenly the door swung open. Odette stood in the doorway. She hoisted up one of her uncle's ancient rifles and aimed it at Paul.

Paul whipped round. "Odette!" he exclaimed. "It's all for you."

Odette fired the rifle. It hit Paul square in the chest and he crumpled to the floor. Odette dropped the rifle. She leant against the doorframe and slid to the ground.

Liz scrambled over to Paul. There was a lot of blood coming from his chest. He raised his hand and touched Liz's chin.

"Such a beautiful sku..." Paul's hand dropped to his side. His eyes went blank.

PC Urquhart rushed to the doorway. "What's happened?" When Odette didn't answer he stepped over her into the kitchen. Liz looked up at him.

PC Urquhart asked, "Is he dead?" Liz nodded.

There was a clatter of footsteps from the hall as the Inspector and Florian entered.

"What's going on here?" asked the Inspector.

The Inspector bent down and studied Paul's body while PC Urquhart made an inspection of the rest of the room.

"Are you okay?" asked Florian. Liz nodded.

Urquhart came across a bloody sack on the table covering something.

"It's my fault. I shot him," sobbed Odette. Florian bent down to help her up. Liz and Florian helped to move Odette into a seat in the hallway.

"I'm sorry," said Odette.

"Don't be. If it hadn't been for you I'd be dead," said Liz.

"Liz!" shouted the Inspector from the kitchen.

"Can you stay with her, doctor?" Liz asked Florian. She nodded. Liz went back to the kitchen. The Inspector was staring at the head lying on the table, from the sack that PC Urquhart had uncovered.

"What's this?" asked the Inspector.

"It was Wilton Grimes. He was a fellow student at the Medical School. Paul said that he killed him," said Liz.

"Why him?" asked the Inspector. He looked around the head, caked in blood, eyes closed.. "I can't see anything particularly different about his head but of course I'm no expert."

Florian came from the doorway. "Perhaps he was a standard. Maybe Dr Love sought out an example of the skull of an intellectual to compare with others?"

"I think Paul went over the edge. In the other cases he had someone do the killing. This time he boasted about doing it himself. That's why I went and got the book for him. He threatened to kill Odette if I didn't do as he said," said Liz. "I would be dead if Odette hadn't shot him."

The Inspector nodded. "I'm sure no jury will convict her."

***

Sergeant Wills pushed the trolley with Dr Paul Love's body into the dead house. Liz stood next to Florian.

"You don't have to be here," said Florian. "I can manage myself."

"I don't want to be here but I'm going to all the same," replied Liz.

"Let's get to it then," said Florian. "Thanks Sergeant. We can manage now."

Wills nodded and left the room.

Florian and Liz started to strip the body of its clothes.

Twenty minutes later Paul's rib cage had been sawn and pushed back.

"Here it is!" said Florian as she held up a bullet between a pair of pincers. She dropped it into a dish.

She put down the pincers and carried on with the examination. A minute later Florian said, "Now what do we have here?" She beckoned Liz to come closer. "Liz. What would you say that discolouration on the left lung is?

"Some kind of pulmonary wasting disease. Could it be consumption?" asked Liz.

"Correct," beamed Florian.

"So what does that mean, doctor?" asked Liz.

"It's pretty far advanced. He'd only a year to live at most, " said Florian.

"I should tell his sister. It might help in the grieving process," said Liz.

***

An hour later Sergeant Wills entered just as Florian pulled the sheet over Paul's dissected body.

"Finished?" asked Wills.

"Yes. Could you bring the carriage to the front? This body's going to the Medical School," said Florian. Wills nodded and left.

Florian washed her hands in the sink. "It's fitting that his body has been donated to medical science."

Liz replied, "I think I need a drink after that. Green Man?"

"Now you're talking!" said Florian.

***

The Green Man was busy. Hector and Campbell were already there at a table in the garden patio. Opposite them sat Amulya, but she seemed a bit distracted and wasn't following their conversation. Florian and Liz joined them.

"Is anyone going to Wilton's funeral?" asked Campbell, as he got up from the table.

"I really disliked him but it was a horrible way to die," said Liz.

"I know," said Hector. "I'll cover it for the paper."

"I'll make a wreath," said Amulya.

"I'll help you," said Liz.

217

"I didn't like him either but he did have some good qualities," said Campbell. Hector gave him a puzzled expression. Campbell shrugged. "Anyway I have to get going."

"Oh you going already?" said Hector.

"Lots of studying to do," replied Campbell. "See you tomorrow." He downed the last of his drink and waved goodbye.

"So you did Paul's autopsy. How did that go?" asked Amuyla.

Florian said, "His body's been sent to the Medical School."

Liz sighed. "Let's change the subject."

An hour later, Florian was feeling a bit tired.

"I think I'll head off now," said Florian.

"I'll accompany you," said Liz. "Are you coming, Amulya?"

Amuyla shook her head. "I'll have one more with Hector. I won't be long."

Liz and Florian made their goodbyes and headed off. It was a pleasant evening and they took their time strolling up Nicholson Street and down to Causewayside.

They reached Florian's house.

"Want to come in for a nightcap?" asked Florian.

"I'd better not, Dr Blyth. I'm a bit tired. I'm just going back to my lodgings," said Liz.

Florian took Liz's hand. "My dear. I know that you've been through a lot the past few days. Doing an autopsy on someone that you know is difficult. You need to step back. Separate your emotions from the task at hand. It's the only way a doctor can function."

"I know, but it doesn't make it any easier," said Liz.

"Well goodnight," said Florian.

"Goodnight, doctor," said Liz. She turned and went back down the street. Florian stood in the doorway and watched her walk off.

Ten minutes later Liz arrived back at her lodgings. She couldn't find her key. She knocked on the door. Sally opened the front door just as Liz found her keys.

"Evening miss," said Sally.

"Sorry I thought I'd lost my keys," said Liz.

"Miss Amuyla's just back too, miss," said Sally. She stood aside to let Liz in.

"Thank you," smiled Liz. She headed upstairs and knocked on Amulya's door.

When Amulya opened it she looked as if she had been crying. She wiped her eyes and said, "Come in."

"What's up?" asked Liz. She sat on the edge of Amulya's bed.

"It's stupid really. Getting upset over nothing," said Amulya.

218

Liz clutched Amulya's hand. "What is it dear?"

Amulya sat down next to Liz. "I had an argument with Hector. I told him what I thought of him."

Liz shrugged. "And what do you think of him?"

"He asked me to marry him," said Amulya.

"Isn't that wonderful. I know you've not known each other very long but you seem to get on well with him," said Liz.

"Yes we did. Until yesterday when I saw..." Liz sighed.

"Saw what?" asked Liz.

"I saw Hector and Campbell, kissing!" stammered Amulya.

"Really?" asked Liz.

"It was after the carriage ran over Dr Love. I went into the garden to find Hector and there they were sitting on the bench, kissing away" said Amulya.

"Maybe it was because Hector was so glad that Paul hadn't killed Campbell?" suggested Liz.

"No. It wasn't like that," said Amulya. "Not like that at all."

"I remember now. That's when you said that you were going to London with me," said Liz.

"I was angry and disappointed at the time. I felt like such a fool, thinking he was the one," said Amulya. "He just wants one of those trophy wives so that he can pretend to act normal in society." Amulya sobbed and Liz gave her a long hug. Amulya straightened up. "So that's what I told him. I'm not going to be a trophy wife."

"Quite right. You don't need a man to make you happy!" stated Liz.

"Liz! I want to try something daft," said Amulya. She grabbed Liz and kissed her forcefully, full on the mouth. She let go and sat back.

"What was that for?" asked Liz.

"Did you feel anything?" asked Amulya.

"Just a bit awkward to be honest," said Liz, looking rather embarrassed.

"Me too. Women don't do anything for me," Amulya sighed. "I wondered if it was me. Had I turned Hector?"

Liz shook her head. "I don't think that it works like that. I knew someone back in the orphanage. Peter, he was called. He said he always knew he was attracted to men."

"But you get people that are attracted to both sexes. Don't you?" asked Amulya. "I heard that it was quite common in India before the Raj."

219

"I don't know. After Paul I think I've had enough of men for a while," said Liz.

"I should go for a more mature man. Someone like Dr Blyth. He's not the best looking but I'm sure that he would be a loving and faithful partner," said Amulya.

"I really don't think Dr Blyth would suit you Amulya. As they say, there's plenty more fish in the sea."

"But I don't want a fish!" grinned Amulya. "Anyway I've got that off my chest. I'll stay friends with Hector but anything else is out of the question."

Chapter 29   Ceremony

A week had passed since the death of Dr Paul Love.
From the look of his eyes Professor Atticus had been experimenting with poison again. He looked like a maniac, with his wide pupils and a massive grin on his face, as he rushed across the courtyard.

Liz sketched a dissected heart as Florian washed her hands in a bowl. Florian dried her hands. She combed her hair in a mirror and said, "What a fuss. Why do they want to have the presentation here?"

Liz crosshatched a shadow to a ventricle and said, "I suppose its publicity for the university."

Florian replied, "But it was one of our own staff ordering the killings."

Liz shook her head. "I still can't believe it. He was so..." There was a sharp knock on the door and Professor Atticus marched in, holding up a letter in his gnarled hand.

With a flourish he handed the letter to Liz and said, "I expect you'll be leaving us soon!" The professor nodded to Florian and rushed out of the room.

Florian sighed. "He should really get a hold on those poison experiments of his." She noticed an angry look come across Liz's face as she read the letter. "What is it?"

Liz huffed. "The senate. They've voted to keep the ban on women graduating."

Florian shook her head. "It doesn't surprise me."

Liz said, "What am I going to do, doctor? I can't afford to go abroad to graduate."

"I'm sure that Odette Love will help out if you want to finish your education abroad wherever, perhaps Paris. As for the immediate future, I received a letter from Sophia Jex-Blake," said Florian. "I gave you both glowing references. She'd be lucky to have you for this new school of medicine for women. "

"Oh thank you, doctor," said Liz.

David Hutchison

"Mind you she won't give you any leeway for being a woman. *A fair field and no favour* is her motto," said Florian.

"I wouldn't want any favour," said Liz.

Florian patted Liz on the shoulder. "I know."

"We'd better go. The presentation is about to start!" said Liz.

"Just a minute," said Florian. She went to a cupboard and took out a glass and a bottle of port. She poured herself a glass. "You?"

"No thank you," said Liz.

Florian downed the glass in a oner. "Let's go!"

***

A crowd was seated in the courtyard. In the front row sat Campbell and Hector. Amulya came and sat next to Hector.

"Hello! I've not seen you for ages," said Hector.

"I had a lot to prepare. I'm moving to London," said Amulya.

"Yes. Liz told me that you're both applying for the London Women's Hospital. I'm sure that you'll get in!" said Hector.

"Thanks," said Amulya.

"Yes, you'll get in, no problem," said Campbell.

"I'll miss you," said Hector.

Amulya smiled, "I'll miss you both. You'll have to come and visit me." Both Campbell and Hector smiled.

"We will do," said Hector. Campbell nodded in agreement.

"Oh here's the rest of them," said Amuyla.

Charles, Liz and Florian were crossing the courtyard. Amulya waved. Liz came and sat beside her. Florian and Charles went and stood off to one side.

Amulya whispered, "I thought you weren't going to make it!"

"I think Dr Blyth was getting a bit nervous," whispered Liz.

Amulya looked over at Florian. Charles was gently patting the doctor's back, obviously trying to calm her down a bit.

On the platform in front sat the Dean of the university, next to Inspector MacLeod and Chief of Police Albert McIntosh. The Dean rose and went to the lectern. He cleared his throat and said, "We are gathered here today at the request of Chief of Police McIntosh."

The Dean bowed and beckoned to McIntosh. The Chief of Police rose and came up to the lectern.

McIntosh began, "Good afternoon. We are here today to celebrate one of your lecturers without whom another of your lecturers would still be causing murder. I'm sure that the irony is not lost on you. Please put your hands together for Dr Florian Blyth."

The crowd applauded as Florian made her way up to the platform. McIntosh shook her hand. Florian smiled as the crowd applauded again. "Thank you. I owe a debt of gratitude to my assistant Liz

222

Moliette, without whom this case would not have been solved." Florian pointed to Liz, who looked around, embarrassed. The crowd applauded.

Florian's smile vanished and she said, "Which makes it even more shocking that today the senate has confirmed that women will not be allowed to graduate."

Amongst the audience a couple of students clapped. Florian stared at them and their claps died out.

Florian reached up and peeled off her fake moustache. "It's about time women were treated equally." There were gasps from the crowd. Florian removed her jacket and lay it on the lectern. She unbuttoned her shirt and removed it to reveal her upper torso swathed in a bandage. Florian unwound the bandage to reveal the stab wound between ample breasts. The crowd gasped. The professor nearly fell off his chair. The Dean looked as if he was having a heart attack. The Inspector and the Chief of Police were both shocked, but quickly recovered. The Inspector grinned.

Florian stared defiantly at the crowd.

Amulya gasped in surprise and grabbed Liz's hand. "You knew! That's your secret!"

"I didn't know that she was going to do this though," said Liz.

"Go on girl!" shouted Campbell.

"My word. What a scoop!" said Hector, as he scribbled down in his notebook.

The professor stood up and shouted, "This is outrageous! I'll have you struck off!" The professor stomped off the platform. Most of the students followed him, some knocking over their chairs as they left. The Dean shook his head at Florian. She shrugged back at him. He left without a word.

The Chief of Police came up to Florian and stood between her and what was left of the crowd. He picked her shirt off the lectern and handed it to her. "I really don't care if you are a doctor or a doctress. You're our police surgeon. Now get your shirt back on doctor!" Florian nodded and dutifully pulled on her shirt.

She said, "Thank you sir. I think I'll need the job as it looks like I won't be lecturing here anytime soon." She draped her jacket over her shoulders.

Charles came up and stood beside Florian. "Are you alright dear?" asked Charles.

"Better than ever," said Florian. "You could say I got it off my chest!"

"You've some sense of humour," said Inspector MacLeod.

"I'm so glad that you did it at last. Maybe we can have a normal life now!" said Charles.

"I don't think that will ever happen. Anyway what's normal?" said Florian.

"Excuse me. I'll leave you to it doctor. Unless you need an escort?" asked the Chief of Police.

"I'll look after her, sir," said Charles.

"Very well," said the Chief of Police. He and the Inspector went off down the platform. "The show's over everyone. Go home!" said the Chief of Police to the few stragglers left. Liz got up and headed past the chief towards the stage. She was followed by Amulya, Hector and Campbell.

Liz went up to Florian, while the others stood back slightly to give her a bit of space. Liz awkwardly hugged Florian as she held her umbrella.

Liz said, "That was so brave!"

The others then came up to Florian. "You're amazing," said Campbell.

"I still can't believe it," said Amulya.

"I'd love to do an in depth interview. I'm sure that I can get the public on your side," said Hector.

"I'll need all the help I can get," said Florian.

"Great!" said Hector. He got out his notebook. "I've so many questions."

Florian shook her head. "Not now. We can arrange to do the interview later. If you don't mind, I need to have a private chat with Liz."

"But..." began Hector.

"Come on you two!" said Amulya. She linked arms with Hector and Campbell. "You can all catch up with us in the Green Man later." The three of them went off down the steps and out of the courtyard.

Florian stared across at her daughter and then at Charles. He nodded.

"Liz, we've got something to tell you," said Florian. "I should have told you before."

"What?" asked Liz.

"I'm ... your mother," said Florian.

Liz was flabbergasted. "What do you mean you're my mother?" asked Liz.

Florian replied, "It wasn't planned. I had to give you up as soon as you were born. I'm so sorry."

"Why didn't you tell me before?" asked Liz.

"I wanted to. I'm so proud of you," said Florian. "I just didn't know how to."

"Oh!" gasped Liz. She was reeling from this unexpected news. She'd always wanted to find out who her parents were, but she never imagined anything like this.

"What about my father. Who's he?" demanded Liz. Suddenly it hit her. She stared at Charles. "Father?"

Charles smiled sheepishly. "I'm sorry. I didn't know either until a few days ago."

Florian and Charles held out their arms to Liz.

"I don't know whether to hug or hit you!" sighed Liz.

Liz hugged them both.

Chapter 30   Back to London

The London School of Medicine For Women sounded a rather grand name for the small building on Henrietta Street that Liz and Amuyla entered. They went up to a young receptionist sitting at a desk.

"Miss Moliette and Miss Patel to see Miss Jex-Blake," said Liz.

The receptionist smiled. "Please take a seat. I'll see if Ms Jex-Blake is ready to see you."

The woman walked off down a corridor, knocked on a door and entered.

Liz looked around the reception area. She was surprised to see that there were several paintings of religious scenes on the walls. She'd expected something more medical.

Suddenly there was a noise of raised voices. The door that the receptionist had gone through opened and a middle-aged woman stamped down the corridor towards them. As she came closer Liz could see that the woman had a scowl on her face. The receptionist came out and ran down the corridor towards the older woman. She caught up with her near where Liz and Amuyla were sitting.

"Mrs Anderson! I'm sure she didn't mean it," said the receptionist. She clutched at the woman's hand.

"Pah! She meant every word. I'm not going to stay here and be insulted by her," said the woman. She shrugged off the receptionist's hand and walked out of the front door. The receptionist stared at the door as it slammed shut. She sighed and then seemed to remember that she had company.

"Sorry. Things are getting a bit hectic here. We've got an eminent doctor arriving from Paris this week to teach some key classes and not everyone was informed," said the receptionist. "Anyway Ms Jex-Blake will see you both now."

The receptionist ushered Liz and Amulya down the corridor and knocked on the door.

There was a muffled, "Come in!"

She opened the door and ushered in the two women.

"Miss Moliette and Miss Patel,"

Sophia Jex-Blake was standing at the window, her dark silhouette framed in the afternoon sun. Jex-Blake turned and gestured to two seats set out in front of an old-fashioned desk.

"Sit down ladies."

The women sat down in the proffered seats but Miss Jex-Blake remained standing at the window.

"So that we are all singing from the same hymn sheet; I expect you to work hard here. I don't expect you to work as hard as a man, but harder. That is the only way we will become doctors. It that clear?" said Ms Jex-Blake.

"Perfectly," said Liz.

"Of course," said Amulya.

"I'm expecting that we will be able to offer you clinical experience on the wards at the Royal Free shortly, but it's not been confirmed yet. In the meantime the dean and I will be teaching classes, bringing in what experts that we can. You should also be aware that you may have to think about applying to gain your degrees abroad if we can't get the legislation through. I am building up contacts with universities in Paris and Berne so one way or another we'll make doctors of you eventually, if you put the work in. Any questions?"

Liz looked across at Amulya.

"I think you've covered everything," said Liz.

"Good," said Ms Jex-Blake, smiling for the first time.

She went across and sat at her desk. She took out a sheet of paper and started writing,

"You may go," she said, not looking up.

"Thank you," said both Liz and Amulya. They got up and left the room.

As they walked back down the corridor Amulya said, "I wonder what we've got ourselves into."

Liz shrugged. "I'm going to the orphanage to visit an old friend. It's just around the corner. Would you like to come along?"

"No. I'm going back to the hotel to get changed. Then I've got some rooms in Earls Court to view. Sure you don't want to come with me?" said Amulya.

"I couldn't afford Earls Court," said Liz.

"Don't worry. I can help you out," said Amuyla.

"No. You've already done enough. Besides I have a plan," said Liz.

***

The Foundling Orphanage looked much smaller than Liz remembered. What a difference a year makes, she thought. The main door was open so she went into the main hall, just as Miss Dante was coming down the stairs.

"Oh Liz. *Ciao!* So nice to see you!" said Miss Dante as she clutched Liz's hand. "How are you?"

"Fine thanks. And you?" asked Liz.

"I've been *occupata* with work. Jane said she'd got a letter from you. You moving back to London?" said Miss Dante.

"Yes. Edinburgh was very exciting but as I feared, the university is determined not to let women graduate," said Liz.

"Liz!" came a shout from the corridor. Jane rushed up and hugged Liz.

"How are you?" asked Jane.

"Oh Jane. It's so good to see you," said Liz. "You're looking well."

"You too," said Jane.

"Jane is teaching *i giovani* full-time," said Miss Dante.

"Yes I'm really enjoying it," said Jane. "How did the interview go at....what was it?"

"The London School of Medicine for Women," said Liz. "I got in!"

"*Meraviglioso!*" said Miss Dante.

"Great! I've got my own room," said Jane. "You're welcome to share it if you like?"

"If you help Jane, fine with me," said Miss Dante.

"Well, I think I could do that until I get something sorted longer term," said Liz.

"Great. That's it settled then. Come and see the room," said Jane.

Liz followed Jane as she rushed up the stairs and along a corridor to a door at the end.

"It's Carrie's old room," said Liz. "Where is she now?"

"I don't know. She just up and left one day. No note. Nothing," said Jane.

***

The next few months went past quickly. Ms Jex-Blake taught them all she knew and the doctors that she managed to bring in for lectures were all very interesting and enthusiastic. Liz and Amulya helped out on the wards at the Royal Free Hospital in between studies. It was hard work but they both enjoyed putting medical theory to good use and meeting patients. Amulya started to go out with Fredric, one of the nice young doctors that she met on the ward.

It was Fredric that came up to Liz one busy day in November and started telling her about a very ill patient on his ward who had asked to see her.

"Who can that be?" asked Liz.

Fredric said, "She won't give her name. She saw you from the window yesterday and asked me if you were from Edinburgh. I said you'd been there for a year."

"I'm intrigued but I've got a lot of work to do today. Tell her I'll come and see her tomorrow," said Liz.

"I don't think she'll last the night," said Fredric.

"Where is she?" asked Liz.

"I've left her in the garden. The far end, next to the apple tree," said Fredric.

Liz nodded. "I'll go and see her but I can't stay long or Dr Williams will be onto me."

"I'll cover for you," said Fredric.

Liz quickly went down the stairs and out the front entrance. It was snowing outside. Who could it be from Edinburgh? She rushed along the path and headed for the apple tree. From the distance across the snow-covered lawn she could see a hunched figure in a shawl. She was in a wheelchair next to the park bench, throwing crumbs to a robin. As Liz came up close the robin flew away. The woman turned. At first Liz didn't recognise her gaunt face but there was something familiar about her defiant-looking green eyes.

"You're Dr Love's assistant aren't you?" said the woman.

Suddenly Liz recognised the wasted face. "It's Bridy Scott. Isn't it?"

Bridy nodded. The robin had returned and with a great effort she pulled a few more pieces of bread off the stale loaf and threw it towards the bird. She didn't throw it far enough and the robin was too wary to come closer. Liz kicked the crumbs farther away and the bird picked up a large piece and flew off. Liz sat down on the bench.

"What do you want?" asked Liz.

"I read about it in the paper. My man Lachie. They've put him in the museum. Well his skeleton, that is," said Bridy.

"Yes his body was given over to the Medical School after the execution," said Liz. "Dr Love too."

"I don't care about that bastard Dr Love. It's him that..."

Bridy had a coughing fit. She wiped her mouth and nose with her dirty shawl.

"Lachie was my love. You should have seen him before he went to war. He never hit me back then. Anyway as I see it, he should be spending eternity next to my side. Buried together," said Bridy.

"I don't think that would be possible. Perhaps if you'd been married you'd have some claim over his body. I'm sorry, I'm no lawyer," said Liz.

"Well there is one thing that you could do for me then. I'd like you to arrange for my body to be sent to the Medical School so I can be with my Lachie," said Bridy.

"I don't know if I can do that. Even if I wanted to. I was thrown out of the place," said Liz.

"You could find a way I'm sure. I have something that may persuade you," said Bridy. She took a dog-eared notebook from a fold in her shawl. "Here!"

Liz took the notebook. "What's this?"

"I kept a list of the jobs Dr Love asked us to do. Always thought it might come in handy," grinned Bridy.

Liz opened the notebook. The first entry was *"Josephine Flett, 24 Kings Road, Aberdeen"*. The second entry was *"Anna Macleod, Velocity"*.

"Anna MacLeod. Inspector Macleod's wife!" said Liz. "That's why Paul said *her*! He recognised her face in the newspaper."

"What?" asked Bridy.

"Nothing," said Liz. "Doesn't matter now."

"That Dr Love bastard never even told us her husband was police!" said Bridy. "We'd never have agreed otherwise. On a bloody ferry too! I hate the sea."

"Velocity? Ah, the ferry!" said Liz. "But why her?"

"He never gave his reasons and we didn't ask," said Bridy. She snatched the notebook back.

"Do you not feel remorse for what you've done?" asked Liz.

"Anyone we did, we did quick! Well is it a deal?" said Bridy.

"I'll do what I can," said Liz.

Bridy handed her the notebook. Liz got up and walked off.

Bridy smiled to herself. She tried to tear off a chunk of bread but couldn't manage. The robin flew down and looked up at her.

***

When Bridy died that evening Liz thought about what she should do with the notebook. She knew that she'd have to get it to the Inspector. As to Bridy's last wish, who could help her at the Edinburgh Medical School? She and Fredric went to visit Amulya and told her the whole story.

"That's so sad," said Amuyla. "We'd better tell the Inspector at once."

"If it was me I'd want to know," said Fredric.

"What about Bridy Scott's last wishes. I know that's she was a murderer but I did give my word," said Liz.

"Well Dr Blyth was sacked so she can't help," said Amulya.

"How about that doctor you told me about, Amuyla. The one that broke his arm in the incident with the sheep?" said Fredric.

"Yes Dr Nicolson. Liz, ask him!" said Amuyla.

Together Liz and Amulya drafted a letter to Dr Nicolson while Fredric arranged for Bridy's body to be stored in the morgue, rather than be buried. Liz wrote to Florian about what had happened. She didn't want to post Bridy's notebook in case it got lost so she handed it into the nearest police station along with a detailed letter to Inspector MacLeod. The station said that they'd despatch it up to Edinburgh right away.

***

The Inspector read Liz's letter again. He wiped his eyes and stared at Bridy's dog-eared notebook. He went to the safe and unlocked it. He brought out the two skulls, each wrapped up in a cloth. He put the one with the bump at the back to one side. According to Bridy Scott's notes this was a Josephine Flett. He picked up the other skull. Was this Anna, in his hands? He imagined her smile. Yes how hadn't he seen it before? There was a knock on the door. He put the skull down.

"Come in!"

Florian walked into the room with a large envelope. "The dental records have arrived from Aberdeen. Are you up to this Inspector?"

The Inspector nodded. Florian sat down. "Let's start then." She took the records out of the envelope and began comparing the teeth of the skull with what the Inspector was certain was Anna's skull. The Inspector filled his pipe and waited.

After a minute Florian looked up at him. "I'm afraid it's conclusive. This is Anna Macleod."

The Inspector's eyes welled up as he tried to light his pipe. He gave up and threw the pipe onto the floor. It shattered into pieces.

"Sorry. I can come back later?" asked Florian.

The Inspector shook his head. "So how did he meet Anna and the other woman Josephine Flett?"

"I looked through some notes Odette found. He had a one off surgery in Aberdeen that they both attended," said Florian.

"She never told me about going to any surgery," said the Inspector. "Mind you she was always worried about her health."

There was a knock on the door and PC Urquhart entered.

"That's a telegram through from the Aberdeen station. They've recovered Josephine Flett's body from her garden shed."

Chapter 31   Christmas in Edinburgh

Dr Nicolson immediately wrote back to Liz that he would do everything he could. Sure enough a few days later the body of Bridy Scott was carted off to Edinburgh.

A week later a letter arrived from Florian asking Liz to come back to Edinburgh to spend Christmas with her. Liz was excited. She'd never really had a family Christmas before. She felt a bit guilty leaving Jane and Amulya over the festive period but Jane had said that she was busy with her suffragette meetings and Amulya was going to visit Fredric's family for the first time.

***

Liz looked out the window, at the castle covered in snow, as the train pulled into Princes Street Station. She took down her travel bag from the rack and picked up her brolly. The train shuddered to a stop. The gentleman opposite Liz opened the door.

"After you miss," he said.

"Thank you." Liz stepped onto the platform. She peered through the mix of steam and smoke, and out of it walked Charles.

"Welcome home Liz!" said Charles. "You're looking well." He shook her hand and then picked up her travel bag. "She's got a carriage waiting."

They weaved through the crowded station. "Working in the new hospital sounds very exciting. Florian read out your letters to me," said Charles.

"It was, but I'm glad to be back," said Liz.

Charles went up to a carriage waiting on Princes Street and tapped on the window. Florian came out of it, dressed in a smart trouser suit. Her hair was slightly longer. No fake moustache. She gave Liz a big hug.

"Welcome home dear. You're looking well," said Florian.

"You too!" said Liz. "I see you've had a shave!"

Florian laughed.

Charles hoisted the travel bag up beside the driver. He opened the door and let the ladies in. Then he got in himself.

"Your letters were wonderful. I want to know all about Jex-Blake's teaching methods," said Florian.

"I've taken loads of notes. I enjoyed your letters too. It sounds like the police work has kept you very busy," said Liz. "How is Inspector MacLeod? I've not heard back from him. It's good that you identified his wife's skull but it still must be difficult for him not having the body."

"I saw him yesterday. He's coping. Told me to give you this," said Florian. "He knew you were coming up for Christmas and didn't want you to miss the post." She took an envelope from her pocket and handed it to Liz. It was an invitation to Frazer MacLeod and Victoria Massey's wedding in January.

"That's wonderful!" said Liz.

"It's the first time Charles and I have been asked to something together," said Florian. Charles nodded and grinned.

"If it hadn't been for the Inspector I don't know how I would have coped moneywise. Professor Atticus made sure that I lost my lecturer job," said Florian.

"You didn't mention him in your letters but I thought as much," Liz frowned.

"Anyway it will be a wonderful wedding," said Florian.

"The twins will make delightful page boys," said Liz.

"I still wonder why Paul picked Anna MacLeod," said Florian. "She didn't have any obvious lumps on her head."

"But neither do I and he tried to kill me too if you remember," said Liz.

"That was because of your mixed race heritage. As far as I can tell from his notes he tried to collect a standard specimen from each race," said Florian. "Maybe Anna MacLeod was the standard for a white European. It's all very disturbing. Like Darwinism gone wrong." Florian sighed. "Perhaps it was because she was a twin and had twins?"

"Oh I didn't know that she was a twin," said Liz.

"Who knows what theories he was coming up with and what he thought important. I've had a more thorough read of his *Book of Skulls* and it still doesn't make much sense. Anyway let's change the subject!" said Florian. "I'm so jealous that you met Professor Coulier. His method of using iodine fuming to show up fingerprints sounds very exciting."

"I'm sure that his technique will be soon used for identification in criminal cases," said Liz.

"You must show me how to do it," said Florian. "I had a case only a couple of weeks ago that it could have been useful in."

"Of course," said Liz. "It was great that they persuaded him to come over from Paris for a few days. I might try getting my degree there when I've finished in London."

Florian nodded. "Oh, I almost forgot. Campbell Preeble came past last week with a note of his new address. He and Mr Findlay bought some old building in Aberdour in Fife. They want us all to come round to dinner when you've settled in," said Florian.

"Yes he did write to say that he was going to go into business with Hector and they were looking for somewhere to start up some sort of clinic. It will be good to catch up with them both," said Liz.

"And Amulya. How is she?" asked Florian.

"She's staying on in London for the break. She's met a new beau. Fredric. He's a doctor at the Royal Free," said Liz.

"How wonderful for her!" said Florian.

"So what's the surprise that you wrote to me about then?" asked Liz.

"We have to stop and pick up someone first," said Florian.

The carriage pulled up at the Medical School. Florian got out of the carriage. Liz followed her.

"I'll wait here," said Charles.

Florian and Liz went up the main steps, crossed the courtyard and made for an entrance on the left, up another set of steps. Florian stopped to speak to an attendant at the doorway.

"Where is the exhibition?" asked Florian.

"Through there. At the end of the corridor." Florian nodded her thanks.

"Come on," said Florian as she dashed down the corridor. They went through a set of doors into a large exhibition area where a multitude of people in expensive clothes were drinking glasses of wine and milling around various paintings and sculptures.

"What is all this for?" asked Liz.

"It's an exhibition on the theme of *Medical Inspirations*. Funded by Odette Love," said Florian.

"She's been so good to me. If it wasn't for you both I'd have not been able to think of applying to London," said Liz.

"We were both delighted to help out," said Florian.

A waiter came up and offered the women a glass of wine.

"No thank you we're not staying," said Florian. She scanned the room. "Now where is she?"

234

An elderly woman with great style came up to them.

"Doctor Blyth. How nice of you to attend. Is this the famous daughter of yours?"

"Mrs McCall. This is my daughter, Liz. She's training at the London School of Medicine for Women. Then possibly off to Paris to finish her studies, unless the law is changed of course," replied Florian.

"It's shocking that women have to go abroad to obtain a degree," said Mrs McCall.

"It is," agreed Liz.

"We really do need more lady doctors. We only have your mother in Scotland so far. I do hope you'll come back here when you finish your studies," said Mrs McCall.

"I do intend to," said Liz.

"Have you seen Miss Love?" asked Florian.

"I think I saw her in the smaller room to the side," said Mrs McCall.

"Thank you. We're in a bit of a rush so I'll catch up later. Still okay to come in next Wednesday for your appointment?" said Florian.

"Of course," said Mrs McCall.

Florian smiled and moved off. As she weaved through the crowd she turned to Liz and said, "My best patient. After Mrs McCall signed up they came in droves. So many women prefer women doctors."

Liz struggled to keep up with her as she headed through the crowd to a smaller room on the right. The room was flanked by rows of tall glass cabinets and was much quieter. Odette sat in her wheelchair at the far end, facing away from them, staring at an exhibit. Florian rushed up to her. As Liz got closer she could see what Odette was staring at. A human skull on a shelf next to an open book. She recognised the book as Paul's *Book of Skulls*. Odette turned round.

"Liz dear!" gasped Odette. Liz bent down and kissed Odette on the cheek. She could see that Odette had been crying.

"How are you?" asked Liz.

"Getting there," said Odette. She clutched both Florian and Liz's hands. "Do you think that he is happy, wherever he is?"

Liz and Florian both nodded. Odette let go off their hands and turned to the skull on the shelf. The note below the skull read "*Dr Paul Love*".

"Paul sums up what one can become when one becomes obsessed. Hopefully others will learn from it," said Odette.

"I hope so," said Liz. She felt sad as suddenly all the good memories of Paul came back to her. All the small moments that she'd forgotten, after his attempt to kill her and Campbell had spoiled everything.

Odette turned her wheelchair around and moved off. "I'll get you outside" she called.

"I think you may find this interesting," said Florian. "This way." She pointed down to two large cabinets standing next to each other. Each contained a full skeleton. Liz looked down at the labels. One was labelled *Adult Male* and the other *Adult Female*.

"Are they whom I'm thinking they are?" asked Liz.

"Yes Dr Nicolson organised it," said Florian. "Come on. I want to show you my surprise now."

"Was that not the surprise?" asked Liz.

"No. Come on," said Florian.

They went back through the exhibition and out into the courtyard where Odette was waiting. Florian and Liz helped Odette down the steps to the carriage. Charles strapped the wheelchair to the back. The carriage went off down the Cowgate.

"I thought we were going to yours?" said Liz.

"Later," said Florian.

"We've something to show you first," said Odette.

The carriage went up Abbeymount and turned into Regent Terrace. It stopped outside Odette's mansion. Charles got out and unsecured the wheelchair from the back.

Liz and Florian helped Odette out of the carriage and into the wheelchair. Liz was just about to open the gate when she noticed it. A brass plaque on the gate.

"Dr F Blyth."

"What's this?" gasped Liz.

"We've turned the ground floor of the mansion into a surgery. I really didn't need all that space," said Odette. "There's space on the plaque for when you qualify too."

"That's wonderful," said Liz. She kissed Odette on the cheek.

"We've already got a huge waiting list of female patients," said Florian.

"You go ahead. Charles will help me," said Odette.

Florian grinned, "Come on then, I can't wait to show you all the new equipment we've got."

Liz and Florian rushed up the garden path to the main door.

Charles was about to help Odette through the gate when he stopped. He spat on his sleeve and polished the brass plaque. He saw a carriage come to a halt in the brass reflection and turned around. Inspector MacLeod descended from the carriage.

"Sir?" said Charles.

"Have you seen Dr Blyth?" asked the Inspector.

"She's showing Liz around the new surgery," said Odette. "Go on ahead."

The Inspector nodded and hastened up the path, through the open door and into the main hall. He heard voices from the dining room, knocked and entered as Florian was showing Liz how the space had been converted into a surgery.

Florian turned and said, "Inspector?"

"Dr Blyth," said the Inspector. "Liz!"

"I'm sorry about the notebook. I.." stumbled Liz, at a loss for words.

"No. Don't be. I've been able to get on with my life now," said the Inspector.

"Well then congratulations on your forthcoming marriage. Thanks for inviting me," said Liz.

The inspector smiled, then his face became serious.

"A yacht. The *Ilvanya*. It's been found drifting in the Firth of Forth. There's a body. Mummified, I think. Could you come and have a look?"

Florian raised her eyebrow to Liz. She grinned.

"Yes, of course Inspector. Lead us to it!"

The End

Printed in Poland
by Amazon Fulfillment
Poland Sp. z o.o., Wrocław

61532270R00139